# INDIA

# DISHONORABLE

WWW.BLACKODYSSEY.NET

Published by

BLACK ODYSSEY MEDIA

www.blackodyssey.net

Email: info@blackodyssey.net

Library of Congress Control Number: 2023919136

First Trade Paperback Printing: April 2024
ISBN: 978-1-957950-39-6
ISBN: 978-1-957950-40-2 (e-book)

Cover Design by Ashlee Nassar of Designs With Sass and Navi' Robins
Photography by Orion Hayes
Model Layout by Julene Fleurmond
Models from left to right: Davina Works, Ty Kruz, Jason Mitchell, and Atiya Johnson.

10 9 8 7 6 5 4 3 2 1

Manufactured in the United States of America

Distributed by Kensington Publishing Corp.

Dear Reader,

I want to thank you immensely for supporting Black Odyssey Media authors, and our ongoing efforts to spotlight more minority storytellers. The scariest and most challenging task for many writers is getting the story, or characters, out of our heads and onto the page. Having admitted that, with every manuscript that Kreceda and I acquire, we believe that it took talent, discipline, and remarkable courage to construct that story, flesh out those characters, and prepare it for the world. Debut or seasoned, our authors are the real heroes and heroines in *OUR* story. And for them, we are eternally grateful.

Whether you are new to India or Black Odyssey Media, we hope that you are here to stay. We also welcome your feedback and kindly ask that you leave a review. For upcoming releases, announcements, submission guidelines, etc., please be sure to visit our website at www.blackodyssey.net or scan the QR code below. We can also be found on social media using @iamblackodyssey. Until next time, take care and enjoy the journey

Joyfully,

Shawanda Williams

Shawanda "N'Tyse" Williams
Founder/Publisher

This book is dedicated to every black girl with a dream.
The world is big enough for all of us!

# PROLOGUE

"Well, little one, it's almost time for us to meet officially." Markita Jones rubbed her round, pregnant belly while staring at her reflection in the mirror on the dresser; she was glowing. "Mommy is very nervous, but I know things are going to be okay," she smiled. "You are so loved and spoiled alr—" The tender moment was cut short by a loud sound.

Instinctively, she walked toward the bedroom door to assess the situation. Initially, she thought her two best friends, Alexis Walker and Kenya Lewis, had dropped something as they made space and moved furniture to prepare for the baby shower they were about to host. Just as she was about to yell downstairs and tell them to be careful, the sound of gunfire erupted through the two-story town house like booming thunder. Fear gripped Markita's heart as she internally processed what was happening.

A barrage of bullets ricocheted off the walls and windows, tearing up everything in their path. Markita dropped to her knees, fearful for her life. That's when she heard her friends screaming for help. They were downstairs in the living room, where she had been no more than ten minutes ago. Had it not been for the baby pressing on her bladder, she'd still be down there.

"Fuck!" Frantically, she searched the bedroom for anything she could use for protection. Unfortunately for Markita, her quest yielded no results. Scared to make a move, yet fearful of being trapped, she crawled toward the bedroom door. Her heart raced erratically as she tried to calm her breathing.

"Where the fuck is the cash at?" a man's deep voice bellowed from the living room.

"I don't have any fucking money in here!" Alexis screamed in agony. It was apparent to Kita that she was injured.

"Bitch, I'm going to ask you one more fucking time. Lie to me again, and you won't like what happens next."

"I'm not lying," Alexis cried. "Please, just leave. Let me call the ambulance before we die in here. I swear to God I won't say nothing . . . just let us live, please."

Though Markita desperately wanted to go downstairs and help her friends, she had an unborn child to think about first. She slowly closed the bedroom door and retrieved her cell phone from the bed. It was lying next to her black Yves St. Laurent Cassandre purse. Quickly, she dialed for help.

"911, what's the emergency?" With a stiff tone, the operator sounded more like a robot than an actual person.

"My name is Markita Jones. I'm at 906 Chene Dr., unit number three. Please send the police and a few ambulances," she whispered through labored breaths.

"What seems to be the emergency?"

"Oh my God, he's coming!" Kita's voice oozed in panic as the sound of heavy footsteps headed in her direction. The pattern of their stride matched the beating in her heart. She felt like she was seconds from passing out. "I'm at my friend's house. Someone just came in shooting!"

"Do you know how many assailants there are? Do you know what they look like?" The operator bombarded her with questions.

Frustrated and afraid, Markita dropped the phone onto the bed. That's when she saw the knob on the bedroom door jiggle. She thought her life was over, but right on cue, the headlights from a car outside illuminated the bedroom window, giving Markita the sign she needed to use the only escape route accessible. Though Markita didn't exactly want to jump two stories to safety, she knew desperate times called for desperate measures.

Quickly, she pried the window open and kicked out the screen. With one leg dangling over the edge, she looked back at the door just in time to see it crack open. Before the assailant could fully enter the room, Markita closed her eyes tight . . . and jumped. Thankfully, she landed on her knees instead of her stomach or back. However, her victory was short lived as the sound of two gunshots whizzed past her head. Without hesitation, she jumped up and frantically ran toward a neighbor's house. *POW!* A missed shot hit the headlight of a burgundy Nissan parked nearby.

"Help!" Markita screamed . . . just before the next shot hit its target. The bullet successfully tore through her left calf muscle and dropped her where she stood. Within seconds, she forced herself up from the ground and shifted her weight onto her right leg, determined to keep pushing. Though hurt and tired, she willed herself to fight for her child, if nothing else. *BANG!* However, the fourth blast was the shot that inevitably put Kita down. The bullet had entered into her back and exited through her chest. The scene appeared theatrical as pieces of her flesh opened and flew out in front of her, sending thick red blood squirting out everywhere.

Seconds after the shot, Markita felt a burning sensation so hot that she began to wonder if she was on fire. The pain was unbearable. She wanted to scream in agony, but her lungs were full of something . . . blood perhaps. She tried twice to get up from the concrete, but it was useless. Her limbs were no longer listening to her brain, as she lay there unmoving. Her eyes fluttered as she tried hard to keep them open. Within a matter of seconds, her body grew cold. Internally, she knew she was losing her fight to stay alive.

"Oh my God!" a lady screamed while another person hollered for someone to call 911.

As Markita lay outside dying beneath the stars, she thought about her mother, Jackie, and how she would feel after receiving the news. She wondered if Jackie would blame herself and go into another bout of depression the way she did when her brother Marlowe was killed. Markita wished she could comfort her mom and let her know that none of this was her fault.

Next, she thought of her fiancé, Rico Richardson, and large tears gathered in the corners of her eyes. Without a doubt, the police would report the incident as being drug-related, and she knew he'd be mad at her for bringing shame to his name and tarnishing his reputation. Markita also knew that Rico would ultimately hate her for losing their child to a street hustle she should have never been caught up in.

Markita wanted to make things right with everyone. She wanted desperately to start over, but there were no second chances in life. It was time to meet her maker and face judgment for how she had been living lately. She wondered if Alexis and Kenya would be at the crossroads to greet her when she arrived. With her friends in mind, she managed to muster a faint smile.

How did three innocent girls from the ghetto get caught up in a life of crime? This simple question triggered a movie to begin playing in Markita's head. With her eyes closed, she began to relax and allow herself to be transported through what felt like multiple dimensions. Flashbacks of her life began in childhood when things were rough for her family. Markita knew this period was the catalyst that undoubtedly turned her from an innocent, sweet girl into an infamous street gangster.

## CHRISTMAS EVE TEN YEARS AGO . . .

Eight-year-old Markita and her mother, Jaqueline Jones, stepped from the semicrowded city bus into the dark, crisp night air. The pair walked in silence down several long blocks toward their run-down, eight-story apartment building centrally located in the middle of the Woodward Housing Projects. The streets were unusually empty this evening, but that was to be expected for the holiday season. Everyone was either inside preparing for Christmas or away visiting family. It was too cold to talk, but that didn't stop little Kita from making smoke rings with her mouth.

When they finally reached their destination, Markita asked her mother if she could make a snow angel. It had snowed over eight inches in Detroit the previous night, meaning heaps of fresh snow were everywhere. Jackie was cold and tired. She wanted to tell her daughter no, but then she remembered her own childhood excitement about playing in the snow and decided not to be a killjoy. With a smile, she relented. "Okay, go ahead, but hurry."

With a smile, Markita fell backward into a fresh pile of snow and began moving her arms and legs sideways like windshield wipers. "Mommy, do it with me, please," she begged through a missing bottom tooth that had fallen out some days ago.

"Girl, no. It's too cold out here for my old bones." Jackie pulled the hood of her coat tighter as Kita begged once more.

"Please, Mommy, just for a minute. We can warm up with hot chocolate and warm cookies when we get inside," she persuaded.

"Who said you were getting hot chocolate and warm cookies, little girl?"

"We always have hot chocolate and warm cookies on Christmas Eve, Mommy," Kita reminded her mother with an innocent giggle. What had started as the only offering Jackie had for her children on the holiday turned into a family tradition over the years. "It's my second favorite thing about Christmas."

"Oh yeah? What's your first favorite thing?" Jackie leaned against the brick exterior of the building and blew hot air onto her bare hands.

"Making Christmas wishes and seeing if they come true is my most favorite thing," Markita continued.

"Is that right? What did you wish for this year?" Jackie asked although she'd found her daughter's secret list a few months ago. It was written in crayon and slightly misspelled, but Jackie had gathered enough information to know that her daughter wanted a traveling doll case, a pair of skates, and a gold necklace with her initials.

While listening to Kita blab, Jackie beamed with excitement. She was proud that she could make Christmas special for both of her kids this year with all of the overtime hours she'd put in between her jobs at the plant and department store. Life had not always been kind to the young mother, but thank God she was finally finding her way out of the dark space she'd been in since being kicked out of her mother's home at fourteen with her first child, Marlowe, who was now sixteen.

"Mommy, you know I can't tell you my wishes because they won't come true."

"Can you at least tell me one?" Jackie insisted, still playing the game.

"Well," Kita paused. "I wished my mom would make a snow angel with me on Christmas Eve," she cleverly embellished.

After a few seconds of careful consideration, Jackie gave in. "Wow! That's really specific, but if that's what you wished for, let's do it." She walked over and found a spot next to her daughter. Together, they made angels and then commenced having a snowball fight. This went on for several minutes before Jackie had to call it quits. Her pants were soaked, and Kita's cheeks and nose turned red. "Let's go get our hot chocolate and warm cookies."

"Deal." Kita stood, stomped the snow off her body, and followed her mother into their building.

Upon entrance into the lobby, they were greeted with the strong smell of urine and a fresh puddle of pee. Kita pinched her nose and looked up at her mother, but Jackie wasn't bothered; she'd adapted to it over the years. Kita pressed the button for the elevator as Jackie checked the mailbox. As usual, it took forever for the elevator to arrive, so Jackie used the time to sort through everything in her hand. Right on top of the stack was a pink envelope with a red stamp that read PAST DUE. Without hesitation, Jackie opened the envelope and gasped. "What?" she said to no one in particular.

"What's wrong, Mommy?" Kita asked as they stepped onto the elevator. Her favorite part of riding was to press the buttons, so she flew over to the keypad. "Three," she pressed and said aloud.

"Nothing, baby." With a furrowed brow, Jackie continued looking through the stack of mail while mumbling under her breath. She was perplexed.

Seconds later, the elevator stopped, and the duo stepped off. They were greeted by their neighbor, Mr. Allen, who had difficulty controlling his rambunctious dog, McGyver. "Hey, Jackie. Hi, Markita. I'm glad I got to see you guys before the big move. I'm sure going to miss you and those Sunday meals you send my way occasionally."

"Hi, Mr. Allen." Markita put her hand out to pet McGyver.

"I'm sorry, Allen." Jackie looked up from her bills. "Did you say you were moving?"

"Not me." Allen looked puzzled. "I saw Larry moving stuff out of your apartment not too long ago. I thought you guys were moving, but maybe I was wrong." He paused. "Don't mind me. I'm sorry for meddling."

At the mention of Larry, her boyfriend of five years, Jackie frowned. Though things had been rocky for quite some time, she didn't know why he would have been moving things out of their apartment on Christmas Eve without telling her. She was also clueless about why the water and electric bills hadn't been paid in two months. She and Larry had a joint account to cover all household expenses. Jackie wasn't computer savvy, so Larry was responsible for making the online payments. The entire time they'd lived together, there had never been a problem, so all of this was out of the ordinary.

"I'm sorry, Allen. Let me go and see what's going on. Merry Christmas." Jackie grabbed Kita's hand and flew toward their apartment.

# CHAPTER ONE

As soon as the ladies approached their two-bedroom flat perfectly tucked in the corner with a homemade Christmas wreath adorning the door, they were promptly met with a letter. It was taped to the peephole and read: FINAL WARNING. "What the fuck is going on?" Jackie snatched the letter, read it, opened the door, and immediately flew into her bedroom. In her haste to confront Larry, she had dropped the bills and letter on the dining table. Kita quickly picked up the mail and read through all of the papers, being the inquisitive child she was. She determined that some of the bills were past due and that the rent hadn't been paid in almost three months. The rental office needed all money and late fees to be paid within ten days, or they would proceed with a formal eviction. Kita didn't know exactly what that meant but knew it wasn't good.

Just as Kita began removing her wet shoes and coat, she could hear her mother and Larry shouting at each other. The yelling didn't faze her because she was used to it. Without hesitation, she walked into the kitchen and tried to cut on the lights, but they didn't work. Without giving it a second thought, she walked over to the sink and washed her hands. Next, she opened the freezer door, stood on her tiptoes, and retrieved the package of chocolate chip cookies. She planned to get started on the dessert, but then she remembered that she needed her mom to cut on the oven first.

After trying to wait it out for a few minutes, Kita decided to go to her bedroom, undress, and change into fresh clothes. The apartment was so dark and cold that she had to wear two layers of pajama pants, a long-sleeved T-shirt, and a sweater. Even with all of the clothing, Kita was freezing. Internally, she debated if she should knock on her mom's door and risk getting in trouble for disrupting grown folks' business or just put on more clothes and thug the cold out. Quickly, she decided on the latter.

After dressing in everything she thought would keep her warm, Kita returned to the kitchen. However, the minute she placed her hand on her bedroom door to open it, she could hear her mother's bedroom door open too. Jackie and Larry continued their argument into the hallway. Kita pressed her ear to the door. She really couldn't make out what they were saying, but she could tell it was about money. This went on for the better part of thirty minutes before things escalated in the living room, where physical punches had been thrown.

Scared to death yet worried about her mother, Kita slowly pulled her bedroom door open to see what was going on. Even in the dark, she could see that the living room furniture was now out of place, and a few pictures had fallen off the wall. Markita wasn't sure who'd delivered the first body shot, but it was clear that her mother was on ten and getting the best of her partner. Larry was a tall, lanky man with few muscles and a bald head. He was bleeding from the nose while Jackie bled from the mouth. Though the couple's relationship wasn't perfect, Kita had never seen things get this bad between them.

"So, are you just going to fuck up the rent and bill money, then come home and pack up your shit like nothing happened?" Jackie dug her nails into Larry's eyes. He backed up, trying to put some distance between them. "What the fuck are me and my kids supposed to do, bitch?"

Markita had never heard her mother curse this much; she knew Jackie was pissed.

"I know I messed up, but I didn't come home like nothing happened. I came home to tell you that I am leaving. You just won't let me go." Larry raised his hands in surrender.

"Let me get this straight." Jackie made a show of her shock by grabbing her chest as she continued. "You go out and smoke up all the money we had for rent, food, bills, and every gotdamn thing else, and think you're just going to come in here and tell me you're leaving? You gotdamn right. I'm *not* making this easy." Swiftly, she extended her arm like Ali in his prime and hit Larry right in the center of his face. Blood oozed out like red slime.

"Bitch! I should kill you." Larry lunged at Jackie and began choking her.

She gasped for air and tried desperately to pry herself free. "Stop," she mumbled.

Seeing her mother fight for her life, Kita ran into Jackie's room and opened the second drawer of her nightstand. She searched until she found a small box labeled KEEP OUT. Without hesitation, she opened the box and retrieved the gun she knew would be hidden there. It was a compact, nine-millimeter handgun, but Kita was too young to be concerned with the logistics at the moment. All she knew was that she had to protect her mother.

"Larry, get off her," she returned to the living room screaming. "Get off her right now!" With tears running down her face and unsteady hands, Markita approached the couple.

Larry's eyes widened in surprise. Maybe he realized what he was doing, or perhaps he just didn't want to get shot. Either way, he released Jackie from his grip. "I'm sorry. I'm sorry."

Jackie fell to the ground and tried hard to catch her breath. Kita ran toward her mother but never took her eyes or the gun off of Larry. Larry looked like he wanted to say something, but he didn't. Instead, he reached for his winter coat lying across the couch and grabbed the duffle bag resting on the floor. After throwing the luggage over his shoulder, he walked over to the sparsely decorated Christmas tree sitting in the corner. He stood there momentarily before kneeling and grabbing a few presents from beneath the tree. Kita couldn't believe what she was seeing. Larry had gone from someone she cared for to being the Grinch in human form as he stole Christmas.

"Really, Larry?" Jackie coughed, trying to catch her breath while removing the gun from her daughter. "As if you haven't done enough, you're going to fuck up Christmas too?"

"I'm sorry," he said while heading toward the door like a thief in the night.

Jackie tried with all her strength to get up off the floor and go after him, but it was useless. She knew if she were lucky enough to catch up to him, things would only get worse. On top of everything else, she couldn't afford to be locked up for Christmas. "I'm sorry, Kita," she whispered.

"Why did he do that to you . . . to us?" Kita had big crocodile tears dancing in the ducts of her doe eyes.

"Larry has a problem, baby." Jackie held her daughter tightly and tried to make sense of things for both of them. In reality, Jackie knew nothing about Larry's bad habit until now, and she felt so stupid for missing all of the signs her intuition should have told her were there.

"What do we do now, Mommy?" Kita continued to cry.

"Christmas is not about gifts, baby. That stuff is just material things that make us feel good. Jesus is the reason for the season; always remember that." Jackie wanted to chastise Kita but relented. She knew the girl had been through a lot today.

"I wasn't talking about the presents. Where are we going to live now?" Kita's words hit Jackie like a ton of bricks as the severity of the situation started to kick in.

# CHAPTER TWO

There was no time for Jackie to wallow in her sorrow before she had to put out yet another fire.

"Mama! What the fuck happened to your face?" sixteen-year-old Marlowe asked from the doorway of the apartment. His handsome brown face looked concerned and angry as he stood there wearing a white hoodie, denim jeans, and an old pair of Nike's. He'd just returned from the local activity center, where he spent most evenings playing basketball.

"Larry hit Mommy." Kita released her mother and ran over to her brother. Since day one, he'd been her protector.

"I'm okay, son." Jackie used the bottom of her shirt to wipe the blood from her face.

"Did he hurt you, Kita?" Marlowe inspected his little sister, whose face was still immersed in tears. Without waiting for her to reply, he stormed to the back of the apartment and into his mother's room. Frantically, he searched for the gun he thought would be hidden. When his search came up empty, he marched back into the living. "Where's the nine? I'm about to kill this nigga."

"I gave it to Mommy after I told Larry to stop hurting her," Kita replied, giving her brother a full report.

"Marlowe, baby, I'm okay. We're okay." Jackie used her strength to get up from the floor. She placed the gun on the coffee table and went to console her children. "Calm down now, and let's all take a minute to breathe."

"Ma! That nigga put his hands on you. I told you I am never letting another one get away with that shit. So, right now, calming down is *not* a fucking option." He was seething. Even at five foot eight, Marlowe had the soul of a giant; nothing and no one scared him. "Give me the gun!"

Unsure of what else to do, Jackie lovingly wrapped her arms around her children. She knew this was bad, but she didn't need Marlowe making matters worse. "I know you want to protect me and Kita, baby, but I got this." A single tear fell down her face as she continued. "I'm sorry I let another no-good, nothing-ass man into our lives. I may not always get it right, but I promise to make better choices from here on out. Please, baby, calm down."

"But, Ma—"

"Marlowe, if you go to jail for doing something crazy tonight, who will be here to look after us then?" Jackie let her words sink in as she noticed her son calm down. "Now, I'm about to go take a shower. Marlowe, please promise me that you will not leave this apartment to go after Larry. Let God deal with him."

"I don't like it, but I promise." Marlowe couldn't even look his mother in the face because the minute he saw her bruises, he knew all bets would be off.

"Thank you, son. Now, pull out some candles from the drawer, then turn on the oven and help Kita with the cookies. It's a gas stove, so it should work even though we don't have electricity. That heat will also warm up the place." Jackie kneeled and kissed her daughter's forehead. "Thank you for helping your mommy. I promise you will never have to do that again, and I will work triple time if I must to replace what he took from you, okay?"

"It's okay, Mommy. I'm just glad you're all right." Kita kissed her mom back and proceeded to enter the kitchen behind Marlowe. Once Jackie was out of sight, Kita grabbed the bills before showing them to her brother. "I think we have to move."

With a frown, Marlowe held the papers close to his face and read over everything twice before placing them back on the counter. "Nah, we ain't moving nowhere. I can promise you that. I'm going to figure out this shit, Kita."

"Marlowe, I was so scared. Do you think Larry is going to come back and get us?"

" As long as I have air in my lungs, neither Larry nor anybody else will ever touch you." Marlowe rubbed his sister's head.

"How can you be sure that Larry won't return, though?" Kita wanted to be reassured.

Like a man on a mission, Marlowe walked over to the coffee table and grabbed his mother's gun. "I'll be right back, okay?"

"What are you going to do? Mommy said not to leave." Kita could tell by the scowl on her brother's face that something was up.

"Kita, I'm the head of this family now. That means I might not always do what's right, but I will damn sure do what's necessary. I'm going to make this shit right so you never have to be scared or worry about him ever again." He tucked the gun beneath the band of his Levi's.

"How long will you be gone?"

"I don't know." Without another word, Marlowe headed for the door, leaving Kita a nervous wreck. She didn't know what Marlowe's definition of "making it right" was, but she hoped it didn't get him into trouble.

For nearly forty minutes, she sat in the living room alone. She wanted to check on her mom, who was still in the bathroom crying with the water running. However, she didn't want to be asked about her brother, so she didn't move. Just as the urge to pee hit her, the front door opened. She looked up to see Marlowe. His white hoodie was now covered in dirt and a dark red substance. He was holding two neatly wrapped gifts Larry had stolen from under the tree. Kita jumped up with excitement. Though she was happy about the returned gifts, she was happier to see her brother. "What did you do? Did you kill him?" Kita quizzed with her eyes as big as saucers.

"Some things you just don't need to know, okay?" Marlowe handed Kita the gifts and removed his hoodie before entering the kitchen and opening the cabinet door beneath the sink. He reached inside and retrieved a black garbage bag. After stuffing his hoodie into the bag, he poured the garbage from the kitchen can on top, then up tied the bag and set it in the corner.

"Where's Mommy's gun?" Kita whispered before placing the gifts back under the tree.

"It's gone," Marlowe replied nonchalantly.

"If it's found, will Mommy get into trouble?" Kita loved forensic mysteries. She knew that most guns could be traced to their owners.

"Nah. Mommy didn't have that gun on papers. She got it off the streets, but check you out. Let me find out my little sister is book smart and street savvy." With a proud smile, he patted her on the head, washed his hands, and proceeded to bake the Christmas cookies.

# CHAPTER THREE

**M**inutes after Marlowe closed the oven door, Jackie returned to the kitchen wearing an old set of Christmas pajamas and a torn robe. The redness in her face, swollen eyes, and lips were very noticeable, but no one mentioned it. "Who's up for hot chocolate?" she asked with her best fake-it-until-you-make-it smile. When neither of her children said anything, she sighed. Out of the corner of her eye, she spotted the past-due letters and eviction notice resting on the counter. Deciding to address the elephant in the room, she grabbed the papers, folded them, and placed them into the kitchen junk drawer.

"I know this is not how any of us planned to spend Christmas Eve, but we're here now. I promise I will figure this mess out after Christmas, but for now, let's please just enjoy the holiday."

Without a word, Marlowe walked out of the kitchen, leaving Jackie crushed. As her oldest child, he'd weathered many storms because of her, and she hated that for him. All she ever wanted was to give her children a better life than she had, but in reality, it seemed that all she'd done was fuck up shit. Despite her best efforts, as a single Black, poorly educated woman living in poverty, the odds were always stacked against her. She wished her kids could see how hard she was trying. She wished they could truly understand her sacrifices, but she knew they probably would never know how her life started and why she ended up here.

It was the fall of her ninth-grade year when she found out she was pregnant with Marlowe. His father was an eighteen-year-old senior who lived in the neighborhood. His name was Marshawn, and he was Jackie's first and only true love. Once Jackie's mother, Dorothy, found out her daughter was pregnant, she beat her like she'd stolen something and then took her to get an abortion. Jackie wanted to keep her baby, so she pleaded with her mother to spare her child's life. However, her cries fell on deaf ears. Dorothy told Jackie that if she decided to keep the baby, she would have to move out and see what being grown meant. The decision was a no-brainer. Jackie moved out of her mother's home and in with Marshawn's family the same day.

Though Marshawn's parents didn't want the young girl and their son playing house under their roof, things went smoothly for a while. Marshawn worked full time at a shoe store and part time at a grocery store to save enough money for the couple to rent an apartment. However, days before Marlowe was born, the shoe store was robbed, and Marshawn was murdered. His parents blamed Jackie for their son's death. They believed he wouldn't have worked so many late hours at that shoe store if it wasn't for her. Needless to say, they kept the money Marshawn had saved and put Jackie out. Days later, she gave birth to her son . . . and things went downhill from there.

Jackie had lived in homeless shelters and rent-by-the-week hotels for the better part of her and Marlowe's life. In addition to working jobs that paid under the table, Jackie dated guys with money, but most of them were no good, and Kita's dad was no different. His name was James. He was a dope boy who didn't know how to keep his hands to himself. Not only was he one of the biggest hoes on the East Side of Detroit, but he was also very abusive. He kicked Jackie's ass on more than a few occasions, but he'd also inadvertently taught her how to defend herself. Right when Jackie found out she was pregnant, James was sent upstate to serve a forty-year sentence for a multitude of criminal charges related to his drug business. Jackie wasn't sad to see him go, but it did mean she'd have to start all over again.

For three years, she and her kids had been living from pillar to post as she tried to make ends meet. Finally, she met Larry, an automotive plant worker with good intentions. The couple fell into a serious relationship very quickly. For Larry, it was love; for Jackie, it was convenience, but they made it work. Larry encouraged her to obtain her GED and provided the stability Jackie needed to get her feet on solid ground. Despite his sporadic behavior, occasional mood swings, and what she thought was a gambling addiction, she felt like Larry was the one. Yet, here she was, feeling like a failure for, once again, choosing the wrong man and letting her kids down on Christmas Eve.

"Ma, did you hear me?" Marlowe was now back in the kitchen holding a Nike shoe box full of money. "I said I got the money we need. We don't have to move."

Snapping back to reality, Jackie looked down at the box as Marlowe lifted the top to reveal several small wads of cash. Each wad was rubber-banded with a big face on top.

"Marlowe, where in the hell did you get this money? And you better not lie to me." Judging by a quick assessment, she believed about $8,000 was in the box.

"I hustle from time to time." Marlowe saw no need to lie. He knew the risks he was taking would be worth the rewards in the end.

"Hustling what?" Jackie hollered. "Boy, I know you ain't selling drugs!"

"Ma, you've lived your life; now, I'm living mine. Please, just take the money and settle the bills and the rent. Merry Christmas," he smiled proudly.

"Marlowe, this game is dangerous. I can't have you out in the streets like this, baby."

"Ma, do you watch the news? It's dangerous going to the store for candy. It's dangerous walking down the street with friends. It's dangerous driving in the wrong neighborhood or knocking on the wrong door. Hell, it's dangerous calling the police for help these days, so the way I see it, I might as well live the kind of life I want to live before I leave this earth. I'm sick of watching you count change. I'm tired of struggling. Stop looking for niggas in the street to save you, Mama, because I got us! As long as I live, you and Kita ain't gon' want for nothing! Now, let's get this hot chocolate going so it starts to feel like Christmas up in here." His large smile was contagious.

Jackie wanted to be mad, but how could she? She was fresh out of options and couldn't let her children end up on the streets again. "Thank you, son." She took the shoe box with tears running down her face and hugged her child for several long seconds. "Once I get us squared away, you won't need to hustle anymore. This is only temporary, you hear me?"

"Mommy, I smell the cookies," Kita interjected.

"You go ahead and handle that. I'll be right back." Marlowe grabbed the garbage bag from the floor.

"Where are you going?"

"I'm going to take the garbage out. It's starting to smell," he lied.

"Come right back." Jackie eyed him suspiciously, then turned toward the oven.

Kita peered at her brother while her mother wasn't looking. With a solemn smile, she placed her little fingers up to her mouth and made a show of locking her lips and throwing away the key. This was the first of many secrets held between the siblings. Though eight years apart, their bond was unbreakable. Marlowe returned the gesture before taking his bloody clothes down to the dumpster, where they would disappear into a sea of trash like a magic trick, never to be seen again.

# CHAPTER FOUR

## CHRISTMAS EVE TEN YEARS LATER

Kita and her best friends, Alexis and Kenya, stretched out on Kita's bed. The latest hip-hop music blared in the background as the high school seniors discussed celebrity gossip, school drama, and the boys they thought were cute. Alexis was a beautiful, chocolate girl with a grown woman's body. She kept her hair and nails on point, so all the local dope boys checked for her. Kenya was beautiful too, with fair skin and a vibrant smile. Though she hadn't come all the way out of the closet, everyone knew she was bisexual. Her style very much gave the soft stud vibe. Though she didn't care for makeup and nails, she wore lots of fitted and revealing clothes. Kita had also grown into herself quite well. No longer was she the little, light-skinned girl with pigtails and a soft voice. At five foot seven and 145 pounds, she was now a curvaceous boy magnet with model looks. Her slanted eyes and full lips complemented her face and made her the apple of many eyes.

"So, Kita . . ." Alexis sat up on the bed and peered inquisitively at her friend.

"Oh shit. Here you go." Markita already knew her girl was on some bullshit.

"What I do?" she laughed.

"Bitch, they don't call you crazy for nothing." Kenya chimed in, reminding everyone of their nicknames. Ever since the girls started hanging out in ninth grade, they'd been referred to by other students as "crazy," "sexy," and "cool." Kita was labeled sexy for the aura that she oozed. Kenya was labeled cool because she got along with everyone, and her vibe was so chill. Alexis, who had set her boyfriend's car on fire, fought damn near the whole school and almost got expelled for stealing from the teacher's lounge. She was labeled crazy for obvious reasons.

"I've changed. I'm grown now," she giggled.

"Ho, didn't you just pull a gun out on Taja from the science class last week?" Kita hollered.

"In my defense, she owed me money for some weed I fronted her. Anyway, bitch, I wasn't going to say anything wild. I just wanted to know who you were going to the prom with. A little birdie told me that Keith Harris asked you before school went on winter break."

"Wait, what?" Kenya was now excited. "Keith Harris, as in the quarterback, homecoming king, and most popular nigga at the school? I barely like niggas, but that one is fine. Did you say yes?"

"I told him I'd let him know after winter break." Markita got off of her bed and walked over to the dresser mirror, inspecting her twenty-six-inch bust and hairstyle with a middle part.

"Are you serious, Kita? Opportunities like that don't come around often. You are cute and all, but that nigga is top tier. You better call him now and tell him yes." Kenya was invested.

"She ain't gon' do that." Alexis smacked her lips. "She is still dick whipped over Rico's ass."

"Girl, I know Rico Richardson was your first love and the first piece of dick you got, but that nigga is long gone. Get over him and get under Keith." Kenya made a show of slapping fives with Alexis.

"First of all, keep y'all voices down before my mama hears y'all. Second of all, ain't nobody pressed about Keith or Rico."

"If you aren't pressed about Rico, tell us why you never dated after he graduated. Let's face it, Kita. He was a senior, and you were just a punk-ass sophomore. He probably went to college and found a real woman or two or three. Ain't no need in holding out hope that your first love will come back to you like it happens in the movies." Alexis laughed, but Kita did not.

Sensing the tension in the room, Kenya removed the blunt behind her ear. "While Mama Jackie is preoccupied in the kitchen, do y'all want to step outside and blow one with your girl?"

"Hell yeah!" Kita and Alexis replied in unison.

As they exited the bedroom, the smell of holiday food hit them smack in the face. "Dang, Mama Jackie, you got it going on up there." Alexis walked into the kitchen and took inventory of what was on the stove.

"Thank you, baby." Jackie took a sip from her wineglass while stirring the steaming pot. "It ain't nothing but a little mac and cheese, greens, yams, and dressing. I'm going to put the turkey and ham on tomorrow morning. You girls be sure to come over, okay?" Jackie was in such a good mood. Her home was covered to the nines with gold and silver Christmas decorations, and the tree overflowed with gifts. Her bills were paid, and the apartment she shared with Kita was filled with love and the sound of Motown music. Though her son had moved out some years ago, she knew he'd be gracing them with his presence soon, and then her heart would be full.

"Mama, I'll be back. We're going to check on Alexis's sister, Talia."

"Um-hmm." Jackie sensed that something was up but decided not to pry. "Marlowe should be here soon, so come right back."

"Yes, ma'am." With her friends in tow, Kita headed for the door.

"Speaking of Marlowe, I hope I'm here when his fine ass shows up." Alexis made a show of lifting her breasts to make them appear more appealing.

"Girl, not you but me. His little ass is fine," Kenya added.

"Y'all know my brother is off-limits, and besides, he ain't checking for either one of y'all jail-bait asses." Kita opened the door to the stairway and ascended to the rooftop toward the trio's secret smoke spot.

After opening the door, Kenya removed the blunt from her ear and sparked it up. She took three puffs, then passed it to Kita, who was peering over the building at the awesome view of her neighborhood. From up there, everything seemed so beautiful that it was sometimes hard to tell that this was the ghetto and everyone in the neighborhood was struggling to make ends meet.

"Y'all are my sisters for real. I know we fuss and fight, but I love y'all so much."

"Every time Kita smokes, she gets emotional." Kenya looked at Alexis and laughed playfully.

"Damn, can I have a moment?" With a smile, Kita wiped a single tear as it fell from her eyes. "I've just been thinking about how close we are and how things will change once we graduate in a few months."

"Yeah, that shit does suck." Alexis looked down at the ground. "From the first day of freshman year, we've been as thick as thieves. Y'all held me down when my mama died, and my sister and I had to move in with my grandma. Y'all even made sure my homework was done when I started skipping school after that." She paused.

"Truth be told, I probably wouldn't even be on track to graduate if it wasn't for y'all."

"Why do things have to change, though? We gon' be best friends until we're in the nursing home or the graveyard." Kenya smacked her lips.

"Facts," Alexis added.

"Yeah, those are facts, but in reality, people pull apart when they move in different directions. I'll be headed to Howard in the fall." Kita sighed. "And as much as I've dreamed of going there my whole life, I don't want to leave y'all."

"Kita, we ain't going nowhere. Trust and believe me and Lex will always be close by." Kenya wrapped an arm around her friend. "I'll be here at Wayne State, and Lex will be—" she was cut off by Alexis.

"Lex will be under the next hood nigga on the come up," she stated as a matter of fact.

"Girl!" Kita smacked her lips.

"What? Shit, don't judge me. Y'all hoes can keep the big dreams and career plans. I'm just an around-the-way girl, addicted to the fast life." Alexis extended her hand and admired her yellow stiletto nails bedazzled in rhinestones.

"Don't you want your own out of life, though?" Kenya frowned. She was disappointed that her friend didn't want more for herself.

"Baby girl, stay in your lane. I know what I'm doing, okay?" Alexis hissed. "Go be a nerd and live your life."

"Okay, y'all, let's not start." Kita clapped her hands like a mother would do her children. "Come on, it's time to head in." She walked toward the door.

"Y'all can slide out, but I want to chill up here a little longer." Alexis reached into her pocket and pulled out her cell phone.

"It's cold as hell as up here. Don't be like that. Come on." Kenya pulled her friend's arm, but it was useless. Alexis was knee-deep in her feelings, and both girls knew the best thing to do was to let her be.

"Okay, girl. I'll catch you later." Kita chimed in.

"Later." Alexis spat.

Kenya and Kita descended the stairs back down to Kita's floor. "Was I wrong for what I said?" Kenya was nobody's yes-man, but she hated to be on anyone's bad side, especially one of her best friends.

"No, you weren't wrong, but you know Lex. She's not like us, and that's okay. You want to be a teacher, and I want to be a lawyer. Lex is content being the real hood wife of a baller. She loves that lifestyle, and we love her, so we gotta let it ride."

"I just see her potential and want more for her, but you're right. I'm going to chill for now." When they reached Kita's floor, Kenya's phone rang. Though the caller ID read UNKNOWN, she smiled from ear to ear. "I've been waiting for this call. I'll catch you later, sis."

"Damn, who is that?" Kita inquired.

"Bye, girl." Kenya pushed Kita out of the stairwell and then answered her phone.

Kita wanted to hang back and eavesdrop, but the smell of Creed indicated that Marlowe had walked past recently. It was his signature scent. Instantly, Kita ran down the hallway and flew into her apartment. As suspected, Marlowe sat on the couch talking with Bernard, their adopted cousin and best friend, for as long as Kita could remember. "What's up, bro? Took yo' ass long enough. What's up, B?"

"Kita, I heard that." Jackie hollered from the kitchen.

"My bad, sis. We had to handle some business first, but I'm here now, so fix your face." Marlowe stood and pulled his sister in for a tight hug.

"Damn, y'all always make me wish I had a sister. Y'all be so excited to see each other that if I didn't know any better, I'd think y'all ain't seen each other in months." Bernard was leaning back on the love seat, glancing down at his cell phone with his crisp dreadlocks hanging near his waist. He was dressed in a denim outfit, white T-shirt, and vintage Gucci boots. A platinum chain hung around his neck with a small pendant that read *"Money Talks."* Marlowe, on the other hand, was dressed down in a very simple pair of black jeans, tan Timberland boots, a white thermal shirt, and a custom Detroit Pistons' coat.

"It ain't too late. Tell Aunt Rhonda you want a sibling," Marlowe laughed.

"Negro, she barely wants my grown ass. What the fuck is she going to do with a baby?" Bernard had been adopted when he was three by Jackie's sister, Rhonda, after her husband's mistress died giving birth. Initially, Rhonda wanted nothing to do with the child conceived via extramarital affairs. However, when her husband found out he was terminally ill and only had a short time to live, he'd made Rhonda promise not to let Bernard end up in foster care. Rhonda agreed to raise Bernard only if her husband took out a hefty insurance policy and made her the beneficiary to help cover the cost of raising the baby. Rhonda received a payout of $500,000 when he died, but almost none of it went to Bernard. At max, she provided her stepson a roof over his head, food to eat, a winter coat, eight outfits, and two pairs of gym shoes per school year. There were no special treats like toys or summer vacations, and Rhonda would die and go to hell before she celebrated anything with Bernard, like Christmas or his birthday. In her mind, those were extras she did not sign up for.

Over the years, Bernard learned to adapt and began spending time with the OGs in his hood. Eventually, they put him on to hustling weed, and soon enough, he was making the money he needed to buy the extra shit that he wanted. Not long after he got on, he put Marlowe on, and the rest was history. Bernard was made for the grind, but Marlowe was made for the business. Together, they combined their skills and went on to take over the drug trade in Detroit. They moved everything from weed to cocaine and occasionally heroin when the prices were right, and they were willing to take the risk that serving "dog food" came with.

"Are you staying for cookies and hot chocolate, Bernard?" Kita took a seat next to her brother.

"As tempting as that sounds, little cuz, I got my own traditions that I'm about to go participate in." He reached into his pocket and removed a small bottle of liquor and a blunt. "Matter of fact, I guess I'll go get my party started right now." He stood. "I'll catch y'all later."

"Aww, B, are you leaving so soon? I just knew you would be my spades partner tonight like you used to be back in the day." Jackie popped into the living room. "Kita and Marlowe didn't stand a chance against us."

Over the years, Bernard had spent so much time at Jackie's house that she felt like he was a second son. Although his stepmother was her sister, Jackie disapproved of how she raised him, but she'd never spoken her mind aloud. As an attempt to alleviate some of that evil shit Rhonda was doing, Jackie always provided a safe place for the young man to come and receive some good old-fashioned love. Now that he and Marlowe were grown men making lots of money and major moves on the streets, she often missed the days when they were younger.

"Kita, they must be delusional." Marlowe rolled his eyes.

"Mama Jackie, we used to bust they ass, didn't we." Bernard smiled, thinking about all the times he'd spent with his aunt and cousins. Those had been his favorite childhood memories.

"Sure did!" Jackie laughed. "All right, baby. Well, you be safe, and Auntie will see you tomorrow, okay?"

"Yes, ma'am. Dinner is still at three, right?"

"You know it." Jackie gave Bernard a tight hug and returned to the kitchen.

"All right, fam. I'll catch y'all tomorrow . . . at the spades table with yo' losing ass."

"Bye, nigga!" Marlowe hollered.

# CHAPTER FIVE

After indulging in Christmas cookies and hot chocolate, Kita, Jackie, and Marlowe sang and danced to Black Christmas songs around the apartment. They'd even done a mini Soul Train line. After an hour of cardio, Marlowe plopped down on the couch, and his mom and sister followed suit. "Mama, I don't know what it is, but you look so pretty tonight." Marlowe peered at his mother.

"Damn, what are you trying to say?" Instinctively, Jackie placed a hand on her hip.

"You are gorgeous every day, but today is different. You got a little glow about you."

"Mama, you bet not be pregnant," Kita joked.

"Girl, bye. That ship sailed years ago." Jackie paused. "I don't know. Maybe this glow is because, for the first time in a long time, I'm finally happy . . . like *really* happy," her eyes got watery. "I don't have to remind y'all that Christmas Eve for us was hardly something to celebrate not too long ago."

"Look at us now, though." Marlowe tried to prevent things from getting sad.

"I know that's right." Jackie wiped her eyes. "I'm here with my two beautiful kids, who are happy and healthy. Life is good."

"It's midnight, guys! Merry Christmas!" Kita had been watching the time on her phone like a hawk. "Are y'all ready to open gifts?"

"No, let's wait until morning. I don't feel like dealing with all that wrapping paper and stuff tonight," Jackie fussed.

"Let's do at least one gift, Mama, please." Without waiting for a reply, Marlowe went to the tree and grabbed an envelope for his sister and a box for his mother.

"Well, hold on before you pass out gifts. Let us give you one of yours." Jackie produced an envelope of her own, and Kita grabbed a gift from beneath the tree.

"You go first." Kita handed Marlowe a box.

He made a show of lifting it up and down, then shaking it before tearing into the paper. "Oh snap, a dash camera. This is dope. Thanks, sis."

"You're a Black man with a Benz. I just want you to be able to record if you ever get stopped by the police." Kita always worried about her brother. Though the gift was for him, it also gave her peace of mind.

"Here is mine." Jackie handed Marlowe an envelope.

"Thanks, Mama," he said before even knowing what it was. "You got me a trip to Dubai? Wow! Thank you."

"The flight and hotel accommodation credit can be used anytime within the next two years. I know you're busy, but promise me you will go. The world is so much bigger than Detroit, son."

"I promise I will go, Mama. Maybe we all can go?" It was just like Marlowe to want to include his mom and sister on his trip. Any good thing he experienced, he wanted them to experience too.

"No, baby, this trip is all yours. Maybe by then, you'll have a steady girlfriend. That way, you can take her and get started on me some grandkids."

"Anyway," he paused and handed Kita the envelope to change the subject, "here, Kita, it's your turn."

She wasted no time ripping into the gift to reveal a postdated check for $30,000. It was made out to Howard University. "Oh my God, Marlowe! This is a lot of money. Thank you so much."

"It's enough to cover your first semester's tuition in full." Unbeknownst to Kita, he'd been saving that money since the day he got into the dope game. He knew the path that he'd chosen for his life didn't lead to many places. Therefore, he wanted to ensure that the destinations on his sister's path were plentiful. "That's just to get you started. I plan to pay as you go. We ain't taking no student loans over here."

"I must be one of God's favorites to have been blessed with such a wonderful son like you. Thank you for doing that for your sister." Jackie beamed proudly.

"It ain't no thing, Mama. Merry Christmas." Marlowe handed his mother a big box.

"Baby, after Kita's gift, I don't need anything," she said while unwrapping the box to reveal another box and then another. "Boy, what is all of this, a prank?"

"Mama, you have invited so many people to Christmas dinner. I don't know how all of these people will fit in here." Marlowe continued to watch as his mother unwrapped her gift.

"Well, we may be cramped, but it'll work itself out."

Finally, Jackie had gotten to the last box. With anticipation, she opened it to reveal two silver keys. Puzzled, she glanced at Marlowe.

"I bought you a brand-new, fully furnished house. It has four bedrooms, three bathrooms, a deck, and a finished basement."

"Marlowe," was all Jackie could say as she was overcome with emotion.

"I told you, as long as I'm living, you and Kita can have the world, Mama!"

# CHAPTER SIX

Christmas Day was one for the books. To her amazement, Jackie had damn near tripled her original guestlist overnight. After seeing the 4,000-square-foot home with hardwood floors, cathedral ceilings, and a three-car garage, Jackie sent out a massive dinner invite to several close friends and even a few distant relatives. Though she was usually very humble and private, there was no way she would miss using the holiday as an opportunity to show off her new home. Jackie had something to prove because the young, fourteen-year-old version of herself, who had been put out, dissed, and forgotten, wanted to let everybody know that she wasn't a failure after all.

To ensure all of her guests had enough to eat, Jackie had to put in an emergency order with her favorite hood chef, Erica, who came through as always with ribs, chicken, dressing, macaroni, green beans, and a banana pudding. All of this was in addition to what Jackie had prepared. Needless to say, the spread was massive.

"Not right there. Slide it over some," Jackie instructed Kita, who'd already moved the same glass jar of cranberry slices three times.

"Ma, all these people are coming in less than an hour, and you got rollers in your hair." Kita placed a gentle hand on her mom's shoulder. "I know you're a perfectionist, but this layout of food looks like something from a magazine. I promise everyone will love it." She knew her mother was nervous, and for some reason, Kita was too. Due to the feud between her mother and grandmother, she'd never been around any of her family members except for Bernard and sometimes Rhonda. Over the years, she'd often wondered what her other aunt and uncle looked like and if she had cousins around her age. Jackie hadn't shared anything about her family with her children, and Rhonda hadn't either.

"Okay, I'm going to go get dressed. Please put the silverware and cups near the punch bowl and then turn on the speaker system. I need to hear The Temptations." Hastily, Jackie scurried out of the kitchen and up the hardwood stairs into her bedroom.

Instinctively, Kita moved around the beautiful, tan and white chef's kitchen in search of serving utensils.

"Damn, I can't tell you the last time I saw Mama so nervous," Marlowe spoke from the doorway of the kitchen, startling his sister, who had her back to him.

"Boy, you scared the shit out of me." Kita grabbed her chest.

"You should be scared." His brows furrowed. "What did I tell you about lacking?" Removing a gun from his waistband, he waved it in the air and placed it on the countertop. "I told you to always have that heat on you when you ain't on school premises."

"Marlowe, give me a break. We've only been in this house for three minutes. It's upstairs in my room," she whispered so that her mother wouldn't overhear the conversation about the pink .22-caliber handgun hiding under her bed. "Besides, this is the city of Novi, not the hood. We're safe here," she naively added.

"Sis, you ain't safe nowhere. How many times do I have to remind you of that?" Walking over to the built-in refrigerator system that looked like the cabinets, he reached inside and grabbed a bottle of water. "You'll be a college girl soon and living on your own. If your big brother taught you nothing else, just remember these two things." He held up two fingers. "Don't trust nobody, and keep your head on the motherfucking swivel!"

"I got you." Kita nodded, halfway listening. The cell phone vibrating across the counter had stolen her attention.

"This week, we'll be hitting the gun range, so I can show you how to use that gun I got you too."

"Okay, okay." She walked over to the phone and glanced at the name Rhonda on the screen.

"Don't be blowing me off for some little knucklehead nigga."

"Boy, chill. This ain't even my phone. It's Mommy's." She held up the phone. "Hey, Auntie Rhonda," Kita answered on the third ring.

"Hey, baby," a warm, sultry voice spoke into the speaker. "Where is your mother?"

"She's getting dressed." Kita peered at Marlowe, who was doing his best to eavesdrop.

"Oh shit!" Rhonda paused. "I was calling to tell her that I accidentally invited our mother and brother to dinner at your house today. Bernard bought me a new phone for Christmas, and I haven't figured out how to use it yet. Girl, I thought I was sending the invitation to my neighbor, Mr. Harris, because your mother said I could bring a plus one, and I fucked around and sent the message in a family group chat this morning. Please, tell her I'm sorry."

Kita's eyes widened in surprise, and so did Marlowe's. They both knew Jackie was going to lose her mind.

# CHAPTER SEVEN

Jackie returned to the kitchen thirty minutes after Rhonda's call to find her children whispering. "Kita, where's the music? And, Marlowe, you look nice, son."

"Thanks, Mama. I figured I'd play Santa and pass out a few dollars to the kids today." He laughed nervously. Aside from the Santa hat on his head, he dressed as usual in a white shirt, plain jeans, a red Gucci belt, and red Gucci loafers. Though Marlowe had money, he was far from flashy. Occasionally, you might catch him wearing an iced-out pair of Cartier buffs or Cuban link, but that was it. He hated attention because he knew it almost always brought bad news.

"What's going on in here? What's the secret?" Jackie eyeballed everything around the kitchen and then retrieved her cell phone. "I bet you Rhonda's ass called to cancel on me, didn't she?" She asked no one in particular, utterly oblivious to the tension in the room.

"Mama, Kita has something to tell you, and you might want to sit down first." With a straight face, Marlowe threw his sister directly in front of the bus.

"Markita Jones, you bet not tell me you're pregnant." The look on Jackie's face was as serious as can be. She placed her phone down and stared at her daughter for several seconds. "Girl, you better spit it out."

"Aunt Rhonda called to say she accidentally invited your mother and brother over for dinner today," Markita spewed.

For several seconds, Jackie stared off into space before shaking her head. She wanted to be mad and call her sister every messy bitch in the book, but she figured if there was ever a time to face her mother, why not do it today in her brand-new house, with her two successful children by her side? Jackie knew that even on her worst day, she was doing better than her mother, who still lived in the same run-down house and was now receiving Social Security as her only means of income. "Fuck it! The more, the merrier, right?" Her voice oozed with sarcasm. Right on cue, the doorbell rang.

After turning on the music, Jackie headed toward the door. Kita and Marlowe trailed behind, doing their best to act naturally. They both eagerly anticipated meeting their estranged relatives, but their excitement faded when Jackie opened the door. The first group of guests included Mr. Allen and some of Jackie's friends from the old building. The next wave of people to arrive consisted of Kita's crew: Kenya, Alexis, and her sister and grandmother, Ms. Barbara. Jackie proudly served her guests beverages and showed off the main level of her new home to each group. Everyone was in awe of the modern home, high-end appliances, and swank décor.

"Cheers to making it out of the hood. May we all follow suit." Allen raised a bottle of water to toast his neighbors, and the crowd erupted in applause and well wishes. The room was filled with lots of love and sincerity. Just as Jackie was about to sit on the white sectional sofa in the living area, the doorbell rang, and she went to answer.

"Oh my goodness, girl. You look so good," a tall man with a medium build, salt-and-pepper hair, and a goatee said before grabbing Jackie around the waist and lifting her a good four inches off the ground.

"Donald, I'm not the little girl you used to pick up all the time. You better put me down before you throw your back out." Though Jackie was caught off guard by his big energy, it was apparent that she was happy to see the man.

"Girl, hush up. In my eyes, you will always be little JJ." He placed Jackie back down. "Let me introduce you to my wife, Carla, and our son, DJ." He gestured toward a small-framed lady with a bob cut and adult acne and a little boy who was slightly overweight but had the cutest face. He appeared to be about seven or eight.

"Please, come in and let me introduce you to my kids." Jackie smiled. "This is my son, Marlowe, and my daughter, Markita. Guys, this is your uncle Donald."

"Wow!" Donald stared at his niece and nephew in awe. "It's so good to meet you both finally. Come give your uncle D some love." With the front door still open, he walked over and picked up Kita like he'd done Jackie. After putting her down, he extended his fist to dap Marlowe. "I ain't gon' pick you up, big fella. I already know you ain't going for it."

"Nice to meet you, man," Marlowe said in a cool tone while sizing up his uncle. There was no beef between them at the moment, but Marlowe wasn't a fan of giving people too much credit up front. He liked to catch their vibe first and then govern himself accordingly. If you were solid, then he fucked with you. If you weren't, he had a way of making you feel uncomfortable.

"JJ, you got a nice place here! I'm so proud of you."

"It's all thanks to my son." Jackie looked at Marlowe lovingly as the next group approached the doorway.

"D, I knew I heard your loud ass in here." Rhonda walked into the house carrying two bottles of wine. A man and an older woman accompanied her. Kita knew instantly that the other woman had to be her grandmother. She shared very similar features with Jackie. Aside from the gray hair and mole over her lip, she and Jackie could've been twins.

"Now, there you go with the jokes." Donald smiled. "If I was to get started on your fat ass, you'd be mad."

"Nigga, shut the hell up and take this shit to the kitchen!" Rhonda passed the bottles to her brother and then hugged her sister. "Please forgive me, girl," she whispered.

"You know you did that shit on purpose," Jackie mumbled.

"Don't be like that, Jackie. It's Christmas." Rhonda released her sister with a sly smile and hugged her niece and nephew. "Merry Christmas, y'all."

"Merry Christmas, Aunt Rhonda," Marlowe and Kita replied in unison.

An awkward silence fell upon the room and lingered for nearly a minute until Jackie decided to speak. "Dorothy," she addressed her mother.

"Jaqueline," the older woman's voice was raspy and sounded cold. Though she was dressed nicely for the festive occasion, her body language was anything but joyful. Her back was stiff, and her face was like stone. It was hard to tell if she was angry, judgmental, or both.

"Is that all you're going to say to me after all these years?" Jackie's voice was unsteady as she held back tears. Over the years, she'd often wondered how this moment would go. In her mind, her mother would be so happy to see her and practically beg for forgiveness. However, it was clear now that an apology would probably never happen.

"I know you ain't expecting me to feel sorry for you," the older woman scoffed. "Shit, you need to be thanking me."

"For what exactly?" Jackie was flabbergasted, and her voice raised an octave, causing several side conversations in the rooms to cease.

"You wanted to be grown, so I let your grown ass find your way." Her eyes wandered around the upscale living space. "Seems to me like everything worked out in your favor."

"Are you fucking ser—"

"Mama," Marlowe gently touched his mother's shoulder, "let's go eat before the food gets cold," he whispered.

"You're right, son. Let's go eat, everyone." Swiftly, Jackie ushered everyone into the dining room, temporarily putting the feud to rest.

# CHAPTER EIGHT

The room was calm for the better part of fifteen minutes as everyone helped themselves to the large spread of food. Jackie ate her meal at the head of her twelve-seat dining table, along with Marlowe and her adult guests. Kita, her friends, Tahlia, and DJ, sat on the bar stools at the kitchen counter. The home's open layout made everyone feel like they were in the same room. "Mama, you outdid yourself with this menu."

"Yeah, Mama, it's bussin'," Kita added as the other guests cosigned.

"Well, this turkey is a little dry." Dorothy leaned toward Donald, attempting to whisper. "Your sister never could cook," she laughed.

"Say it again, but a little louder this time so we all can hear you." Jackie dropped her gold, decorative fork onto the white ceramic plate with a fancy gold trim and pushed back from the table.

"Jackie, girl, can you pass me the gravy?" Rhonda tried to steer everyone away from the fire she saw starting to rise.

"Jacqueline, it seems like you want to say something, so let's clear the air." Dorothy pushed back from the table too. "What is your problem with me?"

"Bitch, *you're* the one with the problem." Jackie stood from the table, and everyone stared intently, waiting for things to escalate.

"JJ, don't call Mama out of her name," Donald added his unwanted two cents. "No matter what she did or how you feel, she's still your mother."

"Nigga, please! That bitch ain't been my mother since I was fourteen."

"Little girl, I'm not going to be too many more bitches." Dorothy slapped her hand down on the table, causing it to rattle the dishes.

"A little girl was what I was when you threw me out of your house and left me to the wolves! A little girl was what I was when I pushed my son out, afraid and alone. I needed a mother, and you said fuck me, so you know what? Fuck *you*!" Jackie spat.

"Now, wait one gotdamn minute, JJ." Donald stood from his seat at the table in defense of his mother just like he always did, even when he knew she was in the wrong.

"Nigga, what are you going do?" With a scowl, Marlowe stood too. "For a nigga that ain't got no teeth, you sure do have a lot to say!"

"Am I supposed to be scared, little nigga?" Donald made a move toward the other side of the table where Marlowe was.

"You *should* be scared!" Marlowe spat.

"Maybe I need to take my belt off and show your young ass some manners like your daddy should've done."

"What the fuck did you say?" Instinctively, Marlowe proceeded toward his uncle like a raging bull in a china shop. Everyone's eyes widened in anticipation, knowing it was about to go down.

"Son, you got five seconds to get your shit together, or it's going to be some smoke in the city. Five." Donald began counting.

"One, nigga." Without a second thought, Marlowe threw a jab so hard it sent Donald flying to the floor and commenced beating his uncle's ass all over the dining room. "Don't ever come up in here disrespecting my mother or me!" He threw several more punches. "Do you know who the fuck I am? I will *kill* you."

Jackie jumped in between the two men and begged Marlowe to stop hitting his uncle. At this point, Donald no longer posed a threat as he lay there bloody and barely able to move. "Coming here was a bad idea. Please collect your things. It's time for y'all to go."

Without being asked, Kita hopped up from her chair and quickly grabbed Dorothy, Donald, and his family's coats and belongings. One by one, she passed them out to everyone like consolation prizes.

"You should be ashamed of yourself for allowing your son to act this way. It's apparent you didn't raise that boy with any type of home training." Dorothy hastily threw on her coat. "He ain't never gon' to amount to shit, and neither will you."

"Bitch, you've been asking for an ass whopping." Jackie began marching toward her mother.

"Ma!" Kita jumped in between the women. Turning toward her grandmother, she pointed at the door. "You better leave before you end up like your son."

Without another word, Dorothy turned on the balls of her feet and marched out of the house with Donald and his family in tow. He would need medical attention from the looks of things, but Kita offered no sympathy as she slammed and locked the door behind them. Jackie apologized to the remaining guests for the altercation before grabbing some paper towels to clean the bloodstained floor, but no one seemed to mind. Marlowe apologized to his mother for disrupting her party before stepping outside on the back patio to cool off. Rhonda went into the kitchen and started filling cups with wine to get everyone back into the spirit. Everything returned to normal within minutes, and the party continued for several hours with lots of cocktails, conversations, and card games.

# CHAPTER NINE

Just as the night was ending, the doorbell rang. "Who could that be at this hour?" Jackie looked over at Rhonda, who was making a to-go plate of leftovers.

"Maybe someone came back because they forgot something." She walked over to the door and peered through the glass. "It's nobody but Bernard." She opened the door.

"Damn, is that any way to treat your favorite son?" he joked while following her through the house toward the kitchen. "What's up, Auntie?"

"Hey, B!" Jackie hugged her nephew tightly. "Where have you been, boy? I needed you on the spades table."

"My bad, Auntie. I got caught up with this chick," he smirked.

"I told you Nae had your ass pussywhipped." Marlowe entered the kitchen and gave his cousin a dap.

"Shidddd," Bernard rebutted. "I whip the pussy, not the other way around, my boy."

"Yeah, okay. Let me find out you over there playing house and keeping secrets." Marlowe laughed along with Rhonda and Jackie.

"Never that, nigga. I don't keep secrets, but apparently, *you* do." Bernard wasn't laughing.

"What the fuck is that supposed to mean?"

"Look, I've had enough family brawls today, so I'm going to leave y'all to it." Rhonda collected her belongings, hugged her sister, and told the men a good night.

"Do I need to stay and referee this shit?" Jackie gave a knowing glance at her son and nephew.

"Auntie, it ain't nothing like that. This is my man, one hundred grand. We just need to clear the air, that's all." Bernard walked over to the food and started making himself a plate.

"Okay, well, I'm going to lay it down. B, put the food up for me when you're done, and, Marlowe, please run the dishwasher. Kita already loaded up everything."

"Yes, ma'am," they replied in unison, waiting for Jackie to leave. After being sure they were alone, Marlowe sat at the kitchen counter.

"So, what's up, nigga?"

"Nigga, why didn't you tell me you upgraded the crib for Auntie Jackie?" Bernard cut to the chase. "How much did this shit hit for? At least four hundred thousand, I know."

"Since when do I need to clear my purchases by you?" Marlowe was confused. "The last time I checked, we are partners in business, not our personal lives. Did you hit my line to ask for permission when you bought that ho from the strip club a Birkin bag?"

"Ain't nobody saying you got to ask for permission, but I feel like the math ain't mathing."

"B, use your fucking words, my nigga. What exactly are you saying?" Marlowe stared hard at his cousin, trying to figure out the problem.

"I know the profit we bring in, and it ain't enough to cop this place without taking a loan, and I know you ain't putting your name on government documents." Bernard returned Marlowe's glare.

"Again, nigga, I ask, what exactly are you saying?"

"Did you make a side deal with the plug behind my back to get fronted with extra work?"

"If you must know, I used almost all of my savings to buy my mama this house outright, and the rest I gave to Kita for tuition." Marlowe was offended. "While you go around tricking your money on hoes and flashy shit, I save mine. The only reason I got into this game was to get my family out of the hood. The only reason you got in this game was to rock some ice." As Marlowe exited the kitchen, he lightly tugged at Bernard's chain. "We are *not* the same."

Bernard didn't feel bad for accusing his cousin of making a side deal because he knew that was the game, and nobody could ever be 100 percent trusted. Instead of chasing after Marlowe, he sat at the kitchen counter and silently ate his food. Markita and her friends joined him in the kitchen a few moments later. They were hunting for leftover dessert to take back to the room since Jackie said they could spend the night.

"What's up, B? When did you get here?"

"Not too long ago," Bernard said after shoving a forkful of food into his mouth. "What's up with this family brawl I heard about?"

"It went down!" Kenya chimed in.

Alexis took a seat beside Bernard. "Marlowe beat y'all uncle's ass, and Mama Jackie almost put the smack down on your grandmother."

"Word." Bernard looked to Kita for confirmation, and she nodded. "Who the fuck invited them anyway?"

"I'll give you one guess." Kita gave a telling look. "Your messy-ass mama."

"Oh shit," he shook his head. "Damn, this Christmas was lit. I hate I missed it."

"Yeah, where were you? I was looking for you." Alexis eyed him seductively.

"Is that right?" Bernard looked her up and down.

"Lex, grab what you came for, and let's head back upstairs." Kita cleared her throat. "Good seeing you, cuz. Be safe out there." She didn't wait for a response before leaving the kitchen with Kenya on her trail. Alexis got up from the bar stool and placed her hand on Bernard's dick.

"Call me sometime, B. I gave you my number a while ago."

"Man, chill. I can't do shit with your young ass." Bernard smirked in amusement.

"I'm young, but this pussy got an old soul." Flirtatiously, she removed her hand from his manhood and sashayed out of the kitchen.

# CHAPTER TEN

The holidays had come, then gone, and before Kita knew it, school was back in session. For some reason, this semester felt different than the last. Maybe it's because she was closer to being done or because she no longer lived in the neighborhood. Either way, she felt like she had mentally checked out and was no longer connected. Just as she exited the school and began walking down the sidewalk, she was tapped on the shoulder by someone with a heavy hand.

"What's up, Kita?"

"Hey, Keith." She looked up to see her potential prom date. He was holding a colorful bouquet of roses. "Aw, these are beautiful."

"I realized when I asked you to the prom the first time I just blurted it out. My sister said I should redo it with a big prom-posal, but I don't think you're that kind of girl, so I got you these instead." He handed her the flowers. "Markita, will you go to prom with me?"

"Of course I will," she said with a smile. She wrapped her arms around Keith's muscular body, and he pulled her in closer.

Suddenly, in the distance, a horn started honking loudly and for so long that Kita pulled away from the embrace and began searching for the cause of the noise. "Oh my God," she blushed.

"Is that your brother?" Keith asked nervously. He'd heard rumors about Marlowe from around the neighborhood, most of which gave him a reason to be apprehensive.

"Yep. That's him," Kita began walking toward the waiting black Infinity with triple black tint and black rims. After noticing Keith didn't move, she turned with a smile. "You may as well come and meet him if you want me to go to prom with you."

"Aww, shit, who is this nigga buying you roses and shit?" Marlowe stepped from the vehicle and teased his sister.

"You might want to ask him for some tips since you need help finding a girlfriend," Kita teased back.

Marlowe gave his sister the finger before turning his attention to Keith, who was doing his best to play cool. "What's up, homie? I'm Marlowe," he held out his fist for a dap.

"I'm Keith, bro. Nice to meet you." Keith extended his fist.

"So what's this?" Marlowe pointed toward the flowers. "Are y'all dating?"

"Nah, man, not yet anyway. I just asked Kita to the prom, and I wanted to make sure that was cool with you too."

"Prom?" Marlowe frowned. "Don't people be fucking after prom? I mean, I know I was fucking after prom."

"Really, bro?" Kita slapped her brother's arm.

"Nah, man, I'm just messing around. My sister doesn't need my permission to do anything, but I appreciate you asking. If y'all ever start dating, you'll get some cool points from me." Marlowe dapped Keith again.

"I appreciate that, Marlowe." Keith's shoulders dropped. "All right, Kita. I'll see you tomorrow."

"See you later." Kita headed over to the passenger seat and got inside.

"Check you out, sis. You got a nigga buying you flowers and shit. That's dope." Marlowe got inside the car, turned down his music, and pulled off.

"Why did you have to embarrass me like that?"

"Baby girl, I know how niggas think, so it ain't no reason to dance around the subject." Marlowe skillfully weaved in and out of traffic. "Every nigga wants pussy, but the power is yours, so be careful who you give it to. The minute you give up your pussy, you relinquish your power, remember that."

"Anyway, I didn't know you were picking me up today. Where's Mommy?" Though Kita knew she could talk to her brother about anything, sex was a topic she often steered clear of.

"She's at home, but I told her I wanted to pick you up." Marlowe looked over at his sister. "I know our sister-brother time will be coming to an end soon, so I'm just trying to savor the moment."

"Damn, don't say it like something bad is going to happen."

"Sis, I live a fast life. I don't know what will happen from minute to minute."

"Marlowe!" Kita hated it when he talked like death was around the corner.

"Girl, chill! I don't plan on leaving here anytime soon, but the fact is that you will be leaving and heading to college in less than eight months. I'm beyond happy for you but sad at the same time. These streets are no joke, Kita. I just want to use the time we've got left and give you as much game as possible." Marlowe wasn't scared of much, but the mere thought of his mother and especially his sister living in a world without him shook him to his core.

"Okay, cool, so give me the game then." Kita reached into her book bag, retrieving a notebook and a pen.

"Rule number one, never write important shit down." He removed the pen from Kita's hand. "Important shit needs to be memorized. Writing it down creates a paper trail."

"And rule number two?" Kita placed her notebook into her book bag.

"Don't trust nobody but your damn self."

"What about Mommy or my best friends?" Kita frowned.

"What did I say?" He paused. "Don't equate love with trust. You can love everyone but trust nobody. You are the only person in the world that will have your back 100 percent."

"Number three?"

"Always have an exit strategy." Marlowe brought his car to a stop at the red light.

"What does that mean for someone who isn't in the streets?" Markita paused, taking a moment to ponder rule three. "I don't sell drugs, and I don't have street beef. As a future lawyer, I doubt I'll need an exit strategy."

"Everyone needs to have a safety plan." Marlowe wasn't amused with his sister's naivety. "Let's say when you become a lawyer, you are forced into defending a client with lots of money and mob ties. The client tells you if he's found guilty, he will have someone come to your house and kill you." Marlowe watched his sister begin to get uncomfortable. "If you wait until he tells you that, it's too late to create a plan because he already has someone watching you. However, if you have a plan in place already, all you have to do is put that shit in motion, and then you'll be ten steps ahead of your ops."

"Okay, that was a good one. What's rule number four?" Kita had suddenly found value in her brother's guidance.

"It's an oldie but goodie." He paused, looking down at the cell phone vibrating in his lap. "Believe none of what you hear and half of what you see, meaning—"

"I know that one already. It means that people lie, so if I didn't see that shit with my own two eyes, it didn't happen."

"Very good, Grasshopper." He patted his sister's head as the cell phone vibrated again. This time, he answered. "What up, doe?" he paused. "Right now, I'm in the car with my sister. Can you give me about an hour?" He paused again. This time, he looked at Kita while waiting for his caller to continue. "All right. I'm on the way." He ended the call and did a U-turn in the opposite direction.

# CHAPTER ELEVEN

**K**ita rode in silence for nearly forty minutes as Marlowe sped toward his destination. She wanted to ask where they were going but decided to find out when they arrived. She knew her brother hated being asked too many questions, and it wasn't often that she got to go to important places with him, so she kept herself busy by playing DJ with the songs on Bluetooth. Although Kita was young, she had an affinity for old music. Hence, the DMX, Jay-Z, and Biggie banged nonstop through the speakers. On some songs like "Song Cry," she rapped word for word, while in other songs like "Damien," Kita simply listened to the melody while envisioning the rapper's lyrics.

"Okay, look." Reaching for the knob on the dashboard, Marlowe turned down the music. He'd just come off of the I-75 freeway. "When we get in here, don't say nothing, don't do nothing, and don't look at nobody too hard in the face."

"Damn, with all of those rules, you may as well leave me in the car." Kita peered out of the window as they drove down several back roads.

"Nah, you coming in. I need to have my eyes on you at all times." Marlowe pulled his vehicle up to the gate of a property densely covered in trees and bushes. From the main road, the three-story farmhouse was barely visible.

"Name?" A tanned foreigner wearing a black suit and wool coat appeared from behind the brush before approaching the car. Though no weapon was visible, Kita knew the man probably had something concealed.

"Marlowe," he replied while looking straight ahead.

"Who's the girl?" the man leaned closer into the car to get a better look.

"This is my sister, Markita. Arman knows she's coming."

"Hold tight." The man disappeared into the bushes for several seconds. Though he was no longer visible, his voice could be heard.

"Is he Armenian?" Kita whispered.

"Yeah, they all are. This place belongs to my connect, who is never in the States, so I'm curious about why he called this meeting," Marlowe whispered back.

Arman Vardanyan was now the head of one of the Armenian mafia families—a very powerful man. However, when he was introduced to Bernard and Marlowe, he was desperately trying to rise through the ranks and prove his worth to the heads of the other families. Those families controlled local unions and gambling commissions. In an attempt to add value to his family's name, Arman set his sights on America, hoping not only to enter but also dominate the drug trade. Quickly, he set up shop in all of the major cities in America and became the number one supplier of cocaine. His strategy was to employ young men of color who weren't afraid of risks and knew how to grind. While in Detroit, he was introduced to Bernard and Marlowe, two hustlers on the rise. Arman didn't care for Bernard, but he saw fire in Marlowe's eyes and could feel the hustle pumping through his veins. The nineteen-year-old kid was something special, and Arman took him under their wings, training him to be a kingpin one day. People within the organization questioned Arman's loyalty to the Black man, but for nearly a decade, Arman had never wavered.

As Marlowe's mind raced about why he'd be summoned, the guard returned and waved the car forward to the gates that were beginning to open. "How did you know that guy was Armenian?" Marlowe asked while driving slowly down a winding road to the main house filled with security guards.

"My favorite YouTuber is Armenian." Kita shrugged. "I can pick up on some words but not many."

"YouTube. Who would have thought." Before exiting the vehicle, Marlowe removed the gun from the waistband of his jeans and placed it into the glove compartment. "Come on. This shouldn't take long."

Together, they exited the vehicle and approached the house. Waiting on the wraparound porch were six men in similar black suits as the man at the gate. Most of them wore scowls on their faces, but one man was smiling when Marlowe approached.

"What's up, my guy?"

"Davit, what's poppin', baby?" Marlowe embraced the young man with a light hug. "This is my sister, Markita."

"Nice to meet you," Markita said to the ground as she curtsied like a fool because she was so nervous. Marlowe had told her not to talk to or look at anyone, and the first thing he does is make introductions.

"Come, follow me to my uncle's study." Davit walked into the home and headed through the living room toward the back. The modern home was decorated with colorful balloons and party streamers. Kita tried not to look at anything in particular, but with several small kids running around, it was hard not to. Just then, a little girl with pigtails and a floral dress ran right into Davit, almost knocking him over. She giggled as he spoke to her in Armenian.

"Sorry about all this, guys. As you can tell by the decorations, it's my cousin Lucine's birthday today." Davit looked back at Marlowe and Markita before reaching the study. He knocked on the brown door twice. A short Armenian man with gray hair opened it. He wore gray slacks, a white-collared shirt, black loafers, and suspenders.

"Give me one second, please." He covered the receiver on his cell phone while walking toward the bar cart in the corner of the dark room, where he removed the lid of a crystal bottle containing brown liquor and poured two drinks. Still holding the cell phone, he returned to where Kita and Marlowe were standing.

"Okay, I understand. Goodbye." After ending the call, he handed Marlowe a drink. "My wife is mad that I had to come to America this week, but it's my child's birthday. What am I going to do?" He shrugged. "Anyway, thanks for coming out here on such short notice and sacrificing time with your family, Marlowe."

"It ain't no thang, man," Marlowe replied.

"This is your sister, right?" Arman looked at Kita, who was trying her best not to look at him. "What's your name, sweetheart?"

"Markita," she answered.

"Such a beautiful name. Well, Markita, if it's okay with you, I'm going to steal your brother for a second to talk a little business. My nephew Davit will take you to the party. Please enjoy some food and cake with the other guests. We'll be done here soon, okay?"

"Okay." Without much of a choice, Kita reluctantly agreed.

"Marlowe, my boy, let's talk about your promotion." Arman closed the door.

# CHAPTER TWELVE

**W**ithout a word, Kita nervously followed Davit toward the party in the all-season room attached to the back of the house. Upon arrival, she was met with more children, a clown, and several adults sitting at a table covered in food that didn't look familiar. "Markita, this is Lucine's mother, Grace." Davit introduced the women who appeared to be similar in age.

"Help yourself, Markita. We have more than enough." Grace's smile was stunning as she pulled Kita closer to the table of food. "There is manti, dolma, lavash, lamb, harissa, and cake."

"Um, cake is fine; thank you." Kita didn't want anything but didn't want to appear rude, so she accepted the one thing on the menu that sounded familiar.

"Chocolate or vanilla?" As Grace reached for the knife to cut the cake, Lucine ran past the table. Another little girl was chasing her. Grace yelled something in Armenian, and the children slowed down momentarily.

"How old is she?" Kita wondered aloud.

"She's three," Grace replied. "Arman wants more children, but I don't know if I could keep up. Do you have kids?"

"Me?" Kita pointed at herself. "No, I'm still in high school."

"Me too, well, sort of." Grace handed Kita the cake. "I was supposed to graduate next year, but Arman has arranged for me to get my GED instead."

"So, you've been with him since you were about what . . . fifteen?" Kita was so invested in the tea that she forgot she wasn't supposed to be talking.

"Thirteen, actually," Grace coyly admitted. "My dad owed Arman money and decided to use me as payment."

"I'm sorry." Kita had heard about arrangements like this but never thought that they existed.

"Don't feel bad for me, girl. Lucine and I live here alone for the most part. We see Arman maybe six times a year, but he stays in Armenia with his wife and older children. He takes care of our needs, and he doesn't ask for much except for a little ass now and then when he's in town." Grace whispered, careful not to let her other guests hear her. It had been a long time since she'd been around someone her age. She was happy to be able to joke and gossip a little.

As the ladies continued to laugh over slices of cake, Arman and Marlowe joined them. The group watched the clown make balloon animals for the children gathered at his feet. While no one was looking, Lucine inched her way over to the table and snuck a grape. Afraid that someone would catch her, she swallowed the whole thing and instantly began to choke. No one saw the little girl in distress as she tried to throw up. Finally, Grace looked down at her toddler, who was turning blue, and screamed. "Oh my God, please, someone help!"

Without reservation, Markita dropped to her knees and began performing the Heimlich maneuver on the little girl. After several abdomen compressions, the grape flew across the room, and Lucine began to cry. Grace cried too as she picked up her baby and consoled her. Arman pulled Kita to her feet and grabbed her tightly.

"Thank you so much! You saved my daughter without hesitation, and for that, I will forever be indebted to you." Instinctively, he reached into his pants pocket and retrieved several crisp hundred-dollar bills. "What you did for me is priceless, but please, let me give you something."

"No, please, don't." Kita insisted, looking the older man in his face for the first time. "I'm just glad I was here."

"Oh my God, I was so scared. How did you know how to do that?" Grace wrapped her arms around Kita.

"I took a class last summer." Kita looked over at Marlowe, who was smiling because he'd been the one who forced her into taking the safety class.

"Markita, I owe you one, I really do." Arman looked back at Marlowe. "Your sister is welcome here anytime. Hell, I prefer her over that fuckup you call your cousin, but anyway, that's another story," he laughed. "I know you guys have got to get going, so take this." He placed the stack of money into Kita's hand. "I'll be seeing you soon."

"Thank you, sir," Kita extended her hand, and Arman shook it. Next, she hugged Lucine and said goodbye to Grace before leaving with her brother the way they'd come.

Once in the car and out of the gate, Kita pulled the money from her pocket and counted. "He gave me almost $3,000!"

"That was a cool thing you did back there."

"Did you know that girl Grace is younger than me?" Markita sat back in her seat.

"I kind of figured, but that ain't none of my business." Marlowe glanced out of the window.

"Her father sold her to Arman to pay off his debt."

"Damn, what happened to not talking to anybody?" Marlowe gave his sister the side eye.

"I didn't ask her. She volunteered that information." Kita crossed her arms in a matter-of-fact way.

"That's all fine and cool, but she ain't your friend, Kita, so I hope y'all didn't exchange numbers and shit."

"No, we didn't."

"Those people in there might seem friendly, but they aren't." Marlowe's tone indicated that he meant business. "Those people will kill everybody you know and hide the bodies where no one will ever find them."

"Why doesn't Arman like Bernard?"

"You know B. He's too flashy, and he doesn't take shit as seriously as he should. From the moment we started getting work from Arman a couple of years ago, he made it clear that Bernard gets no access to him. Cuz is cool with that, though, as long as we split the profits 50/50. Arman wants to take over the world's drug trade, and B is just content with being the King of Detroit."

"What do you want from this game?" Kita had never sat down and discussed the drug business with her brother. However, she figured now was the best time to ask since he was talking.

"All I ever wanted was to take care of you and Mama. Now that y'all don't need me as much, a nigga been thinking about ways to turn this street money into legal streams of income." He paused. "I guess what I'm trying to say is that I want to create generational wealth for my kids, your kids, our family."

"You don't have to be in the streets to do that."

"Shit, the streets are the only thing I know, and I'm good at what I do." Marlowe turned on his blinker and merged onto the freeway while turning up the volume on the radio, indicating that the conversation had ended.

# CHAPTER THIRTEEN

It was Friday night, and Alexis convinced Kenya and Kita to sneak into a twenty-one+ club called Mirage with fake identification. As someone who stayed in the streets, Lex knew everybody, and tonight was no exception. At least three people had come over to greet her in the past ten minutes.

"Bitch, it's thick as hell out here tonight." Kita surveyed the line; it was damn near wrapped around the building.

"The flyer said Young Z would be performing." Lex moved from side to side, trying to stay warm. She wore a fishnet bodysuit with a black bra, denim shorts, and black thigh boots.

"I see your ass shivering," Kenya laughed. "I told both of y'all to put on some clothes. This Detroit winter ain't no joke." She was dressed warmly in a fitted black, long-sleeved top, army fatigue pants, and combat boots. "We got at least another hour in this line before we reach the door."

"All I know is," Kita's teeth clicked together, "when we do get to the front of the line, these IDs better get us through. I ain't trying to be embarrassed." She pulled her long-sleeved, red, bodycon minidress closer to her knees. The sheer pantyhose and suede thigh boots did nothing to comfort her cold skin.

"Bitch, don't ever doubt me." Alexis was offended. "Your black ass just better make sure you remember the year of your birthday."

The ladies all cracked up laughing as the line inched forward slightly. They talked and took pictures for several minutes until, finally, the line moved again.

"Sexy Lex, is that you?" The voice came from the group of men bypassing the entrance line.

"What's up, Breeze?" Alexis wasted no time wrapping her arms around the fine thug she'd met at the gas station a few months ago. At the time, he was outside selling CDs, hopeful for a come-up, but it looked like he'd already made it tonight. "I love the Amiri fit, and I see your ice," Alexis complimented in a sultry voice.

"Are these your girls?" Breeze stared at Kenya and Kita.

"Yeah, I finally got them to come out with me, but tonight might be a loss by the looks of this line."

"Nah, y'all ain't going home." He pulled Alexis by the hand. "Y'all can roll with me and my niggas. We got a booth and some bottles."

With a large smile, Alexis followed Breeze with his boys and her girls in tow. As they approached the bouncer, Kita and Kenya peered at each other. Neither wanted to be embarrassed, especially in front of Breeze's crew. Luckily for them, the bouncer didn't ask to see IDs. He simply asked Breeze how many people were with him, took a head count, and let everyone pass. Kita and Kenya were thrilled to be out of the cold as they walked through the dimly lit club to the reserved section and took a seat. On the other hand, Alexis hit the dance floor because her song was on.

"I got vodka, tequila, and Hennessy. What are y'all drinking?" Breeze leaned down and whispered between Kenya and Kita.

"I'll take Hennessey," Kita announced.

"Oh, so you a Cognac lady. I can fuck with that." Breeze poured Markita's drink and handed it to her. "What about you, slim?"

"I'm good. I don't drink. I smoke." Kenya replied.

"Say less." He tapped his boy's shoulder, whispered something, and was handed a blunt.

"Can we smoke in here?" Kenya asked.

"Man, y'all with me. We good over here."

After making sure the ladies were straight, Breeze joined his boys. They were leaning over the railing, getting turned up to the music. The club was packed, and everybody was vibing. After about twenty minutes, Alexis finally joined her friends in the section. She helped herself to a double shot of Hennessy and plopped down on the leather seating.

"Bitch, look at you drinking Hennessy." She held her plastic cup toward Kita.

"Marlowe always says, 'Hennything is possible.'" Kita clicked cups and toasted as Kenya blew out smoke rings.

The ladies danced, laughed for almost two hours, and had a ball in their section. Breeze and his boys made it rain on everybody standing below them, and then Young Z hit the stage. Though he was a new rapper, his songs were widely known. Damn near the entire club rapped with him word for word. His last song, "Dance," was a banger that had strip clubs worldwide going crazy. Alexis took this as an opportunity to show Breeze what she was working with. She knew Breeze was an up-and-coming hustler. Therefore, she wanted to secure her spot before he reached his full potential.

Like an exotic dancer, she shook her ass like her life depended on it. Making a show of moving her hips from left to right, she had Breeze caught in the *Matrix*. For a second, he forgot where they were as he grabbed Alexis's stomach and pulled her down on his rock-hard dick. "Damn, baby, I want to fuck you bad right now."

"Then do it." Alexis grabbed the Hennessy bottle and poured some liquor into her mouth.

"Right here, in the club?" Breeze had dealt with some freaky bitches in his lifetime, but he'd never done anything this wild.

"Hell yeah, right here in the club, but you know this pussy ain't free. You got to pay to play, my baby." She never lost the rhythm as she threw her ass back.

Breeze reached into his pocket and removed a wad of cash and a condom. After placing the money into Alexis's bra, he quickly put on the Magnum condom and ripped the crotch of her shorts. Before she had time to say anything about that, his dick was beating up her insides like sound coming through the speakers. Kita and Kenya looked at each other in awe at what was happening. They knew their friend was different, but this was wild.

For fifteen minutes, Breeze fucked Alexis in multiple positions until she climaxed. When she was done, she lifted herself off of his dick and began giving him head with the condom still on. It was at this point that both Kita and Kenya lost their minds, and Breeze lost his load right in Alexis's mouth. After taking a minute to clean up and gather himself, he leaned down and pulled Alexis close. "You know you're my bitch now, right?"

"I wouldn't have it any other way, baby." With a look of satisfaction, she wiped her mouth and reapplied her lipstick.

# CHAPTER FOURTEEN

It was a little before two in the morning when Kita decided she was ready to leave the club. Growing up, her brother had always warned her about being in the parking lot after a club closed. In Detroit, everyone who had beef in the club wound up fighting in the parking lot, and those fights would almost always end in gunfire, with an innocent bystander being hurt.

"Are you ready, Lex?"

"Nah," Alexis spoke while planting soft kisses on Breeze's neck. "Y'all go ahead. He got me."

"Girl, you are tripping." Kenya was irritated. "We came together, we leave together. You know the deal."

"She said she's good!" Breeze looked Kenya up and down. "My boy Al will walk y'all to the car, but I got Lex." He slapped Alexis on the ass.

"Fuck it then." Kita rolled her eyes and exited the booth with Kenya and Al. No one said a word as they walked out of the club and toward the street, where they waited for car service. Outside was now a ghost town; other than the muffled sound of club music, the streets were eerily silent.

"So, what's good? Are y'all trying to get into something tonight?" Al grabbed his dick while trying to shoot his shot.

"Yeah, my bed, nigga," Kenya laughed.

"Bitch, who the fuck are you laughing at?" Al hollered, catching both ladies by surprise.

"Damn, it ain't that serious, nigga. Calm down!" Markita snapped.

"You bitches are all the same. Y'all wanna kick it in a nigga's section, drink off a nigga's bottle, and smoke a nigga's weed, but always end up shocked at the end of the night when a nigga wants some pussy. Your girl in there knows what time it is, but you bitches are lame as fuck!"

"We can't be no lamer than your ass out here begging for pussy! Nigga, if you had some real game, you—" Kita didn't get the chance to finish before Al backhanded the fuck out of her face, sending her to the ground.

"You a dead nigga!" Kita fumbled with her phone.

"Yeah, whatever, bitch!" Al gave Kita the middle finger before heading back inside the club.

"Are you okay, girl?" Kenya tried to inspect her friend for damages. Other than a leaking eye, she was fine.

"Yeah, I'm good, but I hope this shit doesn't swell." She inspected her face in the reflection of a car window while managing to dial Marlowe. He answered on the second ring.

"Please tell me why your ass is on the East Side of all places at two in the morning." He used his best big brother voice. Several hours ago, he'd gotten a notification from a tracking app on his phone that his sister was on the go. Although he despised the East Side, he didn't call her and trip because he remembered what it was like to be young and adventurous.

"Marlowe," she whimpered.

"Stay on the phone. I'm on the way!" He didn't need to know what the problem was. All that mattered was that his sister was in trouble.

Within thirty minutes, an old-school, white Impala pulled up to the club on two wheels. Quickly. Marlowe spotted the girls waiting near the building and pulled beside them. The clubgoers were beginning to flood the parking lot. With rage in his eyes and a nine-millimeter handgun in his jeans, he walked up to the car and tapped on the window. When Kita opened the door, the interior light came on, and Marlowe could see that her left eye was swollen. "Aw, hell no! What happened?"

"It was Al," was all Markita managed to say because she was still in shock that he had hit her. As she began to cry again, Kenya took the opportunity to fill in the blanks. Just as she finished the story, Breeze, Al, Alexis, and the rest of Breeze's crew were headed toward them.

"It was him with the braids," Kenya pointed.

"Aye, nigga," Marlowe removed the gun from his jeans before walking up to the crew of young boys. "You got five seconds to tell me why I shouldn't kill your ass for hitting my sister."

"Man, fuck that bitch!" Al dismissed the situation and kept walking. His boys began reaching for the weapons they had concealed. In their minds, this showdown was going to be easy. It was one against many.

"Breeze, you better tell these niggas who the fuck I am." Marlowe took the time to look every nigga in the pupils, one by one. "Right now, this beef is between me and this nigga, but if y'all niggas want the smoke, we can get active!"

"Y'all chill. Put them guns up," Breeze said reluctantly. He hated to betray his boy, but he knew that Marlowe had the drug trade in the city on lock. Though Breeze didn't get his supply directly from Marlowe, he knew that with one call, Marlowe could turn his connection off and make his pockets dryer than the Arizona desert.

"For real, Breeze, it's like that?" Al couldn't believe what he was hearing.

"Nigga, you made it like that when you hit this nigga's sister. I told you about that temper."

"Fuck it then, nigga; let's go." He squared up, but it was a little too late. Marlowe came with a jab that Al had never seen coming. It was followed up with several uppercuts and stomach punches. Although dazed, Al managed to rush Marlowe, taking him by the waist and lifting him off the ground before slamming him on his back. Everyone in the parking lot began to surround the men. Several people started hollering side bets on who they thought would win. It didn't take Marlowe long before he could regain control of the fight. He finished his opponent with three blows to the face and a swift kick to the head.

"Don't ever fuck with mine again, or you'll be a dead nigga next time!" Marlowe spat blood on the ground before walking back toward his car. He stopped abruptly and turned toward Breeze's crew. "Alexis, get your ass in the car, and don't make me repeat it!"

# CHAPTER FIFTEEN

The ride was silent as Marlowe pondered what to say. He wasn't mad that his sister and her friends snuck into a club with fake identification and got wasted. He wasn't even angry that he had to fight a nigga. However, he was highly irritated that he was in the middle of moving weight when he had to come to save the day. Usually, when he transported his product from the warehouse to the trap house, he would do so alone, quickly, and discreetly. He always used a rental or a borrowed car, and he would always go to and from his destination with no stops in between. However, here he was with a trunkful of cocaine, riding his drunk sister around like a gotdamn Uber.

"You could have left me with Kenya when you dropped her and Lex off." Kita was reclined in the seat with her eyes closed.

"Nah. Y'all have had enough fun for the night." Marlowe shook his head. "I'm going to make a quick stop, and then I'm taking you to my crib to sleep off whatever you drank."

"Can we stop and get some coney dogs and chili cheese fries?" Kita's munchies were kicking in, and she knew Coney Island was the perfect late-night spot.

"Aye, why was your girl coming out of the club with Breeze and not outside already with y'all?" Marlowe bypassed her food request. He was trying to get to his destination and then get home.

"I guess that's her new man."

"Since when?"

"Since tonight," Markita slurred her words.

"Tell Shorty to be careful. There's something about that little nigga that I don't like."

"Bro, it ain't too many people that you do like, so that's not saying much," she giggled before frantically lifting in her seat and rolling her window down.

"Aw shit! Are you about to throw up?"

Before Kita could respond, the contents of her stomach violently escaped from her mouth all over the side of the car. Instinctively, Marlowe pulled the car to a stop so Kita could open the door and get out. For several minutes, he listened to her call Earl outside. Every time she thought she was done, her stomach began to bubble, and more liquid erupted. Marlowe was just about to lose his shit and tell her to hurry up when a black patrol car passed by them and did a U-turn.

"Fuck! It's five-o, Kita; be cool," he whispered, but Kita was in a world of her own.

Time seemingly went in slow motion as Marlowe waited for the officer to approach his vehicle. He knew the cop was probably running his plate, but he wasn't worried because the title and registration were clean. He just hoped the officer didn't get too nosy and search the vehicle. In Detroit, Marlowe knew his permission was a nonfactor, and warrants and protocol were a myth.

"Good evening, Officer," he said calmly when the officer approached the window. It was too dark to see the officer's face, but Marlowe could see he was in full uniform.

"License and registration," the officer spoke to Marlowe while looking at Kita. "Is everything okay with your friend over there?"

"That's my little sister. She thought it was a good idea to sneak and have a few drinks with her friends tonight. I went to pick her up, and now I'm about to take her home."

"Does she have identification?" The officer walked over to Kita, who was throwing up yet again.

"Probably not, but her name is Markita Jones," Marlowe hollered, not wanting to take a chance on her volunteering more information than was needed while intoxicated, but it was too late.

"I have ID in my purse." Kita tugged at the wristlet hanging from her arm and produced an identification card.

"This here says Candace Miller." With a puzzled expression, the officer looked from Kita to Marlowe and back again. Nervously, she wiped the mascara and tears falling down her face, and that's when he noticed her swollen eye. "I don't know if I believe this young lady is your sister," the officer paused. "I don't know if you watch the news, but sex trafficking is at an all-time high. How do I know this isn't one of those situations?"

"Officer, I'm sure this looks crazy, but I assure you this is my sister. She and her friends used fake IDs to get into the club tonight. That's what you're holding."

"Hold tight." He began to walk away.

"Sir, please call Detective Douglas from the Fifth Precinct. He'll vouch for me," Marlowe hollered out of the window while glaring at Kita. Though the corrupt cop was the last person he wanted to see tonight, he realized he was fresh out of options.

With his hand on the radio attached to his uniform shirt, the officer stared at Marlowe as he thought about what to do. He'd only been on the beat solo for a little over ninety days and knew his decision could affect how the rest of his tenured colleagues saw him. On the one hand, he wanted to be the hero who trusted his gut and apprehended a would-be trafficker, but on the other hand, he wanted to be a team player. He knew climbing the ranks to make detective was more about who you knew than what you knew, and perhaps making this call would be the introduction he needed to build the alliances he required.

"A'ight, I'll call him. Sit tight."

Twenty minutes later, a silver Dodge Challenger with tinted windows pulled up to the scene. Stepping from the vehicle was an older white man with balding, grayish hair and some serious razor bumps. He was dressed in a cheap, wrinkled suit and smelled of Newport cigarettes and Trident gum. "I'll take it from here, kid."

"Here is what I collected, sir." The younger officer handed over the ID cards and registration. "He said this is sister, but I don't think so."

"Barkley," Detective Douglas leaned close to read the officer's badge, "I said I'll take it from here." Reaching into his pocket, he pulled out a twenty-dollar bill. "Take this and go buy yourself something to eat."

"How should I write up the paperwork?" Officer Barkley asked while reaching for the money.

"What paperwork?" Detective Douglas looked at his colleague.

"Sorry; got it." Officer Barkley nodded his understanding before returning to his vehicle and pulling away.

Detective Douglas walked up to the car with a smug look. "Moneymaking Marlowe . . . Do they still call you that these days?"

"Nah, man, nobody ever called me that."

"You're pretty far from your neck of the woods tonight, wouldn't you say?"

"Yeah, something like that," Marlowe shifted his gaze to Kita. "Look, man, I needed to get that cop off my ass so I can get my sister home. Let me pay you for your time so I get the fuck out of here."

"Whoa, man, slow your roll. What's the rush?" He began looking in the car's back windows before resting his sights on the trunk. "For you to have called me for help, I know there is something in this vehicle you didn't want Barkley to find."

"It ain't nothing like that. I was just tired of wasting my time with that beat cop trying to play detective."

"Cute, but pop the fucking trunk," Detective Douglas demanded.

"Suit yourself," Marlowe bluffed. Just as he was about to open his trunk, an older Black woman appeared on her porch with a cell phone aimed in their direction.

"This boy has been pulled over for too damn long and ain't gone to jail yet, so it leads me to believe that DPD ain't got nothing else better to do than to harass him." The woman began walking closer. "Young man, I am recording for your protection. You will not be shot for driving while Black on my watch!"

"Ma'am, please go back in the house," Detective Douglas instructed.

"This is my property, and I know my rights. I can record, and there is nothing you can do about it."

"Thank you, ma'am. I surely appreciate your kindness," Marlowe smiled harder than a fat rat in a cheese factory.

"Okay, sir, you're good to go. Have a good night." Detective Douglas leaned into the window and handed Marlowe his documents. "I'll be sure to catch up with your ass soon."

"Stay safe out here, Detective!" With those words, Marlowe tossed two hundred-dollar bills out the window and pulled off into the night, putting as much distance between him and the East Side as possible.

# CHAPTER SIXTEEN

**M**arkita hadn't seen much of her brother or her friends since their wild night at the club two months ago. Though Marlowe didn't say it, she knew he was pissed with her, and she couldn't blame him, but it did make her sad, especially today of all days. "Girl, why are you still in here sulking when there's a whole party going on downstairs for you?" Kenya entered Kita's room without knocking.

"It doesn't seem like much of a birthday if you ask me." Kita was lying across her bed, staring at the ceiling with her hands across her chest.

"Bitch, it's your eighteenth birthday . . . you know . . . the biggest birthday milestone you'll ever have in life besides turning twenty-one." Alexis entered the room holding a small gift wrapped in pink paper.

"Who invited you?" Kita sat up and glared at Alexis. "This whole this is *your* fucking fault anyway."

"Now, hold up. That shit ain't fair." Alexis plopped down on the bed. "If I recall, this whole thing happened because your spoiled ass just had to call your brother that night."

"What was I supposed to do?" Kita snapped. "Your boyfriend's friend fucking hit me, or did you forget *that* part because you were too busy being fucked in the club with your nasty ass."

"Bitch, call it what you want, but I do what I have to do to secure the bag." Alexis stood. "Some of us don't have brothers to bankroll our lifestyle or mothers to tuck us in at night." A tear ran down her cheek. "While your privileged ass is in la-la land, the rest of us live in the real world, and it's cold as a motherfucker out here."

"Look, y'all both have valid points, but it's not that deep." Kenya walked closer to her friends and grabbed their hands. "Because of this shit, we haven't kicked it like we used to, and that doesn't feel right to me. Life is too short to have my besties beefing, so can we please put this behind us and go party?"

"I only fight with y'all because y'all are my sisters. I'm sorry for the part I played." Kita hugged her girls.

"I'm sorry too. I would kill or do time for either one of you because I love you that much. Y'all are my sisters for life." Alexis returned Kita's embrace.

"Yeah, yeah, sisters for life . . . Now, let's go eat!" Kenya broke the embrace and led the women out of the bedroom.

Downstairs, the party was in full swing as the partygoers danced to the music blaring through the speakers. "*Wobble baby . . . wobble baby . . . wobble baby.*" Several women were in the middle of the floor, shaking and gyrating their ample frames, trying to outdo one another.

"Come on, Kita, let's dance. This is the one hustle routine I know! If they put that Tamia on, it's over for me." Alexis tugged on the tail of her friend's shirt.

"Nah, you go ahead. I'll be outside checking on the food." Ever since her mother lit the grill, she had her mind set on eating a rib tip sandwich.

"Boring!" Alexis pulled Kenya into the crowd and tried to teach her the moves.

As if her mother knew she was coming, she prepared a plate of rib tips and a piece of white bread. "Happy Birthday, baby."

"Thank you, Mama." Kita took a bite of the flavorsome meal, getting barbeque sauce all over her lips and fingers. "Bussin'!"

"Girl, you always say that. I'm beginning to think you're just gassing me up." Jackie tried to sound hip.

"Mama, you outdid yourself with this party. Thank you again."

"After the way Christmas went, I figured your birthday would be the perfect time for a redo," she laughed. "This time, I only invited friends from the old neighborhood, though. I can't do that family drama again." Just then, the Wobble ended, but the DJ kept the momentum going by transitioning into the Cha-Cha Slide. Jackie flew inside. "This is my jam!"

"These Detroiters love to hustle, don't they?" Markita joked with one of her mother's friends sitting outside having a smoke break. Together, they shared a laugh before returning to the house.

While Kita finished her food in the kitchen, she took a moment to survey the colorful décor her mother had strategically placed throughout the house. There was a giant Happy Birthday banner hanging from the ceiling. Jackie also had streamers and balloons everywhere. There was even a large card resting on an easel for all to sign.

"Kita, come over here and stand next to these balloons." Jackie waited patiently beside a giant one and eight balloon, with her cell phone ready.

"Mama, I'll take the picture, but I can't with the balloons. I'm eighteen, not eight," she complained.

"Girl, come on and take the picture! You know I'm not letting up. I did the same thing when Marlowe turned eighteen." Jackie began clicking away.

"Speaking of Marlowe, have you talked to him?"

"Not since this morning, but he promised to be here. You know that boy has been busier than the president for the past few months." Jackie stroked her daughter's hair. "Don't worry. Knowing your brother, he's probably out trying to purchase you some elaborate gift or something."

"I hope it's a car! I'm tired of being picked up and dropped off at school." She had been circling ads in the Auto Trader magazine for nearly a year but never outright asked because her brother had already done so much for them.

"It wouldn't surprise me. Your brother would give you the world if he could."

"Hey, Jackie, I'm sorry I can't stay, but I appreciate the invite and the plate." Terri Frisk, an old neighbor, reached out for a hug. "Happy Birthday again, Kita. I hate I will miss my boy Marlowe, but please give him my love. That boy is a godsend."

"He sure is!" Mr. Allen added. "Just an all-around great person and blessing to the community."

"Thank you, guys. Hearing you say those things about my son means a lot." Jackie beamed with pride. Kita wanted to remind everyone that it was *her* birthday, and if anyone should be praised today, it should've been her, but she had to give credit where it was due. Marlowe was all of what people said he was, and then some. He took care of people in the old neighborhood. He paid the youngsters to assist the elderly and disabled with odds and ends around their homes, like cleaning and running errands. He'd also randomly gift homeless people with money or hot meals.

"Thank you again, Jackie. Happy Birthday, Kita," Linda Harris, one of Jackie's old coworkers, walked out with the others.

"He better show up before the party dies down, and nobody is going to get to see my car," Markita pouted.

"He will be here; don't worry," Jackie winked.

# CHAPTER SEVENTEEN

Though Kita did her best to enjoy her party, two hours had passed, and Marlowe still hadn't arrived. Looking at her call log, she noted that she had called his cell phone over thirty times, and each call went to voicemail. "Something isn't right." Markita paced the living room floor. Her spirit told her that her brother was in trouble. Jackie wanted to calm her daughter's nerves, but she had to admit that this wasn't like her son. When he said he was going to do something, he did it. Just as Kita was about to dial her brother again, Alexis hollered, "It's Marlowe!"

"Thank God!" Jackie shouted, and a sense of relief came over the room. Everyone eagerly rushed outside to greet him as if it were his birthday.

Kita flew outside with the crowd to see what surprise Marlowe had waiting for her. However, the minute she stepped foot onto the driveway, her whole world shattered. Marlowe was behind the wheel of a black Yukon Denali that had rolled onto the sidewalk and collided with a green electrical box. From her position, she could see that the body of the vehicle had been riddled with bullets. In sync, several people started screaming for help. "He's been shot!" "Somebody, call an ambulance."

Markita frantically screamed her brother's name as she ran over to the vehicle, which was now smoking. She pulled on the door, but it was locked. Thinking fast, she grabbed a rock near her feet and broke the glass. The windows were tinted, so it wasn't until the glass shattered that Markita saw her brother slumped over toward the passenger seat. Hysterically, she reached in, unlocked the door, and pulled him out. The tan Versace hoodie Marlowe was wearing had turned bright red.

"Dammit! Don't die! Please, don't die," Kita screamed. "Marlowe, what happened? Who did this shit?"

"I don't know." He coughed, and blood spilled down his chin. "Right now, that doesn't matter. I got some work and two guns in the back. Grab that shit and hide it for me, Kita." Marlowe spoke with strenuous breaths and continued to cough up blood. Kita was elated to see that her brother was alive.

"Marlowe, baby, what happened?" Jackie ran up to the SUV and dropped down to cradle her son. One of her worst fears had come true. Knowing the life Marlowe lived, she always wondered when the day would come that something like this would happen. No mother ever thinks of burying one of her children. However, staring down at her firstborn covered in blood made the scenario too real. "Where are you hurt, baby?" she cried while nervously searching his body for wounds.

"Kita, handle that shit." Marlowe momentarily ignored his mother. He was ambushed when he'd been on the way to make a drop. Never in his right mind would he have taken drugs into his mother's home. However, the adrenaline of being shot and the fear of dying alone led him straight to his safe haven. "Kita, do you got me?" He needed reassurance. If the police found all the drugs in the trunk, he would surely be going upstate for a very long time.

"OK. OK, I got you." Kita wiped the tears off her face and went to the back of the vehicle to retrieve the product as instructed.

Popping the trunk of the truck, she saw a large duffle bag. After struggling to remove it, she closed the trunk and carried the bag into the house. Several people gathered around the scene, but no one was paying her any attention as their eyes were on Marlowe. Once inside the house, her mind raced. *What if the police come with a raid? Should I flush the dope?* Markita knew that the police would have to have a warrant to search her mother's house. Therefore, she decided to hide the bag instead of flushing it.

Flying toward the basement like a madwoman, she grabbed one of the large Rubbermaid containers her mother used to store Christmas stuff. After dumping the contents to the ground, she tossed the bag inside. Thinking fast, she slid the container into the utility closet, covered it with old blankets, and then headed back outside to check on her brother. When she got to the scene, the ambulance and one squad car were present. Kita was relieved. Typically, in the city, the police took forever to respond, but this was the suburbs. "Is he going to be all right?" she asked her mother as they closed the ambulance door. Kenya and Alexis were consoling Jackie.

"He's been shot multiple times." Jackie could barely get her words out. "Due to the nature of the situation, they said I can't ride with him, so I'm going to drive."

"Mama Jackie, let me drive you," Kenya volunteered.

"Okay, thank you, sweetie." Jackie was dazed.

"Are you coming, Kita?" Kenya asked.

"No, I can't." Kita began to cry as fear gripped her heart. She felt like being at the hospital would make the thought of losing her brother more real than it already was. "Just take care of my mother and keep me posted."

# CHAPTER EIGHTEEN

After the ambulance and Jackie pulled away from the house, the party guests slowly dispersed too. For the better part of an hour, Kita looked out of the front window as the police collected as much evidence as they could from the crime scene. A news van from Channel Two had also arrived on the scene after news of the suburban incident went viral on social media.

"I can't believe this bullshit!" Alexis paced back and forth in the living room. She wanted to be out in the street collecting information about the shooting, but there was no way she could leave her friend. Although Kita wasn't showing it, she knew her friend was devastated. How could such a beautiful day of celebration turn so tragic?

"Me either." Kita sat on the couch, staring down at her blood-covered hands. Silently, she wondered why anyone would want to harm Marlowe and knew whoever did it would probably turn up dead tonight. Marlowe was a well-loved individual. Once word got out about what happened to him, his people would most likely comb every inch of Detroit and its surrounding cities until the perpetrator was found.

"Have you heard anything from your mother?"

"No," Kita replied solemnly. She wanted to remind Alexis that she had been sitting there with her for the whole hour her mother had been gone, but decided against it. It was no use starting an argument with Alexis when she was just as concerned as she was. "Let me call Kenya and see if they know anything yet."

Just as she reached for the phone, someone knocked at the door. Kita wasn't in the mood to speak with any nosy neighbors, so Alexis went to open it. Aunt Rhonda sashayed in, wearing a frightened expression as she dropped beside her niece. "Is he all right?"

"I don't know, Auntie." Kita shrugged. "I haven't heard from my mom or Kenya since they left."

"Well, no news is good news, baby." Rhonda patted Kita's knee. Just then, there was another knock at the door. "That's Bernard. He drove me over here."

Alexis opened the door, and Bernard walked in. He looked a mess and smelled like liquor, with tears in his eyes and his jowls clinched tight. He didn't say anything to anyone as he walked over to Kita and wrapped his arms around her. "I know real niggas ain't supposed to cry, but that is my fucking brother, man! He has been my right-hand man since we were pups. I'm fucked up behind this."

"I know, B!" Kita consoled her cousin while Rhonda and Alexis shed silent tears.

"I was supposed to do the drop today, but I was running behind, and Marlowe insisted he go so everybody got what they needed on time." Bernard wiped his face. "Those shots were probably meant for me."

"B, do you know who could've done this?" Alexis asked the question everyone wondered about.

"We've been running these streets for a long time, so it could've been anybody. Please believe I'm on it, though; when I find out who it is, it's over. Did Marlowe say anything or mention any names?"

"Lord, have mercy!" Rhonda shouted. "The last thing this family needs is more blood on our hands. You all need to take this situation with Marlowe as a sign to repent and start living right."

"Rhonda, I can't have this conversation right now!" Bernard stood abruptly and exited the house.

"Girls, I don't know what to say about all of this. Lord knows I've tried to do my best with Bernard and the same as your mama did with Marlowe. Maybe we should have taken them to church or prayed a little harder. The Bible tells us if you live by the streets, you'll die by the streets. They need to get right with God and walk the straight and narrow."

"Auntie," Kita sighed, "I don't know where in the Bible it says that, but can we hold this conversation another time, perhaps when I know my brother is all right?"

"I'm sorry, baby." Rhonda stood. "I didn't mean any harm."

"It's all good. I'll call you when I get an update." Swiftly, Kita ushered her aunt toward the door.

Once the girls were alone, Alexis reached into her purse and retrieved a blunt. "You know I can't stand that bitch, right?" After lighting the marijuana, she inhaled and passed it to Kita.

"Join the club." Kita laughed, then inhaled. Before she could exhale, there was another knock at the door. For a second, she thought about not answering, but she knew it was probably her aunt or Bernard returning for something they had left. Without checking the peephole, Kita swung the door open and blew out a big smoke cloud. She did nothing to conceal the blunt because she needed it on a day like today for medicinal purposes. Besides, recreational weed was legal in Michigan.

"Hello, I'm Detective Traci Knox, and this is my partner, Detective Brice Walters." A plainclothes female detective lifted her badge for Kita to see. "We're here investigating the shooting of Marlowe Jones. It's my understanding he was your brother, right?"

"He *is* my brother, bitch!" Kita corrected her. Unless she knew something Kita didn't, how dare this bitch use past tense like Marlowe was dead.

"My apologies, Ms. Jones. May we come in?"

"Why?" With the blunt hanging from her mouth, Kita folded her arms. She knew better than to let anybody into her house without a warrant.

"We would like to discuss what happened to your brother." Traci looked agitated.

"Lady, I don't know what happened, and I didn't see anything. He showed up here shot."

"Did he say who did this?" Detective Walters was holding a notebook and pencil. "Several witnesses on the scene told us that you two spoke briefly before he was taken to the hospital."

"I asked him who did this, but he said he didn't know."

"Okay," Detective Knox reached into her pocket and produced a business card. "Here is my number. Please call me if you hear something that might be valuable to the case."

Kita hesitated before taking the card and then closing the door. She stared briefly at it before entering the kitchen and throwing it away. As she tried to collect her thoughts, the doorbell rang again. With an attitude, she hastily pulled it open. "What?"

"Hi. Sorry to disturb you, but I have a delivery for Markita Jones." A bald, white man stood on the porch wearing a suit and an awkward smile.

"That's me," she frowned.

"My name is Jack." He extended a small box. "Your brother Marlowe gave me instructions to deliver your birthday gift today. Happy Birthday!"

With sadness in her eyes, Kita peered behind the man to see a large vehicle trailer backing into the driveway. She couldn't tell what kind of car was being delivered, but it didn't matter because she couldn't get excited. Right now, the only birthday gift she wanted was for her brother to be okay.

# CHAPTER NINETEEN

It took nearly four hours after Marlowe had pulled into his mother's driveway for the police to wrap up the crime scene. Markita watched out the window as his Denali was towed away and the yellow crime scene tape wrapping their property line was pulled down. Aside from a text message from Kenya saying that Marlowe was rushed into surgery, Kita had no other updates.

"All right, girl, the food is put up, and the kitchen is clean. What else can I do?" Alexis was too anxious to sit and play the waiting game, so she used her nervous energy to be productive.

"I appreciate everything, but you don't have to babysit me. I'll be okay. As my aunt said, no news is good news." The very second Markita had finished her sentence, the cell phone in her lap started ringing. "It's Kenya." Her stomach sank, and she hesitated before answering. "How's Marlowe? Is he okay? Did his surgery go well?"

"Hey, sis!" Kenya sighed; her voice was unreadable. "Marlowe is still with us, thank God, but he's not out of the woods yet. The doctor said the bullets did a lot of internal damage. He also lost a significant amount of blood, and they are worried that he may have mobility issues. They will know more in the coming days."

"Thank you, Jesus!" Kita shouted. Alexis didn't know what was being said over the phone, but she jumped for joy anyway.

"They have Marlowe sedated right now and told your mom to go home, but you know Mama Jackie wasn't going for it. She's going to stay overnight."

"Kenya, thank you so much for being there today. I don't know what I would do without you or Lex."

"It ain't no thang. We are sisters for life," Kenya added.

"I have an idea." Alexis smiled. "Since Mama Jackie will be at the hospital all night, let's have an old-school sleepover like we used to. We can watch movies and eat junk in bed until we fall asleep."

"No, I've already taken up your day. I won't monopolize your evening too." In all honesty, Markita wasn't in much of a mood for company. She needed time to process her feelings and sit with her emotions. Though today hadn't ended in tragedy, it was still a traumatic situation that would always live rent-free in her head.

"Girl, bye!" Alexis and Kenya said in unison.

"Guys, I love y'all for wanting to stay with me, but I think I'd rather be alone."

"Okay, let's compromise then." Alexis took a seat beside Kita. "Kenya and I will camp out down here and watch movies. You can stay in your room and act like we aren't here."

"Do I have the choice to decline?" Kita smirked.

"Nope," Kenya replied.

"Okay, fine; movie night it is." Kita gave in.

It took a little less than an hour for Kenya to return to her crew. When she did, the girls took turns showering and dressing in a pair of Kita's pajamas. Collectively, they decided that the movie theme of the night would be old school. The lineup included everything with Denzel. He was Kita's favorite actor. The ladies watched all the movies in silence until the movies began to watch them. Each girl drifted off that night, praying hard for Marlowe's recovery and replaying the day's events in their heads. Aside from Alexis, neither of the other two had been this close to death. Though no one spoke it, they knew this situation had robbed them of an innocence they didn't know existed until now. Their lives were undoubtedly changed forever.

Morning came, and Kita was the first to wake up. She checked her phone for missing calls and messages; there were several, but none from her mother. Standing from the sofa she'd fallen asleep on, she stretched, walked over to the window, and opened the blinds. The sun shone brightly at the front of the house, casting a beautiful glow over the spot where Marlowe had crashed his car.

"Good morning." Kenya was the second to stir. "Any word from your mom?"

"Not yet." Kita paused. "Do you think Marlowe is going to be okay?"

"That's my hope and prayer." Kenya joined her friend at the window. "Marlowe is a fighter, Kita. He'll get through this."

"Yeah, girl, you got to have faith," Alexis said in her baritone morning voice.

"I do have faith, but I also know we all must leave here at some point." Kita turned away from the window. "I've never lived in a world without my brother. He's my provider, my protector, my everything." Her voice began to crack as she was overcome with emotions. "I've never had to worry about shit because I've always had Marlowe. What am I going to do if he leaves me, y'all?"

"He's not going anywhere any time soon, but when that fateful day comes, you will live the way he taught you. You will be strong and carry his legacy with you always." As Alexis spoke, she thought of her mom and how she never felt prepared to live life without her. However, here she was, making a way for herself and helping to raise her little sister. Alexis knew she wasn't perfect, but she was doing her best with what she had.

"Okay, y'all, I hate to break up the pity party, but my nigga Marlowe ain't dead, so enough with all of the sad shit!" Kenya walked over to the kitchen and searched the cabinets until she found what she was looking for. "Bingo," she whispered while retrieving a bottle of Hennessy and three shot glasses. "Here's to Marlowe's recovery because, like he always says, 'Hennything is Possible!'"

# CHAPTER TWENTY

Almost two weeks had gone by, and the city of Detroit was still buzzing about Marlowe's shooting. Some people speculated that the shooter was a young hustler looking to make a name for himself, while others thought the shooter may have been someone who knew Marlowe personally. Either way, there were no solid leads, and the police hadn't made any arrests. Marlowe was still in intensive care with tubes all over his body. His mobility was limited to hand and neck movements, and he was paralyzed from the waist down. A bullet had entered through his rib cage and exited his back, severing his spinal cord. The doctors performed multiple surgeries to repair it, but in the end, even their efforts weren't successful.

"Kita, baby, when will you return to school?" Jackie entered the kitchen wearing a tired expression and a pink robe. She walked over to the Keurig machine in the corner and prepared some coffee.

"Mama, with all that's going on with Marlowe, I can't even think about school right now." Kita sat at the kitchen counter, playing with a bowl of oatmeal. She hadn't had an appetite in days.

Whenever she tried to eat, she never managed to get beyond three bites before feeling full.

"Baby, Marlowe is alive, and we need to be grateful for that." Jackie walked over to her. "Speaking of your brother, it would be nice if you went to see him soon. He misses you."

"I'm afraid to see him like that." Though Kita had talked to her brother on the phone, she still couldn't bring herself to visit him in the hospital.

"I'm sure he's afraid too." Jackie took a seat beside her daughter. "Life for him will never be the same. I'm sure he could use a little reassurance that we will have his back the way he has always had ours." After kissing her daughter's forehead, she went to retrieve her coffee. "You've got one more day at home, and then it's back to school—no ifs, ands, or buts, okay?"

"Yes, ma'am."

"Okay, well, I'm about to get dressed to go see your brother. I'll be there until the visiting hours are over. There is some frozen pizza in the freezer."

"I'll go sit with Marlowe. You can take the day off." Kita emptied the contents of her bowl into the garbage.

"Are you sure?" Jackie gave her daughter a doubtful look.

"Yes. Mama, go get some rest," Kita knew her mother hadn't slept well since Marlowe's shooting. The bags underneath her eyes and the wrinkles in her forehead had aged the beautiful woman by at least five years.

"I'm proud of you." Jackie hugged her daughter before taking her coffee and returning to her bedroom.

An hour later, Kita was dressed casually in a pair of gray joggers and a matching jacket with her natural hair in a slicked-back ponytail. She didn't feel like jazzing herself up, but she wanted Marlowe to at least know she tried. Nervously, she walked down the hospital hallway, stopping several times to gather her nerves.

She didn't know what to expect and feared that her reaction to what she saw would make him sad.

"Fuck it," she mumbled upon approaching his room door. Slowly, she pushed it open and was relieved to see her brother looking much better than she expected. "Hey, bro," she smiled.

"Aw shit, it's going to snow. About damn time you came to see a nigga." Marlowe gave his sister the once-over with a grimace.

"I'm sorry. I just—"

"Kita, I'm just playing. Don't cry," he laughed. "But I'm not going to lie. I was beginning to think you had written me off. I'm glad to see you."

"Boy, stop!" Kita leaned in and kissed his forehead. "I could never write you off."

"So, what took you so fuckin' long then?"

"I had shit to do. I'm a busy lady, you know," she joked before sitting beside the bed. The private room was filled with every type of flower, balloon, and card you could imagine. Kita's eyes roamed the room, taking in everything from the writing on the whiteboard from the nurses to the IV pole and heart monitor.

"What are you looking so sad?" Marlowe didn't like sympathy. He felt like everyone who visited was staring down at him with pity.

"I just never thought I would see you like this, that's all." She held back the tears she felt forming.

"I'm going to be all right, believe that." Marlowe smiled. "I'm a soldier. You know it will take a lot more than this to put me under."

"I know you're strong, but you got to admit this shit is fucked up." Kita sighed. "You are no angel, but you didn't deserve this."

"How is Mama holding up? When she visits, she tries to act tough, but I can tell by the stains near her eyes that she cries on her way up here."

"This is hard for all of us, Marlowe, but Mama will be all right as long as you're all right." Kita could feel the tears sliding down her face, although she was trying hard to hold them back. "That day when you pulled up bleeding and shit, I thought you were dead."

"Me too, shit!" Marlowe's light chuckle turned into a cough. "I was out minding my business, and in the blink of an eye, my whole world changed, but I swear on my soul when I find out who did it, it's up!"

"So, you don't know what happened?" Kita leaned in close. "Did you have beef with anybody? Who was the last person you were with?"

"Slow down." Marlowe began to cough. Kita walked over to the pale pink pitcher and poured some water.

"First thing first. Did you put up that shit for me like I asked?" Marlowe continued to cough.

"Yeah, it's safe." Before Kita could continue with the conversation, Davit and Arman walked into the hospital room wearing solemn expressions. Recognizing his company, Marlowe attempted to sit up in bed and look as healthy as he could . . . but it was useless.

# CHAPTER TWENTY-ONE

"**W**hat's up, y'all," Marlowe managed to sound more cheerful than he felt.

"My son, how are you holding up?" Arman made his way closer to the bed while Davit remained near the door. "Markita, it's wonderful to see you again."

"Same." Kita handed the water she'd poured to her brother.

"Hey, sis, can you go grab me some lunch from the cafeteria?" Marlowe could've hit the call button and asked the nurse to send a message to the dietary department, but his request was a hint to get lost for a little bit.

"I'll be back in fifteen minutes." Catching her brother's drift, she grabbed her purse and left them to talk, purposely leaving the room door cracked. She pretended to walk away but inched back toward the door seconds later.

Davit pulled the curtain and walked closer to the bed. "Marlowe, what the fuck happened, my boy?"

"Some fuck nigga caught me slipping." Marlowe felt the need to explain.

"*Tsk-tsk*." Arman wagged his finger. "The first thing I ever taught you, young Marlowe, was always to have your head on the swivel."

"I know, I know. I thought I was careful, but a lot was going on that day. B asked me to make the drops, and I was trying to get to my sister's birthday party. In my haste, I let a nigga get too close. I should've been paying better attention."

"Do you have any idea who could've done this? Who knew where you were going to be?" Davit asked.

"Nobody," Marlowe coughed. "Shit, I get my money out of the streets, and I go home. I don't fuck with no bitches like that unless I'm out of town, and I don't even hang with nobody except my family and a few friends."

"You know friends are only enemies in disguise. Everybody is cool until they're not," Arman added. "The only thing you can rely on most of the time is family, and even half of them can't be trusted."

Davit and Arman shared a laugh, but Marlowe remained silent.

"Remember, people are only happy for you until you're doing better than them," Davit chimed in. "Are you sure no one in your crew had a hand in this?"

"Nah." Marlowe shook his head. "They know that taking me out would have only cut off the plug for everybody, and nobody in my crew is dumb enough to do that."

"Well, either way, I hate to see you like this, son." Arman patted Marlowe's shoulder. "It's obvious you're out of the game, and you may not want to hear this, but we're going to have to replace you."

"Bullshit!" Marlowe barked. He had worked too hard for his spot and his reputation just to watch that shit crumble like his legs. "I built my clientele from the ground up, man! I'm eating off this shit. My family *needs* this shit." There was no way Marlowe could part with his lifestyle. He couldn't go from eating lobster back to some damn Ramen noodles.

"Look at you, Marlowe. How can you get out there and hustle? Everyone will use your disability as a reason to try you." Arman stood with his arms folded. He hated it had to be like this, but there was no sugarcoating in the dope game.

"Let me figure something out." Marlowe had been so busy living in the now and dealing with his injury that he hadn't thought much about what he would do when the time came for him to return to the streets, but there was no way he could go back to being broke. "Don't count me out just yet. Have a little faith in your boy."

"OK, son, we will give you some time but only a little, and then the train has to move on without you." Arman patted Marlowe's shoulder again. He knew how hard this must be for his protégé. However, this was business, and if Marlowe didn't come up with a solution soon, they would have to find someone to replace him.

After the men said their goodbyes, Kita returned to the room. She could see her brother knee-deep in contemplation. "Is everything okay?"

"Couldn't be better!" Marlowe's tone was an indication that he was irritated.

"Damn." Kita reclaimed her seat next to the bed. The room was silent for several minutes.

"Sis, my bad. I didn't mean to snap at you. I'm just angry." Marlowe's voice had softened. "I'm angry at the nigga that did this, and I'm angry at myself. Truth be told, I'm mad at the fucking world right now, but I didn't mean for you to get the wrath of any of this."

"It's all good." Markita patted her brother's hand. "I know the state of your health has you dealing with a lot of emotions right now."

"Shit! Believe it or not, that's the last thing I'm worried about." He began to cough. "My only concern right now is getting back on the streets because everything we have depends on that."

"Marlowe, please don't stress about money right now. You need to concentrate on healing."

"That's easier said than done when you're responsible for everybody."

Instantly, Kita felt even worse than she already did for her brother. At this moment, he was a living depiction of the statement, "Heavy is the head that wears the crown."

"I will go and apply for two jobs when I leave here. Please know I got us while you recover."

Marlowe knew even if Kita had five jobs, her income wouldn't compare to his, but he didn't want to burst her bubble. "Nah. You ain't got time for two jobs. You need to keep your head in those books and get ready to leave for college." He switched the subject. "Have you considered what elective classes you'd like to take?"

"I'm not leaving until you're back to your old self."

"I told you I'm good. Your ass better be on that plane headed to college real soon, or me and you will have a problem." Marlowe used his serious voice.

"I was thinking about staying here for the first year and attending a local school. By then, you should be back on your feet." Immediately, Kita felt bad for her analogy.

"Markita, Detroit has nothing to offer you. You better take this opportunity and run with it." Marlowe stared at his sister. "If I was half as smart as you, I would've made some very different decisions with my life."

"Don't talk like your life is bad. Besides this minor setback, you're doing damn good if you ask me."

"You think I'm proud to be selling drugs? Do you think I like constantly having to look over my fucking shoulder? You think I *wanted* to become a cripple?" He wasn't trying to raise his voice, but he was passionate about what he was saying. "Look at what my lifestyle did to me."

Kita didn't say anything. How could she? Everything her brother was saying hit home. After a few seconds of silence, she finally found the courage to ask, "I'm sure you thought about this shit way before now. Why didn't you stop?"

"It ain't that easy." Marlowe looked away. "The longer you do it, the deeper you get. So often, I wanted to walk away, but where would our family be if I did?" He paused. "Me, with no high-school diploma, working at a fast-food joint . . . Mom still trying to make a dollar out of fifteen cents. Or you, chasing after dope boys that just want to use you for your body like your friend? Hell no! For my fucking family, I jumped feetfirst into the belly of the beast, and I will do that shit again and again if I have to. In life, we may not always do what's right, but as the head of the family, I will always do what's necessary." Marlowe began to have a coughing fit just as a shift nurse entered the room.

"Hello," the white nurse wearing a Detroit Lions scrub top smiled. "My name is Amy. I don't think we've met yet, but I am the second-shift nurse caring for Mr. Jones."

"Hi, my name is Kita. This bonehead is my brother." Kita laughed. "Hey, I noticed that he's been coughing a lot. Do you think he might have a cold or an infection?"

"Sometimes coughing after surgery can be very normal because the tube they place in during surgery can cause a lot of mucus to build up," Amy spoke while checking Marlowe's vitals and medical equipment.

"Can you look at his throat, though, just to be sure," Kita wanted to err on the side of caution.

"Of course," Amy nodded pleasantly.

"I'm sorry, but my sister sometimes thinks she's my mom," Marlowe joked, and everyone laughed.

# CHAPTER TWENTY-TWO

After spending nearly eight hours at the hospital watching old shows and having random conversations while eating her brother's food, Markita decided to head home for the night. She didn't want to leave, but Marlowe had been given something that knocked him out almost immediately, so he wasn't much company. "Good night," Kita waved to Amy as she passed the nurse's station. Retrieving her phone, she sent a quick text to her mother with the pictures that she and Marlowe had taken and a message letting her know that she was on the way.

With a smirk, Kita walked down the hallway toward the elevator but then decided to take the stairs. She was glad she'd come to see her brother today because the visit had done them both some good. Though there was a long road ahead, she felt in her heart that Marlowe would defy all the odds stacked against him. She knew her brother would live to be the old nigga on the block telling the young boys his cautionary tale one day.

As Kita arrived at the car, her cell phone rang. It was a three-way call with Alexis and Kenya. They'd called to invite her to hang out for a little while. At first, she was going to decline because she was tired, but then she thought of the great day she had with her brother and wanted to celebrate. After clearing the plans with Jackie and promising to be home by midnight, Kita headed over to be with her friends.

Upon arriving at an unfamiliar block a few minutes from her old neighborhood, Kita reluctantly exited her car and approached the house. The porch light was out, and a stray cat lingered nearby. Before she had the chance to knock on the door, it opened. Standing there was a small, brown-skinned woman who looked like she'd seen better days, although her hair was laid and she had on a face full of makeup. "You here for Lex?"

"Yeah." Kita looked past the woman into the house full of older, unfamiliar people.

"She's in the kitchen." The woman moved to the side, making room for Kita to enter, but she didn't move. "Girl, either you coming in or you staying out. My heat ain't for the hood."

"I'll be in, but let me make a quick call." Before Kita had pulled out her cell phone, the door was slammed in her face. Seconds later, it opened up to reveal Alexis and Kenya. They both were standing there with a blue shot cup in hand.

"Whose house is this?" Kita was suspicious of the scene.

"Girl, this is my cousin, Shyla's, spot." Alexis handed her friend a shot. "She lets me do whatever I want over here as long as I hook her up if you know what I mean." Alexis lifted her pinky finger to her nose and sniffed.

"Shot! Shot!" Kenya pulled Kita into the house and closed the door. "Drink up, bitch! We're celebrating tonight."

Without an argument, Kita took her shot to the head. Kenya handed her another shot, and she downed that one too. "Who are all of these people?"

"I don't know, girl. These are my cousin's friends." Alexis shrugged. "It doesn't matter, though, because they got liquor and weed. I gave her a little cocaine from Breeze as our contribution to the party, so we're good."

"I know this crowd ain't our typical scene. We just figured you needed to unwind after spending the day at the hospital, and this is the only option at the moment because after what happened last time, I know you ain't going to a club for a while."

"That's a big fact!" Kita laughed while looking around the room. It was full of men and women participating in various activities. A game of spades was going on at a card table in the corner, and a few people were dancing in the kitchen. One lady was sitting on the rundown couch eating from a plate in her lap while the man beside her broke down a blunt on the table. The air was thick and smoky, and the lights were dim. The music in the background rotated between hip-hop and R&B from the late '90s.

After an hour, Kita began to relax and feel more comfortable. Not only did she puff on a few blunts in rotation around the room, but she'd also taken a shot with a stranger for her birthday and played several hands of spades. The game was called "Rise and Fly." Whichever team won two out of three hands would stay at the table and face a new team of opponents, while the losers had to rise and fly. She was feeling good and buzzed, but she wasn't wasted. She knew Marlowe wouldn't be able to save her tonight if things got out of hand, and she for damn sure wasn't going to call her mother.

"Oh shit." The time on Kita's phone told her that it was 1:25 a.m. "Y'all, I got to go. My mama is cool, but she ain't that cool."

"Yeah, I need to be leaving too. We have school tomorrow. Well, at least two of us do." Kenya cast a glance at Kita.

"Okay, before y'all leave, let's do one more shot. It won't even kick in until y'all are home." Alexis didn't wait for a response before grabbing an almost empty bottle of vodka and proceeding to waterfall her friends, damn near drowning Kenya.

"Oh, hell no. I'll pass." Kita shook her head. She wasn't trying to go home smelling like liquor.

"Bitch, come on! Take one for Marlowe," Alexis persuaded.

"All right," Kita relented.

After taking the shot, the girls said goodbye and headed in their respective directions. Just as Kita sat down in the car and turned on the engine, her phone rang. It was Jackie. "Hey, Ma," she tried to sound sober. "I'm sorry. I know it's late, but I swear I'm on the way as we speak."

"Kita," Jackie said before silence lingered on the line, "Marlowe's gone, baby."

"What?" was all Kita could say as her intoxicated brain tried diligently to process the information. Hot tears fell down her face, and her ears started ringing as her mother explained the final moments of her brother's life.

"There was internal bleeding. He was rushed into emergency surgery, but his body wasn't strong enough. Marlowe died on the operating table."

# CHAPTER TWENTY-THREE

Exactly five days after Marlowe passed away, Jackie sent off her son with one of the most elaborate funeral services the city of Detroit had ever seen. Everyone was asked to wear white and yellow, Marlowe's favorite colors. Marlowe was dressed in an all-white pair of Amiri jeans, a matching T-shirt, a yellow Versace belt, and a gold Medusa head on the buckle. The Titan Gold Series Glass casket allowed attendees to see the white Louboutins on his feet. Surrounding the viewing area was an array of white flowers from various loved ones, friends, and associates. Greater Mount Hope, a ten-thousand-seat megachurch on the city's West Side, hosted the homegoing celebration, and nearly every seat on the lower level was full. After a trio of sisters from a local gospel group sang two songs, Rhonda read off the obituary and a few cards. Nearly one hundred people stood in line to give remarks—however, the funeral director of A. W. Funeral Home had to cut the line down to fifteen people, or else the service would have lasted hours. As the time for remarks ended, Jackie took to the stage. With a weary smile and her head held high, she grabbed the microphone and spoke one final message to her beloved Marlowe: "In this life and the next, I love you, son."

Pastor Nathaniel King, the fifty-something-year-old officiant of the service, was known for his large following of young wayward people and his hip-hop holy roller Sunday suits. While some praised the relatively young pastor for his ability to keep one foot in the streets and the other in the pulpit, others condemned him for it. He'd been called everything but a child of God by those who didn't understand his mission, but that never stopped him from getting up every Sunday morning and preaching the roof off of the house of God. Today's sermon was no different.

Pastor King had tailored his speech to meet all of the dope boys and around-the-way girls in the audience where they were at in life. He wanted to drive home the point that nobody was too deep in the streets, too broken, or too far gone to give their life over to God. He also spoke on forgiveness because he knew the code of the streets was to almost always seek street justice. At the conclusion of the service, five people had made their way to the front of the church after deciding to give their life over to Christ. In Pastor King's book, that was a win for God and why he did what he did the way he did it.

Ten men eagerly stood to act as pallbearers, although only six were needed, and nearly every woman sitting in the first four rows lined up to carry flowers. Once outside, everyone watched in awe as Marlowe's body was loaded into a custom, white stretch Porsche hearse. Some cheered while others cried as their beloved hood hero was taken on his final ride through the city of Detroit before it reached the funeral home, where his body would be cremated in the morning.

After the funeral service, close friends and a small handful of family members went back to Jackie's house for the repast. Erica and her team had worked diligently to transform the backyard into an elegant space for the solemn celebration. Large tents, chairs, and tables were all decorated with yellow and white floral centerpieces. Balloons and photo backdrops were placed in various corners of the yard, so you'd catch a glimpse of Marlowe no matter where you stood. While Jackie went into autopilot mode, graciously hosting her guests as if she hadn't lost her son, Kita retreated to her room. Though she'd gotten through the funeral without breaking down, the thought that her brother was never coming home was starting to sink in.

"Gotdamn, Marlowe! I can't believe you left me like this!" Kita spoke aloud once she was in her bedroom with the door closed. "I know we all have to leave here one day, but why did you have to go so soon?" Pain dripped from every word she spoke, and tears began to fill her eyes yet again. One by one, she stared at all the pictures of herself, Marlowe, and Jackie around the room. Closing her eyes, she took a moment to reminisce about those times they were together. She wanted desperately to remember what the scene sounded like, what it smelled like, and how it felt to be back with her brother again. For a second, she felt joy . . . but then her eyes opened, reminding her that he was gone. Instantly, her sorrow turned into anger, and her blood began to boil. "Bro, I swear on my life if I ever find who did this to you, I will kill that motherfucker myself."

Suddenly, a knock on the door interrupted her moment. Quickly, she wiped her eyes. "Just a minute."

After a few seconds, the door opened. It was Bernard. He was dressed to the nines in a white ensemble and canary yellow mink coat. "Hey, cuz, I noticed you were missing, so I wanted to check in on you before I left." Closing the door behind him, he stepped farther into the room.

"I'm good; just a little wound up. I don't feel like being out there right now."

"I feel you." Reaching into the pocket of his jacket, he produced a pint of Hennessy. "Don't tell Mama Jackie, but here is a little something to take the edge off." Bernard handed the bottle to Kita.

"Damn, this was Marlowe's favorite drink." She smiled. "Remember when he used to say, 'Hennything is possible'?"

"Yeah, I do," he smiled. "Cheers to my nigga, Marlowe. That boy will forever be missed." Bernard wiped a tear dancing in the corner of his eye.

"B, I'm so hurt, man. I haven't been eating, and I barely sleep these days. I just can't believe he's gone." Kita took a seat on the bed. "I was at the hospital talking to him one minute, and then he was gone."

"At least you kind of got to say goodbye, but I never made it to the hospital." Bernard stared at the floor. "I didn't want to see him laid up like that, but that was selfish of me. I felt in my heart that nigga was coming home, but I should've gone to see him." Bernard reached into his coat pocket again, this time producing a large wad of rubber-banded money.

"Look, Kita, I'm about to slide out of here, but before I do, here is something for you and Mama Jackie. It ain't much, but I will be back every two weeks to drop a little something off to cover bills and shit."

"B, I can't take your money."

"Look, I insist." He walked over and placed the money into her nightstand drawer. "We are family, and I promise to look out for you guys like you have always looked out for me. I owe you more than you'll ever know."

"You don't owe us nothing, B. Like you said, we are family." She paused. "Well, if I could ask for one thing, it would be for you to find the motherfucker responsible for killing my brother." There was fire in Kita's eyes.

"Say less! I've been on that shit." Bernard hollered, "Man, the day it happened, I put some bread out on the street for anybody that brings me a lead. As soon as I find out who did it, I swear on my life I will close-casket that nigga!"

"Thanks, B." Kita felt relieved to know she wasn't alone on her journey for retaliation. "I've racked my brain to figure out who had a motive to do it. Everybody loved my brother, you know, but not too long ago, he got into a little altercation with one of Breeze's boys at the club. His name is Al, and Marlowe beat the brakes off his ass."

"Yeah, Marlowe told me about that." Bernard rubbed the hairs on his chin. "Let me look into that shit, and I'll keep you posted on what I find out. In the meantime, don't tell your girl I'm checking into her man and his people."

"I won't say shit." Kita made a show of locking her lips and throwing away the key. Immediately, the gesture reminded her of Marlowe, and again, tears fell down her face.

"It's going to be all right, cuz." Bernard walked over to Kita and wrapped his arms around her shoulders. "Call me anytime, day or night, and I got you." After breaking the embrace, he left Kita alone in the room with her thoughts.

Nearly an hour passed before she found the courage to leave her sanctuary. Although she didn't feel up to engaging in trips down memory lane with the other guests, she knew it might do her heart some good to laugh. As soon as she exited her room, Alexis and Kenya came down the hallway. "You must've known we were on the way to pull you out of that stuffy room." Alexis ran up and hugged Kita.

"Girl, you and Mama Jackie did so well at the funeral." Kenya joined the hugging circle. "I know Marlowe was pleased with the way y'all laid him out. That see-through casket was fire!"

"Yeah, it was nice." Kita smiled as she led her friends back down the hallway toward the stairs. "My mama spent a pretty penny on it too; it was probably the most expensive part of the funeral." As Kita reached the bottom step, Marlowe's nurse, Amy, walked through the front door. "Oh my God, thank you for coming." Kita ran up to the woman dressed in yellow scrubs and wrapped her arms around her before introducing Amy to everyone.

"I got off my shift and came right over. I wouldn't have missed this for the world. Even in that short time, Marlowe was one of my favorites." Amy was starting to turn red in the face.

"It's so crazy how that shit went, right?" Kita stared deeply into Amy's blue eyes. "We were talking and laughing all day, and then—*boom*, he died." She paused. "Do you think the coughing I told you about had anything to do with it?" After Marlowe's passing, Kita had no contact with anyone at the hospital and had only gotten second-hand information through her mom.

"Is there somewhere private we can talk?" Amy whispered while looking around the house with a concerned expression.

"Yeah, come upstairs to my room." Without hesitation, Kita pulled Amy's hand and guided her back up the stairs toward her bedroom. Kenya and Alexis followed closely.

Once inside the room, Amy stared at the additional guests. "I was kind of hoping we could have this conversation alone."

Kita sensed her worry, but with a firm voice, she said, "They're cool. I trust them with my life."

"Okay," Amy exhaled. "So, that night after you left the hospital, a man came off the elevator wearing a black hoodie pulled tight. When he walked past the nurse's station, I tried to tell him that visiting hours were ending in less than thirty minutes, but he bypassed me, saying he wouldn't be long. As I watched him enter Marlowe's room, something in my spirit didn't sit right, but when I got up to follow him, one of my other patients hit the call button." Amy looked around the room for dramatic effect.

"Well, as soon as I left my patient, the emergency sirens went off in your brother's room, indicating a code blue. The doctor, other members of our team, and I flew into the room, but Marlowe was no longer breathing. The doctor rushed your brother into emergency surgery, and he did find an internal bleed that he felt was the cause, but I feel like that guy in the hoodie did something to cause your brother's death." Amy reached into her pocket. "I found this on the floor in the corner of Marlowe's room. I know for sure it wasn't there before."

Kita's heart damn near stopped when Amy handed her a small pendant that read *Money Talks*. She paused for several long seconds before finding the strength to ask, "What did he look like?"

"He was short and light-skinned. I also believe he had dreadlocks or braids because I could see the imprints of his thick hair through the hoodie." Amy paused and took a deep breath. "Please, Kita, don't tell anyone the information I gave you because I will lose my job. I also don't want to be involved in anything that will bring harm to my children or me. Marlowe was a good dude, so I just wanted you to know."

"Thank you for bringing this information to me." Kita embraced Amy for several seconds. "I swear on my life we will never say a word. This information is more valuable than you will ever know." Kita looked at Kenya and Alexis before reaching into her nightstand drawer and retrieving the stack of money that Bernard had just given her. "Amy, please take this for your troubles."

"I can't take your money." Amy shook her head diligently.

"Marlowe believed in taking care of people, and I do too." Kita placed the money into Amy's hand. "Now, take this and leave.

I don't want the wrong person to see you here and remember you from the hospital." Kita's voice had a sense of urgency that wasn't there before.

"Thank you, Kita." Nervously, Amy backed her way out of the room, closing the door behind herself. Kenya and Alexis eyed Kita suspiciously. They didn't know what was going on but sensed something big was about to unfold. When the coast was clear, Kita dropped down on the bed and closed her eyes. She took several deep breaths and tried to calm her nerves. The palms of her hands became incredibly moist, and she felt a wave of heat come over her as the room spun.

"So, what's up, Kita? What are we missing here?" Alexis took a seat on the bed beside Kita. It was hard to watch her friend experience the onset of what she knew was a panic attack. Therefore, she rubbed Kita's back as she watched her struggle to form a sentence.

"Y'all," Kita spoke through labored breaths while clutching the pendant in her hand for dear life, "Bernard killed my fucking brother!"

# CHAPTER TWENTY-FOUR

The room fell deathly silent as everyone pondered on the bomb Kita had just dropped. They knew if she were right, then Bernard was the biggest snake in the game, and he'd have to be dealt with immediately. However, they also knew if Kita were wrong, her accusations would have serious consequences.

"He called Marlowe his brother!" Kita screamed with a voice full of rage. Her heart was beating so loud everyone in the room could practically hear it. "That motherfucker grew up with us! He ate at our table, shared clothes with my brother, and called my mother his fucking auntie!" Wiping tears from her eyes, she stood from the bed and turned to look at her friends. "After all of that, how could he have taken the life of his best friend?" Kita's heart was shattered into a thousand pieces.

"I hate to be the one to say it, but there is no loyalty in the dope game." Alexis stared at the ground for several seconds before her head sprang up like a Jack in the Box. "You know that nigga needs to be dealt with immediately."

"Absolutely!" Kita added.

"How, though?" Kenya looked around the room. "We don't know how to pull no shit like this off."

"Should we bring Breeze and his crew in on it? Despite that shit between Marlowe and Al, I know they'll help us if I ask." Alexis grabbed her cell phone.

"Nah. This shit is personal! I have to be the one to avenge my brother's death." Kita could see nothing but red.

"You've never harmed a fly, Kita. How in the hell do you expect to body a nigga?" Alexis scoffed.

"Bitch, for Marlowe, I'd take the life of anybody, and you better believe that."

"Let's all take a beat." Kenya could sense that things were about to get too real. "Let's sleep on this and talk tomorrow when cooler heads prevail. Right now, we're all operating off of emotion, and that's a recipe for disaster."

"Kenya, I love you and understand if you don't want any part of this," Kita looked her friend square in the face, "but Bernard is going to die tonight, and I will be the one to pull the trigger." The room fell silent again as each girl pondered the outcome of the situation. Neither girl truly knew what they were signing up for, but each of them felt a sense of loyalty to Marlowe that couldn't be denied.

"So, how do you want to play this?" Alexis was the first to speak up.

"I don't know yet." Kita rubbed her temples; her head was aching. "Y'all should go home. I'll call you in a few when I have a plan."

"Are you sure you want us to leave?" Kenya's voice was soft. "I don't think being alone right now is a good idea."

"I won't be alone. This house is full of people," Kita sighed. "Besides, I need time to collect my thoughts. I should have a solid plan by midnight, so stay by the phone."

"Okay, girl, we love you." Alexis grabbed her friend in a tight embrace, and Kenya joined in. "All for one, and one for all."

"I don't know what I would do without y'all." Kita took several breaths in and blew them out slowly.

"Let's all pray that we never have to find out," Alexis said before following Kenya out of the room.

For the remainder of the day, Kita hid out in her room, leaving her mom to entertain the guests as she developed a plan to take out Bernard. Just before ten, there was a light knock on the door. "Come in," Kita hollered. She was lying across the foot of her bed in the dark. Nothing except the squeaking in the ceiling fan could be heard.

"Hey, you," Jackie spoke lovingly as she entered her daughter's bedroom and turned on the light switch.

"Hey, Mama." Kita sat up. "Is everyone gone?"

"Yeah, the last group left about thirty minutes ago." Jackie yawned. "I just wanted to check in on you before I showered and headed to bed. How are you doing, baby girl? I know this whole thing has been a lot to process."

"I'm not okay, but I will be," Kita sighed. "How are you, Ma?"

"I'm not okay, but I will be," she mimicked and then wrapped her arms around Kita.

"How are you . . . really, Ma?" Kita embraced Jackie and squeezed tight. She knew the pain she felt as Marlowe's sister was nothing in comparison to the pain of her mother.

"Well, in all honesty, I'm hurt and angry, but I know there is nothing I can do about it." Jackie exhaled.

"What if you *could* do something about it?"

"If by doing something like bringing Marlowe back, I'd give my life for his without hesitation." With tears in her eyes, Jackie stroked her daughter's head. "I'd die for both of you, you know that."

"No, I mean, if the person responsible for what happened to him was right here in front of us, what would you do?" After breaking the embrace, Kita leaned up to look at her mother.

"Kita, I know I didn't have y'all in church the way I should have, but you know I've always preached to you and Marlowe both that vengeance is the Lord's." Jackie took a deep breath and continued. "I've been doing a lot of soul-searching here lately and talking to Pastor King. Although we're angry, we must turn the other cheek. We must learn to forgive those who harmed us because that's the only way into heaven."

"God forgives, but I don't, and you shouldn't either!" Kita snapped. "Especially when it comes to Marlowe."

"Markita, you need to calm down." Jackie's tone increased to match Kita's. "Your brother was no saint. We all know when you live by the streets, there is a good possibility that you will die the same way." Jackie stood. "Do I miss my son? Yes, I do, but if you ask me, Marlowe played a big part in his demise. He should have left those streets, and you know that."

"How could he leave?" Kita stood from the bed and stared eye-to-eye with her mother. "Could he have left the streets when Larry left us on Christmas Eve without electricity? Could he have left the streets when he had to play catch-up on all of your bills to keep us from living on the street again? Could he have left the streets when he helped those in need in the neighborhood or when he paid for my college?" Kita began to cry, not because she was sad but because she was angry. "Marlowe might not have been a gotdamn saint according to the Bible, but he for damn sure was an earthly angel!"

"Good night, Markita. Get some rest. Hopefully, tomorrow is a better day for us both." With a sincere expression, Jackie turned on the balls of her feet and headed out of her daughter's room.

# CHAPTER TWENTY-FIVE

**S**till seething from the conversation with her mother, Kita used that energy as the fuel needed to press forward with her plan. She grabbed her cell phone and dialed Bernard. He answered on the third ring. "What's up, Kita? Is everything okay?"

"Everything is fine." Her voice was soft and sensual. "I just needed to hear your voice; it calms me."

"Is that so?" It was apparent that Bernard was taken aback by this conversation, yet he played along nonetheless.

"Yeah, now that the house is quiet and everyone is gone, I feel so alone."

"As long as I'm around, you ain't never got to be alone."

"Can I come over to where you are? I just need some company for a little bit."

"That's not a good idea because I'm at the trap right now. How about I come to kick it with you tomorrow? Me and you can go grab lunch or something." Bernard tried hard to stay in his big cousin role, but then Kita began to cry lightly.

"That's okay, B. I'll call someone else to keep me company tonight," she sniffed.

"All right; look, you can come by tonight, but you can't stay no longer than an hour or two. The trap is no place for you."

"Thanks, B. I'll be there shortly."

"Bet. Call me when you're outside."

After ending the call, Kita contacted her friends and gave them the rundown. Next, she stripped and put on an all-black sweatshirt, black leggings, and black shoes. Quickly, she went to the basement and pulled out the bag she'd hidden for Marlowe. Inside, she found two handguns; one was black, and the other was silver. Carefully, she tucked them into the pocket of her hoodie and made her way back to the kitchen. Just as she opened the fridge to grab some water, someone knocked faintly on the side door. It was Kenya and Alexis, both dressed in all black. "Turn your phones on silent and then give them to me," Kita whispered while opening a random kitchen drawer.

"Why do we have to leave our phones here? What if shit goes sideways, and we need to call for help or something?" Kenya asked while handing over her phone.

"Phones can be traced by every cell tower they hit. Meaning, as we travel to Bernard, our movements can be traced. However, if all of our phones are here, then we can alibi each other, if need be, by saying y'all spent the night." Kita placed the phones into the drawer, grabbed her keys, and led her friends outside to Marlowe's whip. Though they felt weird getting into his car without him, no one said anything.

As discussed earlier, Kenya hopped into the driver's seat, Alexis sat in the passenger seat, and Kita rode in the back. Other than the sound of the engine and the tires hitting the pavement, the car was silent. The journey to the trap took approximately twenty-eight minutes. Kita was the first to speak when they pulled the car to a slow creep down the block. "Look, y'all, it's not too late to back down if y'all ain't with it."

"Are you backing down?" Alexis asked.

"Hell no."

"Well, neither am I." Alexis looked over at Kenya. "What about you?"

"Like I said earlier, all for one and one for all." Kenya found a spot a few doors from the two-story home on Woodlawn Street and brought the car to a stop without cutting the engine.

"Okay, y'all remember the plan, right?" Kita sounded more confident than she felt.

"Yes. You're going to enter the house alone and leave the door unlocked. I will come in after a few minutes and back you up. Kenya will stay with the car in case someone approaches from outside."

"Who is that?" Kenya pointed toward the trap house where a man with a large beard had just opened the door. Standing on the porch, he appeared to be engaged in some sort of altercation on the phone. After several seconds of shouting, he left the porch, got into a white vehicle, and pulled off.

"All right, I think it's go-time. No telling how long before he comes back." Alexis spoke the obvious.

"Do you think more people are in there?" Kenya asked.

"Don't matter." Kita put her hand on the door and exited the car like it was on fire. Quickly, she double-checked her weapon to make sure it had bullets, and then she tucked the gun into the small of her back and proceeded toward the house.

After approaching the porch, Kita knocked softly on the door. Within seconds, the door swung open, and Bernard greeted Kita with the barrel of his gun and a menacing scowl.

"B, it's me," Kita screamed.

"Damn, my bad. I told you to call." He lowered the gun and let Kita into the dingy house. The smell of marijuana filled the air, and the television could be heard in the background.

"My phone died. I'm sorry. I guess with everything going on today, I didn't realize that my battery was low."

"No need to apologize." Bernard closed and locked the door. "My fault for scaring you like that, but you know how it is out in these streets." Bernard entered the living room and placed his gun on the broken card table in the corner. Kita quickly unlocked the door and walked into the living room behind him. There were two sofas with missing couch cushions, a lamp on the floor with no shade, and various pieces of trash scattered about. "Do your mama know you over here?" Bernard took a seat.

"No, she's knocked out cold." Kita tried to relax and not sound so rehearsed. "Can I hit that?"

"Help yourself," Bernard passed Kita the blunt from off the card table that he'd just been smoking with one of his boys.

"You always have the best weed." She swallowed hard. The churning in her stomach was intensifying. "Marlowe too, but he wouldn't let me smoke his." With a giggle, Kita stepped closer to her mark.

"Marlowe was always overprotective when it came to you. I used to clown the nigga for it, but real shit, that was admirable." Bernard began bagging up a white rocklike substance from the coffee table. Kita recognized it as crack cocaine because she had seen Marlowe doing the same thing many times in the past.

"I keep racking my brain, wondering what he did to deserve this?" Kita looked around the scarcely decorated room with chipped paint, stained, torn carpet, and several basketball posters on the wall. "I know we just talked earlier, but have you heard anything since leaving the house?" She took a seat on the sofa across from him.

"Nope." Bernard never looked up from what he was doing.

"Well, shortly after you left, someone from the hospital came by the house and said they witnessed what happened." Kita stared intently at Bernard.

"A witness? I thought he died in surgery."

"That's what they said, but the witness suspects foul play." Kita continued, "The witness said they have proof and will take it to the police."

"What proof?" Bernard stopped fidgeting with the cocaine and placed it back on the table. "Did this witness give a description or name anybody?"

"Yeah, they said it was you, nigga." With a stiff finger, she pointed at his guilty ass.

"Me?" His poker face was strong. "Get the fuck out of here."

"B, why did you do it?" Kita pressed.

"Kita, I know you've been going through some shit, but I need you to be for real right now." Bernard stood. "It's *me* you're talking to. Why the fuck would I kill my brother?"

"He was my brother, nigga, and you just took him from me like he was nothing!" Removing the charm from her pocket, she tossed it over toward Bernard. "I promise I won't let you suffer like you did Marlowe. I will take your life as soon as you tell me why you did it." Kita removed the gun from the waist of her pants and pointed it at her target. Her hand was steady, and she was calm. "My mother fed your ungrateful ass! My brother treated you like family, and *this* is what you do?"

Reaching down to grab the pendant, Bernard frowned. "This shit was staged, Kita. I'd never do any shit like this, and you know that."

"Bernard, that charm never leaves your fucking neck!"

"Fuck it. Yeah, I did it." He shrugged. "So, are you going to shoot me or not because I'm tired of talking?" Bernard's smug smirk turned into laughter to antagonize Kita. Just then, the door opened, and Alexis entered the house with her gun cocked, ready for action.

"Oh shit. You bitches got some heart," Bernard continued, "but it takes balls to play this fucking game." He made a move toward the table where his gun was. Instinctively, Kita shot a bullet right into his hand.

"Why did you do it?" she screamed.

"Kita, we need to do this now and get the fuck out of Dodge!" Alexis looked back toward the door.

"If you're as smart as you think, then you know it's best to listen to your friend." Bernard's hand was bleeding profusely.

"Why did you do it?" Kita began to cry tears of anger.

"Kita, come on," Alexis urged.

"Y'all got two seconds to get the fuck out of here before I body y'all bitches just like I did Marlowe!" Bernard spat.

That statement was all it took to push Kita to the point of no return. *POP! POP! POP!* She closed her eyes tight and let off three shots. When she opened her eyes, Bernard had fallen backward and was sliding down the wall while holding his chest. Kita's eyes widened in surprise as everything around her went in slow motion. Alexis could not believe that Kita had pulled the trigger so many times.

"Are you okay?" Alexis hurried over to Kita, who was standing there in a daze.

"I did what I came to do. Yeah, I'm good." Without remorse, Kita watched as Bernard bled out the way Marlowe had done. The gruesome sight gave her brief satisfaction, but then it was time to finish the job.

With a confident glide, Kita walked up to Bernard and slid her gun into his mouth, between his teeth. "I'm going to ask you one more time. Why did you kill my brother?"

"Marlowe tried to cut me out, but I started this shit, so fuck that nigga!" Blood dripped from his mouth.

"Marlowe would never do that, and you know it!"

"Kita, we have to go!" Alexis urged.

"He wanted to shine, so I gave that nigga a halo." Bernard's eyes pleaded with Kita not to pull the trigger, but he knew his fate was sealed. Karma was a bitch that always came back for what she was owed. "Just do it!" he mumbled, and Kita obliged. *POP!* She sent one final shot to the front of his head, causing it to explode and send brain matter everywhere.

"Let's get the fuck out of here." Nervously, Alexis looked around the room as the realization that she had just taken part in a homicide hit her like a ton of bricks.

"Grab those baggies first!" Kita didn't know why she was concerned with the cocaine lying around, but she felt it was necessary to make the crime scene look like a robbery. Quickly, Alexis began grabbing the drugs and money off the table while Kita checked the house to make sure they didn't miss anything else. The place was mostly empty, but she struck gold when she entered the kitchen. Sitting on the wooden table was a medium-sized box. Inside were two perfectly wrapped bricks of pure white, uncut cocaine. Kita didn't know what to do with the dope, but she knew a lick when she saw one.

"Hot damn! We hit the fucking jackpot," Alexis yelled when she entered the kitchen and noticed the bricks.

"Hell yeah!" Kita grabbed the box and headed toward the door. Just before she placed her hand on the knob, someone knocked. Her heart damn near leaped from her body as she eyed Alexis suspiciously. "What the fuck?" Kita whispered.

Alexis clutched her pistol and proceeded toward the door. Standing on her tiptoes, she looked through the peephole to see a shadowed figure of a woman. She was dressed in mix-matched clothing and was shifting from side to side. "What do you need?" Alexis spoke in a baritone, clearly pretending to imitate the sound of a man's voice.

"Let me get enough for a twenty." The woman stepped closer to the door, waving her money. "Wait. Lex, is that you?" She pressed her face up against the door.

Alexis backed away from the door and stared at Kita. With a whisper, she said, "It's my cousin, Shyla."

"What the fuck is she doing here?" Kita began pacing the floor nervously. "Get rid of her."

"Lex, you and B can finish doing whatever it is y'all in there doing, but I need a hit first. Tell him I got twenty dollars." Shyla began to knock harder. "Did you hear me? Tell him—"

"Bitch, I heard you. Hold on." Alexis stepped over Bernard's body and grabbed some of the cocaine he had on the card table. After grabbing more than enough of the dope, she walked back over to the door and unlocked it. With her face covered, she extended her hand, "Where is the cash?"

Quickly, Shyla placed her balled-up money into Alexis's hand and was handed the cocaine. "Hell yeah!" Shyla snatched up the drugs and jumped up and down in the air for joy.

"Aye," Alexis continued in her deep voice. "If anybody comes asking, remember you ain't seen shit tonight, and you ain't heard nothing either!"

"On my soul, I don't know anything," Shyla added before leaving the porch and running off into the shadows.

"What the fuck was that?" Kita snapped. "She knows that was you, and now her ass can destroy our alibi."

"Calm down, Matlock!" Alexis scoffed. "She's a fiend that got what she came for and then some. Shyla isn't going to say anything."

"I hope not."

After waiting a few minutes, Kita opened the door and stepped out onto the porch. Thankfully, the street was dark and still empty as she and Alexis hurried toward the waiting car.

"What's all of this?" Kenya pointed to the box as they closed the door.

"This is what you call hustling." Alexis smiled. "We got some bricks, and I even managed to make us a little gas money too." She held up the twenty-dollar bill.

"Girl, put the pedal to the metal, and let's go." Kita cautiously checked the windows.

"What about Bernard?" Kenya pulled the car out of its spot.

"Hopefully, they don't find his ass until he's rotting with decay and filled with maggots." Kita fell back into her seat once the car pulled away from the block. A look of satisfaction adorned her face.

# CHAPTER TWENTY-SIX

After bending several city blocks to ensure they weren't being followed, Kita instructed Kenya to drive to Belle Isle, a private island in the city of Detroit with public access to the Detroit River, which flowed between Detroit and Canada. The large park has been considered a staple of the city for decades. People visit the island year-round for various reasons, including family gatherings, auto events, special exhibits, and more. Tonight, Kita decided to visit the island for a unique reason.

"Where are we going? You know I don't fuck around on the Isle at night." Nervously, Kenya drove the vehicle slowly down the winding road. There was nothing in sight except for a few animals that appeared beneath the shadows of the headlights.

"I ain't gon' lie. This shit is kind of creepy." Alexis pointed to gray fog looming in the air. During the daytime, Belle Isle was filled with people, but at night, it was a ghost town and the perfect setting for a horror story.

"Pull up right there." Kita wasn't a bit worried about who or what could be lurking in the shadows. "Give me your gun, Lex." She began dismantling her weapon and wiping off the individual pieces. After doing the same to Alexis's gun, Kita exited the car, ran up to the edge of the pavement, and tossed each piece into the choppy water. The current in the Detroit River was deadly. There are several stories about people being swept away within seconds and torn to shreds. There was also a common joke amongst the city's residents that if you wanted to make something or someone disappear, take them to the Detroit River. Kita knew the weapons she'd just tossed would probably never be found, and if they were, the water would damn near erase any prints that might've been left.

The girls returned to Kita's house just before the clock on the dashboard struck two in the morning. Carefully, Kenya parked Marlowe's car back into its spot. After quietly entering the house, Kita directed them to the basement, where she dumped Bernard's bricks into the Rubbermaid container, along with Marlowe's stuff. "Place your clothes and shoes into this bag. We'll burn it tomorrow in the fire pit when my mom leaves."

"Girl, I need my shoes. You're tripping." Alexis whined.

"I didn't even leave the car. Why do I have to burn my stuff?" Kenya asked.

"DNA transfers, so we have to get rid of everything from tonight." Kita stripped down to her underwear, dropping her clothes into the black garbage bag.

"What about Marlowe's car? Are you going to burn it too?" Alexis glared.

"I'm going to clean it well and throw the tarp back over it," Kita responded in a matter-of-fact tone.

"You just said that DNA transfers," Alexis interjected. "I know his car holds sentimental value, but—" She was cut off.

"Look," Kita sighed, "no one is going to be checking for a dead man's car, but if they do, I promise I will burn it." She looked both her friends in the eyes, so they knew she was serious.

The friends all took turns showering without additional conversations before drifting off to sleep as best as they could that night. Alexis violently tossed and turned while Kenya mumbled softly. Kita tried everything from counting sheep to listening to music on her headphones. However, sleep evaded her, so she stared quietly at the ceiling until the sun began to seep through the curtains. Somewhere around seven, she'd finally dozed off.

It was just after nine when Kita's bedroom door swung open.

"Kita, I know last night was rough, but I thought we could .. . oh." Jackie jumped slightly. "I didn't know you girls were here. It startled me."

"Sorry, Mama Jackie," Kenya was the first to open her eyes. "Our girl called last night, and we came running," she explained.

"That's what I love most about you girls. No matter what, you're always there for one another."

"One for all, all for one," Alexis mumbled with her eyes still closed.

"I'm going to go down and make you girls a big breakfast. I'll come and get you when I'm done." With a smile and a warm heart, Jackie left the girls to their slumber as she went to make good on her promise.

For almost fifty minutes, she busied herself in the kitchen, wrestling with pots and pans while making frequent trips to the fridge from the stove. She had just set the table and grabbed a canister of orange juice when the girls came down the stairs. "Dang, Mama," Kita wiped sleep from her eyes, "you laid it out. What's the special occasion?"

"I don't need a special occasion to love on my girls." Jackie took a seat at the head of the table. "We've got bacon, sausage, mini-omelets, waffles, cheese grits, biscuits and gravy, hash browns, and orange juice. Dig in."

"You don't have to tell me twice." Kenya wasted no time fixing her plate.

"Mama Jackie, if there is any left over, do you mind if I take a plate to my grandma and Talia?"

"Baby, that's no problem at all. You all get started. I'll grab a few containers and make their plates now." Jackie sprang from her seat and retreated to the kitchen.

"What's wrong, Kita?" Kenya asked her friend when she noticed she wasn't eating.

"Nothing. I just don't have an appetite." Kita could barely look at the pieces of sausage or scrambled eggs without images of Bernard's brain matter invading her mind.

"I know what you mean," Alexis added.

Just as Jackie came back to the table, her cell phone rang. "Whoever it is will have to wait."

"Everything is delicious, Mama Jackie," Kenya said between bites of food.

"Thank you, but please slow down before you choke," Jackie teased, and everyone laughed. Seconds later, Jackie's cell phone rang again. This time, she got up to answer it, "Hello . . . wait, slow down. Who? What! Oh my goodness."

At the sound of Jackie's distress, everyone looked her way, waiting patiently to hear the tea. "Mama, what happened?" Kita asked once Jackie was off the phone. However, Jackie didn't say a word. Instead, she ran over to the television and fumbled with the remote. Kita, Alexis, and Kenya stood from the table and joined her in front of the television. Though the reporter's mouth was moving, no one heard a thing. They were all in shock as a recent image of Bernard appeared on the screen, with words below his picture that read: *Body found in a vacant house on Woodlawn St.*

"First Marlowe, now B?" Jackie looked at Kita. "What in the hell is going on around here?" Before anyone could speak, Jackie's cell phone started ringing again, and then there was a knock at the door. As Jackie answered the phone, Kita stared at the door. The room was beginning to spin, and her ears were ringing.

"Somebody, get the door, please." Jackie's voice snapped Kita back into reality.

With each step toward the door, her feet felt heavier. Her heart pounded like crazy and damn near exploded when she opened the door to see the detectives from the other night. "Miss Jones, I wish I could say it was nice to see you again." Detective Knox wore an unreadable expression. "Is your mother home?"

"Yes, I am Jaqueline Jones. Can I help you?" Jackie appeared in the doorway by her daughter's side.

"Ma'am, I am Detective Knox, and this is my partner, Detective Walters." The female officer extended a card that Jackie did not accept.

"Kita, go ahead and eat your breakfast before it gets cold." Jackie dismissed her daughter before continuing. "How can I help you, ma'am?"

On the other side of the door, Kita and her friends were about to shit bricks as each of them replayed in their heads what they'd done the night before.

"I don't know if Markita told you, but we were here the night your son Marlowe was shot."

"Yes, I'm aware." Jackie lied. The truth is, Kita hadn't told her anything. She was just going with the flow.

"Well, we've received word through our colleagues that your nephew Bernard was found murdered this morning, ma'am." Detective Knox tried her best to appear sympathetic.

"Yes, I was just made aware myself a few minutes ago." Jackie shifted her weight from one leg to the other.

"We believe that both of these crimes are somehow related. We just wanted to sit down and ask you and Markita some questions that may help us connect the investigations."

"Detective, I can't do this today. You'll have to come back another day or move on with your investigations without us," Jackie said as she prepared to close the door.

"I know this is difficult, but we only need a few minutes of your time."

"Detective, what you need to do is get your hand off my door and go do your job!" Without another word, Jackie slammed and locked the door. With tears in her eyes, she turned and faced the girls, who were already crying for totally different reasons.

# CHAPTER TWENTY-SEVEN

It had been nearly a week since Kita and her crew felt like they were sitting on pins and needles. Every knock at the door dropped their stomachs to their feet, and every siren they heard in the distance seemed like it was meant just for them. Paranoia was getting the best of them, and today was no different. "Come on, Kita, are you ready?" Jackie called from the landing of the stairs where she'd been waiting on Kita for nearly ten minutes.

"Coming," Kita responded for the fifth time.

"You've got two seconds before I come up there, and when I do, I promise you won't like it," Jackie threatened. With no additional options, Kita opened her door and went downstairs. She was wearing a pair of black jeans, a white top, and a frown.

"Mom, please don't make me go."

"Markita, what is the problem?" Jackie was confused. "Bernard was family. I can't believe you're acting like this."

"I feel like attending the service today is going to make me relive Marlowe's funeral, and I'm not ready for that." Kita tried her best to sound convincing, but the truth was that she'd rather be anywhere today than at the funeral services of the man she'd killed.

"I understand, baby, I do, but Aunt Rhonda is counting on us. She asked me to read the cards and you, the obituary, or vice versa."

"Ma, I can't do either of those things!" Kita protested loudly.

"Come on, girl; let's go." Jackie grabbed her keys and practically dragged Kita out of the house.

The ride to the funeral home was silent because both ladies were deep in thought for different reasons. Jackie tried to summon the courage to be strong for her sister, although she was still grieving, and Kita tried to summon the strength to act like Bernard's sorry ass would be missed. As Jackie pulled her car into the lot, she checked the GPS address to ensure she'd driven to the right place. "It's empty," she said, stating the obvious.

"There is Aunt Rhonda's car, so we have to be at the right place," Kita pointed out.

"Okay, come on. Let's go pay our respects." Jackie grabbed her purse and exited the car. Though taking her time, Kita did the same. On her way to the church, she pulled out her cell phone and shot a message to her friends. It read: This shit is dead . . . no pun intended!

Once inside the funeral home, Jackie and Kita took turns signing in before entering the small room where there were no bells and whistles, just a plain wooden box sitting at the front. Kita smirked because the casket was closed, which indicated that the funeral home had not been able to repair Bernard's head well enough to display his body. The generic sound of an organ playing in the background could be heard over the speakers. Rhonda sat with her boyfriend in the front row. Jackie sat beside her sister while Kita opted for a spot in the back. Unlike Marlowe's funeral, there were no floral arrangements, only one blown-up picture of Bernard, which, ironically, had been captured by Kita on Christmas.

After listening to the sound of the organ for fifteen minutes, Rhonda approached the podium. She tapped it twice to ensure it was working, but in reality, the twelve people in the room would have heard her just fine if it wasn't.

"For those who don't know, my name is Rhonda, and Bernard was my husband's son," she paused. "It's not a secret that Bernard was not an angel. Since he was a young child, he was always hell-bent on doing the wrong thing. I tried to love and guide him as best I could, but I knew in my heart that it would only be a matter of time before we ended up here. I'm surprised he lived this long."

Someone in the audience began to cough. Jackie looked back at Kita, who had her head down. It was apparent by everyone's reaction that no one could believe Rhonda was giving this kind of speech at her stepson's funeral. However, everyone listened as she continued.

"Anyway, I just wanted to say that I know Bernard was a difficult person to love, so I appreciate all of you for showing up today. It shows that each of you loved him. Thank you."

Feeling the need to undo some of the damage that her sister had done, Jackie took to the podium and cleared her throat. "Hey, everybody, Bernard was my nephew, but I loved him like a son. He was funny, charming, and, let's not forget, flashy." Jackie joked, and everyone erupted into laughter. "Bernard was my spades partner too." She began to wipe her eyes. "Above all of that, my nephew was caring. When my son died, he was the first person to call me in the morning and the last to call at night. Sometimes, he would even send me random text messages during the day. We'd share a joke or sometimes an old story, but no matter what, he made sure to tell me that he loved me and that he had my daughter and me . . ."

Jackie began to get choked up on her words. "I'm sad that B is gone, but I find comfort in knowing he has been reunited with my son. Those two were inseparable, so I pray they find each other in the afterlife. Rest well, Bernard. I love you. Now, come on up here, Kita, and say something for your cousin."

Kita began to feel a large lump form in her throat as she stared at her mother. Seemingly, everyone in the room was now looking back at her, so she felt obligated to say something. After taking several deep breaths, Kita willed herself to stand and approach the podium. She cleared her throat before speaking. "Bernard, I can't believe we're here again. This seems like a nightmare, and I pray every night that God wakes me up so things can be normal again. However, every morning, I'm reminded that this is real, and life for us will never be the same again. So, sleep on, dear cousin, and find peace knowing I will look after my mom and Aunt Rhonda."

Kita left the podium and reclaimed her seat in the back. After she spoke, two other people stood and gave remarks. One was a girl Bernard messed with sparingly, and the other was an older man who often hung out at the corner store.

When the service ended, there was no ride to the cemetery or repast. Everyone simply got into their vehicles and left. Jackie and Rhonda talked in the parking lot for a few minutes while Kita sat in the car contemplating the day's events. Though she felt no remorse for what she'd done, it was quite sad to see that Bernard's funeral service had turned out the way it did. Not one person in the whole place loved him more than the person he'd inflicted the most pain upon, which was her mother. "I hope hell is hot, B!" Kita mumbled as Jackie opened the door.

"Well, looks like it's just you and me, kid." Jackie held out her hand. Instinctively, Kita gently placed her hand on top of her mother's.

"Always and forever," Kita replied.

"Promise me that you will get back on track with school and finish what you started. With Marlowe and Bernard gone, things will be different, but you can still go to school and make something of yourself." Jackie gazed lovingly into her daughter's eyes.

"I promise," Kita replied.

# CHAPTER TWENTY-EIGHT

As days turned into weeks and weeks into months, the rumors about who killed Marlowe and Bernard died down, and the investigation had seemingly grown cold. Though they were in the clear, Kita and Kenya still decided to keep a low profile until graduation. They'd kept their heads down in the books and bypassed most senior activities, including prom. The incident with Bernard and Marlowe altered how they saw life and made them more mature. After dealing with trauma like that, the happenings of high school no longer appealed to them.

Alexis, on the other hand, was the complete opposite. As things with her and Breeze got serious, she began hanging out more with his crew, which meant she saw less of her friends with each passing month. When graduation rolled around, the once-best friends felt like distant strangers. Jackie didn't like this for the girls and wanted desperately to intervene, but she was too busy working multiple jobs to do anything about it.

Before long, the summer had passed, and Kita was preparing for her flight to Washington. Though she'd dreamed of attending Howard University her whole life, she was far from prepared to start fall classes. Neither her head nor her heart was in it anymore because, without Marlowe, her dream just didn't make sense. The doorbell rang as she stared at the suitcase sitting on her floor. Thankful for the distraction, she eagerly headed toward the door. To her surprise, Kenya and Alexis stood there holding congratulations balloons, a bouquet of roses, and a teddy bear. "Hey, y'all, what are you doing here?" With a huge smile, Kita hugged her friends.

"Did you think we would let you sneak off to Washington without a proper goodbye?" Alexis handed Kita the bear.

"We have one more gift too." In true Kenya fashion, she pulled a blunt from behind her ear.

"Aww, y'all are so sweet." Kita's eyes began to water. "Damn, I missed the hell out of y'all."

"I missed y'all too," Kenya added. "There is so much that's going on right now."

"Same here," Alexis laughed. "Hanging with Breeze is cool, but he could never replace my besties. There is so much catching up we have to do."

"Come on; y'all are just in time to help me pack." Kita led her friends upstairs, where they resumed their usual positions around the room, pretending to be helpful. Kenya immediately stretched out across the bed while Alexis ran right into the closet to rummage through Kita's clothes. "So, what's new?"

"I got a job!" Kenya declared. However, before her friends could share their excitement, she added, "It's at a cellular company and only makes $15.25 an hour. What the hell am I supposed to do with that?"

"At least you have a job. That's the first thing on my to-do list when I get to Washington. Shit has been tight around here lately." Kita folded up a sweatshirt and put it in her suitcase.

"Is that why you didn't go to prom?" Alexis returned from the closet carrying a red dress and shoes.

"No, I didn't go because it just didn't feel right. How was it?"

"Girl, y'all didn't miss anything." Alexis held up the dress to her body. "I stayed for about an hour. Then I called Breeze to come and get me."

"Speaking of Breeze," Kenya sat up on the bed, "how's that going?"

"Are there any wedding bells yet? You two have been on each other like white on rice these days," Kita giggled.

"Things are going okay," Alexis paused. "I love him, and I think he loves me, although he's never outright said it. He treats me like a queen and gets me anything my heart desires, but I noticed that the more he does for me, the more it seems like he's controlling me." She placed the dress on the bed, then joined Kita on the floor.

"What do you mean by controlling you?" Kenya asked.

"For example, the other day, he took me shopping and then asked where I wanted to eat dinner. I said I wanted seafood, but he said he was feeling steak and that the dress he'd just bought me would look good beneath the lights at Moe's Steakhouse."

"So, you got a new dress and ate steak," Kenya teased. "Sounds like you winning if you ask me." She jokingly laughed, and everyone else followed suit.

"I just wish I had some independence, but don't get me wrong. The steak was good, and I looked bad as motherfucker in that dress!" Alexis fell over in laughter as Kenya playfully hit her with the pillow.

The remainder of the night went like this, and the friends chuckled until their stomachs hurt as they caught up on the happenings in each other's lives for over three hours. It was a much-needed reunion for everyone, and when it was over, the trio was back tight like never before. Just before midnight, everyone said their goodbyes and promised to call soon. After letting them out, Kita returned to putting the final touches on her luggage. When she finished, she grabbed a picture from the wall of her and Marlowe. Over the past few months, she had tried not to think of him, but today, he was heavy on her mind. Grabbing her cell phone, she scrolled to her music app and began to play one of her favorite sad songs over the Bluetooth speaker. *"Although we've come to the end of the road . . ."* Kita crooned along with the music, word for word. When the song was over, she played it again and then one more time for good measure. Though some time had passed, it was still hard to believe that her brother was gone. If her tears could've built a stairwell to heaven, she'd be able to see him daily.

"Kita, please play something else, baby." Jackie poked her head into her daughter's room. The song was wearing her out. She knew this was a part of Kita's grieving process, but Jackie couldn't take it any longer.

"Mama, I didn't hear you come in." Kita stopped the music. "How was work?"

"It was long but not too bad. I'm about to grab a bite, shower, and catch some sleep before I have to get up and take you to the airport in the morning."

"Mama, I could've arranged another ride so you could sleep in a little. I know you have to go to work after taking me."

"Girl, hush! You know there ain't nothing in this world going to keep me from seeing my baby off to college." Closing the bedroom door, Jackie headed back downstairs to the kitchen to eat and open the mail that she'd been putting off reading for a while.

One by one, each envelope contained a bill of some sort. Almost all of them were past due or shut-off notices. "Damn." Jackie rubbed her forehead. This was something she thought she'd never have to worry about again.

"Hey, Mama, guess who stopped by." Jackie tried to cover the bills with her fast-food bag as Kita entered the kitchen. "What's all of that?"

"Never mind this. Who came over, baby?"

"Mama, how bad is it?" Kita attempted to grab some mail, but Jackie blocked her.

"It ain't nothing a little more overtime can't help."

"Do you have any money saved?" Kita asked.

"Kita, I used every dollar I had on Marlowe's funeral. I couldn't give him much in life, but in death, I owed him that kind of service. The rest of the money I've used here and there to keep us afloat. This house and all that comes with it ain't cheap. Part of me wants to walk away from it and find something more affordable. But I just can't bring myself to do it because I remember how happy Marlowe was when he gave it to us." Jackie collected the stack of mail and placed it into a neat pile before rubber-banding it and putting it into her work bag to deal with later.

"Mama, I'm sorry I haven't helped you more." Kita had been in her own world, so focused on graduation, that she'd missed the signs that her mother needed her. "I still have that money from Marlowe for college. Please take that and catch everything up."

"No, ma'am. You need that money for school, textbooks, and everything else."

"Mama, I know you don't want to hear this," Kita sighed, "but I don't think school is for me right now."

"Markita Jones, I *don't* want to hear that mess." Jackie slapped her hand down on the counter. "You will go to that school and make something of yourself, do you hear me?"

"Mama, I promise I will attend school, but not now. You know better than anybody that the last thing I need to do is go to Washington tomorrow. I can't focus enough as it is, and my heart ain't in it. If I go there, I will probably flunk out and be right back here before the end of the semester."

"Kita—"

"Mama, if I go up there and waste Marlowe's money, you will be pissed, so why not just take it and do what you gotta do? I can stay home, help around here for a while, and then enroll in school once we're caught up."

"Baby, I will figure this out regardless of whether you are here, but if you truly need to take some gap time off from school, then take it." Jackie rubbed her temples.

"Really?" Kita squealed.

"I wish you'd go off to school and get that degree, but I do understand if you need some time. The past couple of months have been rough on everyone."

"I promise, Mama, I will help you figure this out, and as soon as I do, I will enroll in school, even if it's not at Howard."

"Okay, Kita." Jackie yawned. "I'm going to head on up and call it a night. I love you."

"Love you more." Kita hugged her mom and watched her leave the kitchen.

After listening closely to her footsteps up the stairs and her door closing, Kita reached into Jackie's work bag and retrieved the bills. Carefully, she inspected them all before placing them back in their spot. For half an hour, she sat in silence, trying to rack her brain for a strategy. That's when her next move hit her like a ton of bricks . . . literally!

# CHAPTER TWENTY-NINE

The next day, once Jackie left for work, Kita called her friends over for an emergency meeting. Initially, she was met with some resistance because Kenya had to work, and Alexis was babysitting her sister. However, they relented once they heard the urgency in Kita's tone. Shortly after ending the call, Kita retreated to the basement and grabbed Marlowe's hidden treasure. Until last night, she'd forgotten all about it.

After carrying the heavy bag up the stairs into her room, she opened it and reviewed the contents. In addition to a few bricks of cocaine, there were two digital scales, a Ziplock filled with clear baggies, an industrial box of baking soda, a pot, a large Pyrex measuring bowl, several pairs of surgical gloves, an N95 mask, and a pink envelope. Kita's heart raced when she saw her name on it. Instantly, she knew it was her birthday card from Marlowe. "Damn," she sniffed as her face became flooded with tears. For several seconds, she contemplated opening the card and reading his final message to her, but instead, she decided to keep it for a day when she needed to feel his presence. The doorbell rang just as Kita tucked the card between her mattress and box spring. As suspected, it was Kenya, Alexis, and Talia.

"What's the emergency?" Kenya asked upon entry into the house. Alexis said nothing as she walked Talia over to the sofa and turned the television on the Discovery Channel.

"I think Disney is on 204." Kita walked into the kitchen and grabbed a bag of chips from the pantry to give to Talia.

"I'm not a baby." Talia plopped down on the couch and made herself comfortable.

"She likes the Discovery channel and the news," Alexis giggled. "She spends too much time with my grandma."

"Anyway, girl, what's the tea?" Kenya checked her cell phone for the time.

"What if I told y'all we had a surefire way to earn some extra money?" Kita glanced around at her friends.

"Shit, I'd say sign me up." Alexis was all ears. "A girl like me ain't never gon' turn down no extra money."

"I'd ask you what's the catch." Kenya folded her arms across her chest.

"Damn, why you always gotta be like that?" Alexis smacked her lips.

"Like what?" Kenya rolled her eyes.

"Calm down, ladies, and follow me." Kita led her friends upstairs toward her room.

"You want to start selling dope?" Alexis replied after finding the bricks of cocaine on Kita's bed.

"I've been holding Marlowe's bricks since the day he got shot, but two of these came from what we stole from Bernard." Kita watched as her friends inspected the wrapped bundles of illegal substances.

"Are you out of your fucking mind?" Kenya gave Kita a stare that said she knew better.

"Hear me out." Kita raised her hands in surrender. "I thought we could sell what we have and split the profit for a quick come-up. Once it's gone, we're done."

"Again, I ask, are you out of your fucking mind? We are motherfucking college-bound bitches, not fucking drug dealers."

"Last night, I told my mom I wasn't going to Howard. I won't attend any university until I get things squared away here first." Kita hated to admit to her friends that she was putting her dream on hold, but it was what it was. "I'll admit, I don't know everything about the dope game, but I know we all could desperately use the money. If we put our heads together and combine our resources, we could rock this shit!"

Though Kita did her best to appeal to her friends, she knew what she asked them to do was nothing small, and they would need time to consider. "You don't have to answer me today, and you don't have to say yes. I've already chosen, but I wanted to bring you guys in if you wanted to be down."

The room fell silent as each girl pondered over what their friend had just proposed. Although the drug trade was a man's game that came with more downs than ups, they knew that Kita was right. Why couldn't they get a piece of the action? Kenya was tired of seeing her mother work so damn hard just to get nowhere, and Alexis was tired of being the flavor of the week. Her only taste of the good life came when she was the arm candy of D's boy, and although she and Breeze were getting serious, there was no telling when he'd be done with her and on to the next like every nigga before him had done.

"You know the game has a funny way of ending friendships, right?" Kenya paused. "Shit! For the paper and clout, Rico switched up Mitch, Nino switched up on G-Money, and Bernard switched up on Marlowe. I'm not trying to lose y'all like that."

Kita extended her arm, holding her hand midway in the air. "So, let's make a pact that we flip these bricks, make some money, and then we're out of the game!"

"I'm in as long as we vow to have one another's back, no matter what!" Alexis placed her hand on top of Kita's.

"There is no 'I' in the word 'team,' and as long as we do this, everybody has a say-so on how we do it . . . agreed?" Kenya waited for a response before adding her hand to the pact.

"Agreed," Kita and Alexis shouted, and the deal was done.

# CHAPTER THIRTY

For several days, Kita and her crew devised a plan to get their temporary illegal business off the ground. They decided to sell most of the product as powder because it was simple, and the profit margin was higher. However, Alexis still finessed Breeze into teaching her how to turn some of the cocaine into top-tier crack rocks just in case there was a market for it.

While she was busy with her man, Kenya and Kita scouted the city to find locations to sell from. Though there were abandoned dwellings on practically every street corner, the ladies had no desire to trap the old way. Instead, they leveraged their connections with local businesses that middle-manned drug sales to specific clientele for a small portion of the profits. Within weeks, they'd secured a potential opportunity for an exclusive deal through Reggie's Exotic Mobile Detailing Service, The Lion's Den Gentlemen's Club, and Star Nails. Each of these businesses had a legitimate side and an illegal one.

The legit side operated normally to keep up appearances and the books clean. However, the illegal side was run by Joey Lenox, a small-time hustler who prided himself on being the go-to guy for everything. Joey didn't care if the client had weird fetishes or risky, middle-of-the-night requests as long as their money was good.

The girls had gone to school with him, and though he'd graduated a year before them, they still ran in some of the same circles. When Joey found out what his old classmates were trying to get into, he quickly offered to work with them as long as their product was right, which Kita guaranteed it was. Joey took her number and promised to call when a client needed blow.

"When I call, you better come correct or don't come at all," he warned. Since then, a day had turned into three, and then five, but there was still no word from Joey.

As Kita lay across her bed, aimlessly thumbing through a magazine, the buzzing of her cell phone captured her attention. "What's up, Lex?"

"Aye, meet me at my cousin Shyla's spot. Do you still remember where she lives?"

"I do," Kita frowned, "but what is this about?"

"I can't say much on the phone; just meet me there," she said. With that, she ended the call. Instantly, Kita's mind began to race as she thought of all the reasons Alexis would summon her over to Shyla's. The first thing that came to mind was that maybe Shyla was trying to shake them down for what she saw at Bernard's spot. The second thing that came to mind was that Shyla and her friends were looking for some party favors.

It took about fifteen minutes for Kita to decide to go and see what was going on instead of overthinking it. When she arrived, she paused at the door to see if she could hear anything, but everything was quiet, so she knocked on the door. Two seconds later, Alexis opened it. Kita stepped into the house and glanced around.

"What's up?"

"I had an idea, but I'll tell you when Kenya returns from the bathroom." Alexis took a seat on a folding chair in the kitchen.

"Where's your cousin?" Kita whispered as Kenya entered the room.

"Probably out somewhere getting drunk or high. Who knows," Alexis shrugged.

"All right, let's get this meeting underway." Kenya took a seat. "Tell us your idea, Lex."

"As y'all know, I've spent several days breaking down the coke, weighing it, and bagging it up into various sizes. I've even rocked some up, and we haven't sold shit. So, while we wait on Joey, I was thinking we can sell some out of Shyla's crib."

"I don't know about that," Kita frowned.

"Think about it before shutting me down. Damn." Alexis stood and began to pace the floor. "We have all of this product ready to go, and we ain't made a sale yet! I mean, wasn't the goal—to make money?"

"She's right, Kita," Kenya chimed in. "Shyla's crib is the perfect spot to trap from if she lets us. She and her friends would be like built-in clientele . . . easy money."

"So let me get this straight. Y'all think it's a good idea to sell drugs out of the home of a crackhead?" Kita's eyes darted from Alexis to Kenya.

"All Shyla would want is some complimentary shit here and there, and we're good. She'll let us do whatever we got to do to get that shit off." Alexis grabbed Kita's arms. "Look, Kita, when it comes to the books, baby, you got it, but in the streets, I'm a straight-A student. A real hustler would never pass on an opportunity like this. While we sit around waiting on a call from Joey that may never come, we could be out making money."

Though Kita didn't think Alexis's plan was the best, she had to admit that she did have a point. "All right, cool. Kenya, it sounds like you're in on this, so I guess I am too."

"I promise you won't regret this." Alexis squealed, happy that her friends trusted her decision-making skills. For as long as they'd been cool, she never expressed it but often felt like the odd one in the group because she wasn't as smart as them. While they focused on books and strengthening their brains, Alexis focused on survival. Life had been her greatest teacher, and the streets had been her favorite classroom. She knew without a shadow of a doubt that if her friends wanted to do well in their new venture, they had to let her take the lead.

# CHAPTER THIRTY-ONE

True to her word, Alexis's idea to hustle from Shyla's house was indeed a great one. With Marlowe and Bernard off the streets, there had been somewhat of a drought throughout the city. Breeze had even mentioned that things for him would be slow until he found a new connection. Alexis felt bad for her man but dared not expose herself to him, especially since things would only be temporary. Once word got out that customers had found a new location to cop from, they began to show up at Shyla's house in numbers. Just like in the fast-food industry, there was a breakfast, lunch, and dinner rush, which simultaneously excited and overwhelmed Kita, Alexis, and Kenya. Though they knew it was safer to stick together, they had to split into three shifts to keep up with the demand. The girls were getting money every hour on the hour like clockwork, and life was finally beginning to look up.

Kita sat at the bottom of the stairs, lacing up her shoes when her mother came through the front door. Due to busy schedules, they hadn't seen much of each other in the past few days, so this encounter was a welcomed surprise. "Hey, Mama. How was work?"

"Girl!" Jackie groaned. "I'm not going to waste my breath talking about that place. How has work been going for you? It feels like I barely see you these days."

"It's been pretty busy," Kita stood. "I'm headed there now."

"Oh no, at this hour?" Jackie glanced down at her watch. "What kind of company has customer service shifts this late?"

"The kind with global customers, Mama," Kita quickly responded. "Did you know it's only one p.m. in Australia right now?"

"What's with the black scarf?" Jackie pointed to the bandanna tied around Kita's neck.

"It's cold in the office, so I wear it to keep my neck warm." The lie had come out so smoothly that Kita damn near believed it herself.

"They still sell sweaters, scarves, and turtlenecks, right?" Jackie frowned. "Maybe I can find you something more presentable in my closet. You look like a little hoodlum with that thing on. You don't want your coworkers getting the wrong idea, do you?"

"Ma, I'm good. This was Marlowe's. I wear it because it smells like him," Kita hadn't lied about that part.

"I'm sorry for giving you a hard time, baby. Sometimes, it's hard to watch you grow up, and no matter how hard I try, I can't stop worrying about you." Jackie pulled Kita in for a hug. "The world is a dangerous place, and I don't want anybody getting the wrong idea about my girl, but I am proud of you because I know this adjustment hasn't been easy."

"Thanks, Ma. I love you."

"Hey, let's watch a movie on one of those streaming apps this weekend if you can spare some time for your old mama." Jackie smiled warmly.

"I'll do you one better. How about I take you to the movies, and if you're good for the rest of the week, I'll even treat you to popcorn too," Kita laughed.

"Oh, can I get McDonald's afterward too?" Jackie mimicked Kita when she was younger.

"Now, Jaqueline," this time it was Kita's turn to mimic, "you know I don't have McDonald's money."

"Girl, stop it! I did not sound like that," Jackie laughed.

"When you get to the theater, don't look at nothing, don't touch nothing, and don't ask for nothing except a small popcorn." With a smile, Kita stared at her mother, who was laughing hysterically. It was nice to see Jackie do something she hadn't done much of lately. When they finished with the jokes, Kita hugged her mother good night, then went to Shyla's house to relieve Kenya, who had class in the morning.

When she arrived at the trap, there was a small line outside of at least six people looking to score their fix for the night. Kita took a second to admire the scenery. She felt proud and wondered if the adrenaline she felt at that very moment was the feeling that had kept her brother in the game for so long. There was something addictive about seeing the crowd with money in their hands that made Kita feel like she was on top of the world, though this was only the beginning.

After taking in the scene at the front of the house, Kita walked around the side and entered through the back door. As usual, the place was quiet. Shyla was nowhere to be found, but Kenya sat on a chair near the front door, reading a large textbook. "Hey, girl! It's been busy as hell tonight. I'm about to start calling us the '*Get Money Girls*.'"

"Yeah, I saw the line outside." Kita walked over to the fridge and grabbed water. "Word must be getting out."

"I've been trying to finish this damn chapter for three hours." Kenya closed her book and reached into her pocket to retrieve the money she'd made. "Alexis made $1,500 this afternoon, and I made $3,200." Kenya counted a variation of green bills. "Here's your cut of everything, and here is Lex's cut of my shift."

"Damn! Hopefully, I can triple that amount for us tonight." Kita pointed to Kenya's book. "What are you reading?"

"It's called *The New Jim Crow* by Michelle Alexander. It's required reading for one of my classes this semester, so I figured I'd get it out of the way early. It's good." Kenya placed the book into her bag and retrieved a black Glock. Breeze had purchased the gun off the street for Alexis to carry as protection, but she let the crew hold on to it during their shift. The gun Marlowe had purchased Kita was legally registered, so she didn't carry it when trapping. After carefully handing the weapon to Kita, the women said their goodbyes.

Once alone, Kita relaxed in the chair by the door and waited for the action. Within the first two hours, the traffic was nonstop, but after a while, things slowed down tremendously, giving her time to catch up on her social media pages. Someone tapped on the door as soon as she placed her phone back into her pocket.

"What do you need?" Kita adjusted her voice to sound deeper and stern.

"Let me holler at you right quick, youngin'." The voice on the other side of the door sounded familiar, but Kita couldn't place it.

"Tell me what you need, or get the fuck on!"

"I need a 50 ball," he said.

Kita pulled the black bandanna over her nose and mouth, grabbed a baggie from the table, and opened the door, prepared to complete the transaction through the mailbox slot on the gated, metal screen door. "Where is the money, nigga?"

"Youngin', I don't have the cash on me right now, but I have a couple of things you might be interested in." The man standing in the shadows reached into his pocket and pulled out a cheap watch and a small tablet with a blue shark case over it.

"Nigga, did you bring your kid's tablet to cover your bill?" Kita was enraged as she thought of her own childhood.

"He'll be all right, won't you, little man?" The customer turned and kneeled to speak with the toddler standing behind him. "You know Daddy is sick and needs his medicine, right?"

"Nah, bro, you're tripping." Kita's heart sank as she saw the sadness in the boy's eyes. "Take his ass home," she demanded.

"Come on, don't be like that. I'm hurting right now."

"We don't take toys, nigga. Cash only. Come back with the money and without the kid, and I got you." Kita closed the door and listened to the customer knock for almost five minutes before finally getting the hint.

Kita felt sad for the child as she assessed his exposure to this lifestyle and even the part she played in his childhood trauma. However, that didn't stop her from serving the next customer. She knew all was fair in the drug game because morals and ethics didn't exist. Yes, these customers had families that loved them and didn't want to see them hasten their demise, but the harsh reality was that if they didn't cop from Kita, they would surely cop from someone else. For that reason alone, she quickly snapped out of her funk and continued with business.

# CHAPTER THIRTY-TWO

It was just before eight in the morning when the sound of Kita's cell phone jolted her awake. She'd fallen asleep in the chair almost an hour ago when the rush ended. "Hello." With one eye closed, she tried to catch the name on the caller ID, but it said UNKNOWN.

"Hey, it's Joey. Can you and your girls join me and my clients tonight for dinner at The Boat House? It's a small gathering, but they like to party."

"What time?" Kita stood from the chair and stretched.

"Let's say around 6:30 p.m. and bring three of your best-looking fat friends. My clients are chubby chasers."

"Bet." Kita ended the call and placed the phone into the back pocket of her jeans. "Hell yeah!" she squealed, elated to finally receive Joey's call.

"About time your ass woke up." Alexis approached the kitchen.

"Bitch, I've only been sleeping for about forty-five minutes. When did you get here?" Kita wiped sleep from her eyes.

"Probably half an hour ago. What's all of the excitement for?" Alexis quizzed.

"Joey finally called. He wants us to meet him tonight at The Boat House. He spoke in code words, but I think he wants three ounces."

"Oh shit, we're about to get paid for real!" Alexis jumped up and down. "For real, if we can get a few more calls like that, we'll be done with this much sooner than we thought."

"Facts." Kita pulled the money she'd collected from her pocket. "I made a little over $2,600 last night." Kita went about the actions of dividing the money three ways.

"Man, it feels good to have money, doesn't it?" Alexis made a show of thumbing through her cash. "It's going to be hard to adjust when we sell out of the product."

"That's why you at least need to save a few dollars." Kita pointed to the new Gucci shoes on her friend's feet. "I wasn't going to say anything, but I peeped the new shit. You better slow down."

"I didn't have to suck or fuck nobody for the money, so I treated myself to a little shopping spree. It was a celebration of my independence." Alexis looked down at her shoes.

"I ain't mad at you, boo." Kita hugged her friend goodbye, handed her the Glock, and headed for the door.

Before going home to catch up on sleep, Kita stopped at the grocery store to grab a few things they were low on at the house, like bread, eggs, cheese, and milk. After paying the cashier, Kita headed outside and popped the trunk of her car. Aside from a white van and five other cars, the lot was empty. Kita smiled as she placed her items into the trunk because it felt good to chip in. Though she hadn't purchased anything major like Alexis had, she felt like the grocery trip was her celebration of independence too.

Just as Kita went to close the trunk, she was forcefully pushed from the back. Before she could understand what was happening, the trunk closed, locking her inside. "Help!" she screamed as the car's ignition turned on and the vehicle began to move. "What the fuck! Let me out!"

As the car sped off, Kita kicked and banged, trying hard to fight her way out. When that mission failed, she reached into her pocket to retrieve her phone. Frantically, she dialed 911, but the signal was nonexistent. Fearing for her life, Kita searched the car for anything she could use as a weapon, but other than groceries, she had nothing. She closed her eyes and tried to listen to anything that could give her a clue about who had taken her and where they were headed, but the car was silent. As the vehicle continued to drive at high speeds, Kita wondered if this was a sex-trafficking situation. She'd recently read that between fifteen thousand and fifty thousand women and children were abducted each year and sold into trafficking rings. Her mind raced as she thought about how to get out of this, and she began hyperventilating. It felt like the trunk space was getting smaller by the second. At any moment, she thought she would suffocate . . . but then the car stopped.

Impatiently, Kita waited what felt like hours but was merely minutes for the trunk to open, and when it did, her mouth fell open. "Arman?"

"Markita, I hate we had to meet like this." He extended his hand and helped her out. Kita's eyes roamed the area, trying to find something that could identify where she had been taken.

"What's going on? Where are we?" Markita was very confused. She never thought she'd cross paths with her brother's connect again, especially like this.

"Relax. This industrial garage is one of my properties." Arman reached into his jacket pocket and removed a pack of cigarettes and a light. Kita thought he was reaching for a gun, so she flinched. "I'm not going to hurt you. I brought you here to talk."

"Talk about what?" Kita's eyes shifted past Arman to see Davit in the distance. He appeared to be on a phone call.

"Well, for starters, we can talk about the drugs you've been pushing on the West Side of Detroit." Arman pulled hard on his cigarette. "*My* drugs."

"Your drugs?" Kita repeated.

"Picture it." Arman held his hands in the air to imitate a screen. "Marlowe picks up a drop of his usual quantity on consignment, drives away, gets shot, and ends up in the hospital. I think this is a robbery attempt, and my product is gone. However, when I visit Marlowe in the hospital, he doesn't say that, so I relax. He tells me he'll be back on the street making money in no time, and I believe him because I know Marlowe. If he said he would do something, I know he'd die trying, at the very least. However, things take the ultimate turn for the worst, and Marlowe dies. Now I'm worried, so I go and shake down Marlowe's partner, your cousin, Bernard. I ask him where my fucking product is, and he swears on a stack of Bibles that he doesn't know. I tell him it doesn't matter because Marlowe's debt is now his debt. After all, that's how partnerships work. I gave him a few weeks to get my fucking money to me, and then you know what happened?" Arman didn't wait for a response. "Bernard is found dead too, so then I had to officially place finding my product on the 'lost cause' list. I even lost a few nights of sleep thinking about that loss, but then I get word that my product or something very similar has turned back up in an unlikely place. Do you see where I'm going with this?" Arman cut to the chase. "Where did you get those bricks from?"

She said, "Marlowe asked me to hold on to the dope the night he got shot."

"Markita," Arman sighed, "I'm going to need the $150,000 that they're worth, and I'm going to need that money today."

"Today?" Kita couldn't believe what she was hearing. Even with the pending sale from Joey, there was no way she could repay a debt that large on such short notice. "Arman, I'm sorry. I had no idea those bricks were on consignment. They'd been sitting in the basement collecting dust, so I decided to flip them with my friends because we all needed the money. My mom and I have been struggling since Marlowe died."

"While I appreciate the heartfelt story, business is business." Arman flicked his cigarette to the ground and stepped on it with the sole of a Louboutin loafer. "I need my money today."

"Arman, I understand the urgency, but I don't have that much money." Kita's eyes pleaded with him to show her some compassion. "Marlowe and Bernard had a system. They had street soldiers and several large buyers. It's just me and two of my friends. I will get you your money, but I need more time."

Arman smiled. "You have so much tenacity, just like your brother, and I like that. With that said, Markita, I dislike how you and your brother use that 'friend' word so loosely. I believe that your brother lost his life because of a friend, and I caution you not to do the same."

"You're right. My brother indeed lost his life because he called the wrong person his friend, but I took care of that. It won't bring back my brother, but it does help me sleep a little." Kita didn't care one bit that she'd just incriminated herself to Arman because she knew the chances of him being wired were slim, especially since he so freely talked about his cocaine.

"It was you that took care of Bernard?" Arman's eyes lit up like a fireworks display.

"Yeah, for my brother, and I'd do it repeatedly if I had to."

"Wow! I'm impressed." Arman stroked his chin. "Markita, I might have underestimated you. How do you feel about taking Marlowe's place beneath my umbrella and picking up where he left off?"

Kita was stunned into silence as she weighed her options. "Arman, I—"

"If you decide to work for me, I will dissolve this debt as my gift to you for saving my daughter. You and your associates are free to take the profits and do what you please. After that, our agreement will mimic the deal Marlowe and I had, which was ten bricks every two weeks. You can either do consignment prices for a 60/40 split, or you can pay wholesale prices upfront, which equate to a 50/50 split." Arman could sense the hesitation on his acquaintance's face, so he continued. "Join my team, and you will become the hero in your story. You can save the day for you and your mother, picking up the pieces right where your brother left them. The money you make in the drug trade can change your life if you know how to do it."

After several seconds of silence, Markita finally spoke. "Will you teach me?"

Arman's smile widened. "I will show you everything you need to know because I see the same fire in your eyes that I used to see in your brother's. It is on you to teach the others because, from this moment on, I will only deal with you, Kita. Don't tell them my name, and I have no interest in knowing theirs. Things are just cleaner this way, understood?"

# CHAPTER THIRTY-THREE

The ride home was silent as Kita tried to digest everything that had taken place in the last hour. She'd gone from a nobody on the streets to becoming a major player in the dope game before noon. As she pulled her car into the driveway, she shot a group text to her crew, letting them know that she wanted to have a big meeting. Without waiting for them to reply, Kita tucked the phone back into her pocket, exited the car, then proceeded toward her door. While walking across the lawn, a tow truck driver crept up slowly. At first, Kita paid it no mind, but then he stopped and reversed into her driveway, and his backup sirens blared. "Can I help you?" Kita asked once the driver was in view.

"Yeah, I have an order from the finance company to repossess this vehicle for defaulting on the loan." The tow truck driver was a tall, muscular, yet slightly overweight man. With a frown, Kita watched him struggle down off the truck and waddle over to her with a clipboard. "I'm showing the name Marlowe Jones on the loan. Is that you?"

"How much do I need to pay to keep you from towing my car?" Kita folded her arms and stood with an attitude.

"Let's see." He reached for the glasses clipped to his neon vest, put them on, and reviewed the work order. "It looks like $5,086.49 is needed to bring the loan current and take care of the additional fees charged for us having to come out here."

"Okay, hold on one second. I'll grab some money and be right back. Please don't tow my shit!" Kita flew into the house like a bat out of hell. She ran to her room and into the closet to retrieve the gold glass jewelry box hidden on the top shelf. Quickly, she grabbed some money and returned downstairs to pay the driver. After counting the cash twice, he filled out the form as proof of payment and provided her with a copy.

"The finance company's information is at the bottom next to your account number. You can call them and set up autopayments to receive a monthly discount. It's probably not much, but a dollar is a dollar, right?" The driver saw that Kita could care less about his suggestion, so he wished her a good day and left without another word.

For the remainder of the afternoon, Markita slept until it was time to return to Shyla's house. She wanted to catch both Kenya and Alexis at the same before they switched shifts. Upon arrival, Kita noticed that Shyla's neighborhood looked very different in the daylight than it did at night, and it was quiet too.

"What's up, girl?" Lex called from the doorway. Her smile was as big as Texas.

"What up, doe?" Kita reached for a dap.

"Are you ready for tonight? I've been thinking about that shit all day." Alexis rubbed her hands together.

"Me too." Kita entered the house to see Shyla sitting on her sofa, drinking from a red cup. "What's up?" she nodded.

"Same shit, different day," Shyla responded without bothering to look in Kita's direction. Just then, Kenya entered the house carrying her bag and the book she had been reading the day before.

"What's up, y'all?"

"Just in time for Kita's meeting and payout." Alexis reached into her purse and produced several green bills. "Today was slow, I only made about $650."

"Damn, that's less than $220 split three ways." Kenya used mental math.

"Um . . ." Shyla cleared her throat. "Don't y'all think it's time for me to get cut in? I've been more than accommodating, wouldn't you say?" She sashayed over to the girls with her hand out.

"What are you talking about?" Alexis smacked her lips. "We break you off something every fucking day." She reached for a baggie of cocaine and held it up.

"Those little twenty-dollar bumps here and there are cool and all, but since y'all been here around the clock, I need some money on my bills."

"You're tripping, Shyla!" Alexis shook her head. "We had a deal. Don't act grimy."

"Grimy?" Shyla repeated. "Bitch, if I was grimy, I would've gone to the police and snitched on your ass for being at Bernard's spot the night he was killed." Shyla scoffed, "Yeah, y'all forgot about that, huh? Well, I didn't, and I think the police would find it too much of a coincidence that y'all miraculously came up on this cocaine after he was murdered."

"Bitch!" Within an instance, Alexis pulled out the gun she was carrying in her bra and pointed it at her cousin. "You, of all people, should know not to threaten me!"

Immediately, Shyla raised her hands in surrender as Kita and Kenya tried to intervene. "What would it take to keep your mouth closed, Shyla?" Kita held her breath while waiting for the response.

"I need at least $10,500 a month," Shyla spat.

"You done lost your fucking mind!" Alexis cocked her gun. "I will kill you right here before I let you hustle me like that."

No one in the room knew if Alexis was serious, but they knew enough not to second-guess her. "Okay, listen, Shyla. That amount is a big stretch, but we can make $4,500 happen." Markita hoped that Shyla would make the right decision. If not, she knew they'd have two dead bodies under their belt.

After several seconds of silence, Shyla nodded her head. "Yeah, I guess we can make that work."

# CHAPTER THIRTY-FOUR

Things at Shyla's house had gotten so intense that Kita decided it was best to close up shop for the night. Though Shyla eventually agreed to the more reasonable terms, Kita knew everyone needed time to calm down. After paying Shyla a portion of her money for the month, the trio decided to discuss business over lunch at The Seafood King on West McNichols. When they arrived, the place was empty, which provided the perfect setting to get down to the nitty-gritty. Within a few minutes, the ladies were seated by their waitress, given menus, and provided with water. Everyone knew what they wanted, so they wasted no time getting right to it. Once all orders were placed, the food hit the table in less than fifteen minutes, and everyone dug in.

"Okay, so should we dress up to meet with Joey?" Kenya asked with a mouthful of food. "I've never been to The Boat House."

"Sorry, Kenya, that will have to wait for right now. We got some other shit we need to discuss first." Kita bit down on her Cajun corn, then wiped her mouth. "When I left the spot earlier, I was forced into the trunk of my car and kidnapped."

"*What?*" Kenya interjected.

"By whom?" Alexis added.

"If y'all let me finish, all your questions will be answered." Kita giggled. "Anyway, it was Marlowe's plug. He came to collect his money for the drugs we've been selling."

"How much?" Alexis placed the crab leg she'd just broken down onto the plate.

"He said $150,000." Kita leaned in closely. "Due at the end of the day."

Kenya began to choke so badly that she needed water. "We don't have that kind of money."

"That's what I told him." Kita nodded.

"Well, obviously, he let you live, so what *did* he say?" Alexis had lost her appetite by now, so she pushed her plate aside.

"After I told him about how I handled Bernard, he said he admired my heart and saw something in me that he'd seen in Marlowe. He offered us the opportunity to take over Marlowe's business, which is ten bricks every two weeks."

"Ten!" Kenya exclaimed.

"Wait, so let me get this straight. You told the plug that you handled Bernard alone, with no help from us?" Alexis couldn't contain her irritation.

"I didn't think it would be smart to implicate anyone else in the murder, but if you want, I can call him back and make sure you get your credit." Kita rolled her eyes. In her mind, it was so typical of Alexis to be concerned with the wrong thing.

"Well, you did right by leaving my name out of it, but I don't know about this deal to continue to work for him." Kenya leaned back in her seat. "We said once this pack was done, then we were done. However, now it sounds like we're far from done."

"Yeah, I'm with her." Alexis began picking at her food. "How could you have made such a big decision like that without at least asking us first?"

"You act like I had a choice?" Now, Kita found herself becoming agitated. "If y'all don't want to continue, I get it, but we will need $150,000 tonight."

"Fuck!" Alexis hit the table, causing the plates to rattle.

"Do you think we can just give him the cocaine and money we have left and call it good?" Kenya tried to devise a solid plan but knew the math wasn't adding up.

"There were only two bricks in Marlowe's bag, plus the two we got from B. Even if we sold all that, we'd still be significantly short because the other six bricks were missing. Remember, Marlowe had made some drops before he got to the house that day," Kita explained.

"Do you know who he might've dropped them off to? Maybe we can run down on them and collect?" Alexis posed the question to Markita but chose to look at Kenya.

"You know, like I do, ain't nobody gon' fess up to owing Marlowe money for drugs he fronted them before he died."

"Fuck it then, I guess we got no choice." Alexis picked up her crab leg. "Now that we know we are doing this, we need to devise an iron-clad plan to get this money!"

"Cheers to the *Get Money Girls*, I guess." Kenya raised her plastic cup for a toast. Markita and Alexis followed suit.

# CHAPTER THIRTY-FIVE

**S**ince Markita felt terrible for having to pull rank and make a decision for the group without asking, she decided to fall back that evening when they went to meet with Joey. She knew it meant something to Alexis to feel like she was in control, so she encouraged her to do all the talking as they approached the door of The Boat House. Upon entrance into the upscale establishment decorated in a nautical theme, they were met with the smell of seasoned seafood and a young waitress who greeted them with a smile. "Your party is right this way." She led the group down a ramp toward the back of a restaurant and into a private dining room.

Joey sat alone at a round table with his back to the wall. "Ah, ladies, thank you for coming." He stood to greet them and pull out their chairs.

"Where is everyone?" Alexis sat, resting the duffle bag on the chair beside her. Kenya and Kita took their seats as well.

"They should be arriving at any moment, but first, let's handle some business." Joey reached into the briefcase under the table and pulled out a sheet of paper with lots of writing on it. The top of the form read "Nondisclosure Agreement."

"Ladies, this legal document binds you to a confidential contract with me and my clients. In essence, when this ink is dry, you are not allowed to discuss what you see or hear while working with me or any of my clients and vice versa. This legal document is enforceable for up to sixty years after your work with my clients and me ends." Joey reached into his pocket and produced a Montblanc ink pen.

Alexis reached for the pen and was the first to sign her name before passing the paper to Kita, who skimmed through it. After determining the paperwork was legit, she signed, and Kenya followed suit. Joey collected the paper and placed it back into his briefcase, then raised his hand to summon the waitress standing nearby. When she approached the table, Joey took the liberty of ordering damn near the entire menu and two bottles of Dom Pérignon on ice. Seconds after the waitress walked away with the order, three large men entered the private room. They were dressed to the nines in a combination of custom casual wear and expensive suits. The cologne drifting off of their bodies smelled like money.

"Ladies, these are my clients, Paul, Kenneth, and Ray. Gentlemen, these are my colleagues, Alexis, Markita, and Kenya."

The men greeted each lady with a smile before joining them at the table. "I thought we signed up to sell party favors, not pussy." Alexis broke the ice with her joke, and everyone erupted into laughter, though she was partially serious.

"Shit, I'm down to pay for that too." Kenneth looked her up and down like he'd pounce on her at any moment if she gave the green light.

"So, what do you guys do for a living, and what brings you to Detroit?" Kita glanced around the table.

Kenya dropped her head with embarrassment. "Forgive my friends. They don't watch sports, so they wouldn't know that you all were professional football players who have now transitioned into various positions within sports media."

"Professional as in the NFL?" Alexis needed clarification as she began to count the dollar signs dancing in her eyes.

"That would be correct." Kenneth smiled, exposing his pearly white teeth.

"I don't mean to be crass, ladies, but we're only in town for two nights, and I'd like to get my party started." Paul rubbed the palms of his hands together. "Can I see what you have?"

Alexis grabbed her bag and passed it over. Paul and the fellows inspected it with anticipation. "Is this all?"

"That's three ounces. How much do you want?" Alexis looked from Kita to Joey, knowing someone had misunderstood the assignment.

"They wanted three pounds." Joey looked at Kita. "That's what I meant when I said three of your fat friends."

"Sorry for the misunderstanding, gentlemen. You can purchase what we have now, and I promise to personally deliver the rest to you within an hour after we leave the restaurant tonight."

"Are you willing to discount us for the inconvenience?" Ray continued to rummage through the bag.

"The last thing I'm trying to do is give your rich ass a discount, but I'll see what we can do." Alexis laid on her charm.

"I like you," Kenneth continued, admiring her from across the table. "If y'all fine asses party with us tonight, then we'll forget the mishap."

"If by 'party' you mean sniff coke, it's a hard pass for me." Kenya shook her head.

"Me too, fellas," Kita raised her hands in surrender. "Coke ain't for me."

"Why? Is your product trash?" Ray sat up in his chair, causing the temperature in the room to change.

"Man, don't insult us. Our shit ain't stepped on. This is high-quality powder, some of the purest shit you're going to find on this side of the map." Alexis rolled her eyes, pretending to be more irritated than she felt.

"Calm down, cutie." Kenneth reached into the inside jacket in his pocket and retrieved a golden straw. He handed it to her, "If your shit is so good, then I think you should have some."

"Nah, baby, I don't play with my nose." Alexis shook her head.

"You know what, Joey? . . . This is beginning to look like a real waste of my time." As Ray raised his voice, the waitress and her staff approached the table with food, so he stopped talking until they left. "We could have done something else with $60,000 other than play with these little girls tonight."

Alexis looked at Kita and Kenya, desperately trying to read their faces. She knew there was no way they should have been willing to let that much money walk away. She also knew they couldn't afford to blow the opportunity to work with more of Joey's clients, especially with a biweekly, ten-brick deal underway. Doing what Alexis did best, she took one for the team.

"Fuck it. Give me the straw." In one swift motion, she grabbed the coke, poured a line on the back of her hand, and sniffed it like a pro. Alexis knew risks like this were necessary to rise through the ranks of the dope game.

# CHAPTER THIRTY-SIX

It was hard for anyone to believe that three months had passed since the girls agreed to take over Marlowe's hustle. However, the money they consistently saw daily made things real. Not only was Shyla's spot still jumping through the week, but also the business with Joey had skyrocketed too. Once word spread through his clientele that Kita and her girls had the best product on the streets, they could barely keep up with demand. Though Joey kept their identities hidden, every other coke dealer in the city began to inquire about who was taking their business. Some speculated that out-of-towners had moved into the city and were now taking over. Others speculated that someone inside the city had foreseen the drought coming and decided to sit on their cocaine until the right time. No one could find proof of either theory, but they knew whoever had the coke was eating well, and they were right.

Kita had been able to settle things at home and save enough to pay off her tuition whenever she planned to enroll. Kenya was thriving in school, and she'd also been able to gift her mother with a ten-day cruise for her birthday, which made her incredibly proud. Alexis was flourishing in her new role as a trap queen as well.

173

She'd finally found something she was good at besides tricking niggas, and her money grew so long that she'd been splurging left and right on Talia and her grandmother. It felt good not having to depend on a man, although she still let Breeze think he was a savior and spoil her with lavish gifts.

For the first time in a long time, life was good. Well . . . It was good until the first of many problems knocked on Shyla's side door one night.

"Who is it?" she asked, daring not to move from her position on the brand-new burgundy sofa she'd just had delivered days ago. It provided the perfect seat to watch all the new Tubi movies on her high-definition, sixty-inch television.

*BOOM. BOOM!* The banging on the door got louder, which pissed Shyla off. "I get one fucking day to myself with nobody running in and out of here, and a bitch can't even finish a movie in peace," she mumbled to herself before sitting up and pausing the movie.

"I said, who the fuck is it?" she hollered loudly, hoping the person would hear her, but this time when there was no reply, she quickly got up with an attitude and went to check the peephole.

That's when the door was kicked off the hinges, and two masked men invaded her space.

"Where's the coke?" the biggest of the men asked with the barrel of his gun pointed inches from Shyla's head while the other began ransacking the house.

"What coke?" Already knowing what kind of situation this was, Shyla nervously held her hands in the air.

"Bitch, don't play with me!" Full of rage, he hit her with the butt of his weapon, causing blood to squirt from her head. "I don't have time for games. Where's the cocaine?"

"There is no cocaine in here." Shyla's hands began to tremble as she held the leaking wound in her head, trying to keep the blood from messing up her shirt.

"I'm going to ask you one last time, and then I'm going to blow your fucking brains out!" He cocked the gun. "Word in the hood is that the cocaine being flooded on the streets—*my* streets—came from here. So, where is it?"

"Ain't nothing in here, I swear! They went dry over an hour ago, but she went to get some more," Shyla blurted out. "She should be back in a few minutes." Shyla was so scared that she farted and accidentally had a bowel movement in her pants. Loose stools were sometimes a side effect of drug use.

"Good girl." The assailant patted her on the top of the head like a dog.

"Man, ain't shit in here!" the second gunman said after returning to the living room.

Just then, Kita approached the side of the house with a small knapsack. She was so busy scrolling social media on her phone that she didn't see that Shyla's door was off the hinges until it was too late. "Fuck!" After noticing the men holding a bleeding Shyla at gunpoint, Kita made a run for it.

"Get her!" the larger man instructed his partner as Kita ran like a track star through the neighborhood. The way her legs moved, you might've thought she was Sha'Carri's twin. However, the guy had caught up to her in no time. He wrapped his long arms around her and tackled her to the ground before landing a hard blow to the side of her face. Kita screamed in pain as she attempted to fight back. He sent another blow to her face and began pulling at the bag on her shoulder. Kita tried to hold on to it as best she could, but when he sent one final blow to her face, she was knocked completely out.

Unsure of where she was or how long she'd been out, Kita awakened in a panic, only to find Kenya and Alexis staring down at her. Quickly, she tried to get up, but her body rocked with pain, especially her face. "What the fuck happened?" she mumbled.

"We were robbed!" Kenya extended a hand to help her friend to her feet.

"Is Shyla okay? They had a gun to her head," Kita recalled.

"That bitch is fine, just a little shaken up. Luckily, after taking the coke, they left. Her place is a mess, but no real damage," Alexis replied.

"Did they take our money?" Kita's heart sank as she tried to calculate how much money they had. Ever since they began making more than a couple of dollars a day, they started hiding money so they didn't have to walk around with large sums on their person.

"No, it's still in the ice cream container in the freezer." The first thing Alexis did after receiving the call from Shyla was check their hiding spot the moment she entered the apartment. Thankfully, their assailants had looked everywhere in the house except the refrigerator.

"We got lucky this time, but now we have to change shit up." Kita knew tonight was just part of the game. However, it provided a valuable lesson for the girls to never keep the money and the product in the same place and never get too comfortable. "I wonder who it was?" she pondered, "It had to be someone from around this area."

"I say we put some bread out on the streets for these niggas. I bet we find out ASAP!" Alexis suggested.

"I say we chuck it up as a loss and just move the fuck on," Kenya countered. After all, everyone had to take a loss at some point in the game. She was just glad theirs happened sooner than later. Now, they knew they had to tighten up.

"Fuck that!" Kita snapped. "If we let this ride, then we become a target for everybody else." Though hitting licks was a part of the game, letting shit slide was a no-no. This had to be handled immediately. Now that word was out about who they were, Kita knew tonight's attempt would become the first of many. As women in this treacherous industry, they had to move faster, think smarter, and go much harder than their male counterparts.

"Okay, I'm with all the smoke if that's what y'all want," Kenya relented. "Meanwhile, we need to close up shop and find a new location."

# CHAPTER THIRTY-SEVEN

After reaching out to a handyman to come and fix Shyla's door, the girls divided their earnings from the day and headed off in different directions. Kita had a splitting headache and wanted desperately to shower, take Tylenol, and lie down, so she headed home. The moment she pulled into the driveway and saw her aunt Rhonda's car, she contemplated driving off. For the past few months, Rhonda had been overcome with grief about Bernard. It was almost like his death brought out the love she never showed him in life, and Kita couldn't stand it. The front door opened just as she prepared to back out of the driveway. Jackie and Rhonda appeared on the porch as they hugged and said goodbye. Rhonda walked past the car and waved at her niece before getting into her vehicle and disappearing down the block. With a smile, Jackie patiently waited on Kita, who was trying to stall.

"What the hell happened to your face?" Jackie went into full mommy mode when Kita finally approached the porch.

"I got into a fight; it's nothing major," she replied.

"A fight with who, Mike Tyson?" Gently, Jackie assessed her daughter's bruised and swollen face.

"Some chick from the projects." Kita shrugged. "Like I said, it's nothing, Ma."

Jackie didn't believe that a girl could pack such a punch. She knew there was more to the story, so she continued to pry.

"Why were you fighting in the first place, Markita?"

"Ma, can we please talk about this tomorrow?" She tried to bypass Jackie, who was blocking the path into the house.

"Does this fight have anything to do with the money I found under your mattress?" Jackie watched the expression on her daughter's face turn from wounded to infuriated.

"Why in the fuck were you going through my shit?" Usually, Markita would have handled her mother with care, but today had been extremely long, and she pressed on her reserved nerve.

"Markita, don't you dare fucking talk to me like that! Are you telling me what I *think* you're telling me?" Jackie snapped.

"I haven't said anything, so how could I be telling you something?" Markita sassed.

"Then answer my question!" Jackie demanded. "Why was there so much money under your mattress? Are you selling drugs?"

"Yes, I've been selling some shit that I was holding for Marlowe because we needed—" Kita never got to finish her sentence. Jackie backhanded her daughter on the other side of her face without so much as a second thought. "What the fuck?" It took every ounce of strength Kita had not to hit her mother back.

"Are you out of your mind? Do you *not* care about your brother losing his life because of this *very* thing?" Jackie couldn't believe Markita could be so damn stupid. "You are too smart for this, Markita!"

"Marlowe taught me that in life, we may not always do what's right, but as the head of the family, you always do what's necessary. He's gone, so now, *I'm* the head of the family because it's *my* job to take care of you." Markita repeated her brother's words on that fateful day at the hospital. It felt like confirmation that she was doing the right thing to her.

"Markita, you don't have to be the head of this house. *I* am your mother; *I* will figure something out."

"Ma, you've been saying that shit since I was a little girl, but you *never* figure it out!" Kita sighed. She hated to wound her mother's feelings, but the truth hurt. "You've never really gone the distance to follow through on a plan to figure things out, have you? You always do just enough to make people want to step in and save you. Larry, Marlowe, me, and God knows who else! Stop pretending to be the perfect mom and just be who you fucking are. Things would be much simpler if you did that."

With tears in her eyes and a quivering lip, Jackie wanted to scream at Kita and tell her that she didn't know what she was talking about, but deep down, she knew her daughter was right. Though she had overcome many adversities and been a hard worker all of her life and who wanted more for herself and her children, she had to admit that over the years, it had become easy to look the other way when Marlowe made bad decisions that were beneficial to helping her portray a lifestyle she was proud of.

"Kita, I received everything you said tonight. It's clear that I'm not perfect, and you're—"

"Mama, I didn't say that." Kita began to backpedal.

"Let's go somewhere and start over, just you and me. We don't need a big fancy house or expensive cars. All you need to do is focus on school, and I promise I will handle the rest."

"Mama, I can't just walk away from what Marlowe built for us because then, none of his sacrifices will have mattered." Kita tried to enter the house again, but her mother blocked her once more.

"Markita, I can't lose another child to these streets." The tears falling from Jackie's face were like wet pleas that fell on deaf ears.

"Mom, I'll be careful."

"Fine." Jackie broke down, sobbing like a baby. She felt terrible for failing both of her children. "If you want to live a life of crime, then you will do so from somewhere other than my house."

"Wow! Are you putting me out like your mother did you all of those years ago?" Kita's eyes widened in surprise.

"I'll give you tonight to decide, but when you wake up in the morning, and you still want to be a gotdamn drug dealer, then you can pack your shit and get the fuck out." It killed Jackie to be anything like her mother, but this was different. She felt confident that her ultimatum would save her daughter's life.

# CHAPTER THIRTY-EIGHT

The sound of the headboard banging against the wall competed with the squeaking of the mattress and the music on the portable speaker as Breeze fucked Alexis from the back. He struggled not to come too quickly, but the combination of her wet pussy and the sight of her beautiful, round ass was mocking his resistance in the worst way. "Gotdamn, bae, I'm about bust."

"Give it to me, daddy." Alexis slid off of Breeze's dick, turned around, and began sucking hard until he came all over her face. His body quivered as the last of his sperm oozed out. Smiling proudly, Alexis swallowed the white cream that had gotten into her mouth.

Satisfied, Breeze fell onto the bed and reached for the blunt on his nightstand. He sparked it up and took three small hits before passing it to Alexis, who did the same.

"That dick was good as hell, baby!" She waited for him to compliment her as they always did, but he didn't. She sat up in bed and turned to face him, "What's wrong with you? You've been acting weird these past few weeks."

"Ain't nothing wrong, bae. I just got a lot on my mind." Breeze blew out a cloud of smoke and put down the blunt.

"Talk to me. What's going on?" Alexis stared at her man.

"It's nothing. Besides, you won't understand." Breeze waved her off.

"Try me. I'm smarter than a lot of people give me credit for." Alexis began rubbing her man's chest.

"It ain't shit, really. I've just been stressed about this cocaine drought, that's all." Breeze sighed. "The shit that I've managed to find from some niggas in Chicago is so stepped on that my customers don't want to fuck with it like that. I hustle other shit too, but cocaine is a big deal for my business. I need a new plug."

Alexis could see that her man was bothered. "What if I told you that I could help you out?" She bit down on her bottom lip while debating silently about how much she should say.

"You can't help me, but I love you for that, Lex." Breeze stared at his girl with a smirk. He thought she was sweet for caring about what he was going through.

"I might have a plug on some pure cocaine," she blurted out.

"From where?" Instantly, his demeanor changed as he sat up on the side of the bed. "How the fuck do you have a damn cocaine connect?"

"I can't reveal my source, but I can get you what you need for a decent price."

With one swift motion, Breeze turned and lunged at Alexis. He didn't put his hands on her, but he did get aggressively close. "Are you fucking somebody else?"

"No! Why would you ask me that?" Alexis tried to stand from the bed, but Breeze grabbed her by the arms and held her down.

"The only way you would have access to some motherfucking coke at a decent price is if you're fucking the plug!" Breeze was seething. "Alexis, grab your shit and get the fuck out."

"Bae," she cried.

"Get the fuck out!" He barked before releasing her arms. "I can't believe I fell for your ho ass."

"Don't talk to me like that, Breeze!" Alexis scrambled to grab her clothes from the floor.

"Who is he, Alexis?"

"There is no 'he,' nigga. *I* am the fucking plug!" Instantly, Alexis regretted spewing too much information.

"You?" Breeze looked like he was caught in the *Matrix* as Alexis made her way toward his bedroom door. "Stop it. Talk to me," his voice had softened as he pulled Alexis into his arms.

"Let me go." She tried to push past him.

"Lex, I'm sorry, bae." Breeze held on to his girl tightly. After several moments, he could see her shoulders drop as she began to relax. "I love you, girl, and the thought that you might've seen someone else had me tripping. Do you accept my apology?"

"Yeah, I do, but you bet not ever do that shit again!" Alexis dropped her head onto his chest. He began to rub her ass and then plant soft kisses from the top of her head down to her toes. Like a dog, he got on all fours and began to nibble at the panties she'd put on. Carefully, he removed them with his teeth and dove straight into her sweet spot with his tongue. Alexis shivered as she came into his mouth. Breeze stood, exposing his erect dick, and gave Alexis a look that was all too familiar. Without protest, she lay back on the bed, lifted her legs in the air, and waited for him to enter her like only he could.

The second session lasted for nearly forty minutes as Breeze made sure to pleasure every inch of her body. When he finished, they lay together in postsexual bliss as he lovingly stroked her hair weave. In the softest voice, he said, "Bae, tell me about the coke."

With a sly smirk and still reeling in passion, Alexis told him everything she wanted him to know about the business she shared with her friends before rolling over and dozing off. Quietly, Breeze lay there pondering what his girl had told him and plotting his next move.

# CHAPTER THIRTY-NINE

**S**lowly but surely, Kita and her crew began taking over Detroit and its surrounding cities one gritty block at a time, so much so that the locals coined their nickname, "The Get Money Girls." Though they tried to keep a low profile, it was hard to do. As the only known squad of female drug dealers of their caliber, they were a big deal. The streets loved their product, but the rival dough boys hated them. It was hard for a nigga to see a bitch taking food off his table and not be upset. Their product had single-handedly tipped the scales of power in a direction opposite to societal norms. Kita and her crew had taken the term "head bitches in charge" to new heights.

More money almost always came with more flexing, and rightfully so. For several months, each girl had stepped up her game in a major way. Alexis moved from the slums into a condo overlooking the riverfront. Kenya was pushing a new, baby-blue 2023 Lexus RX 350 sitting on all chrome to her classes at Wayne State University. Though Markita wasn't much of a stunner, she treated herself to a classic, old-school, cocaine-white BMW 745 and a townhome in Ann Arbor, Michigan. Occasionally, she found other reasons to splurge, and tonight was one of them. It was Marlowe's birthday, and Kita had rented out DUO's entire bar and restaurant. The place was packed, and everyone dressed in yellow at her request. Though seeing her brother's face on the T-shirts and buttons was hard, times like this made her feel his presence.

"Let's give it up for my nigga, Marlowe, one more time!" the DJ yelled on the microphone, and the entire crowd began cheering and clapping. Markita watched from her seat in the VIP section that was roped off. She wasn't in much of a social mood. However, being amongst people who loved her brother brought a strange sense of peace.

"Excuse me, young lady, is this seat taken?" An older Italian man wearing vintage Armani slid into the booth beside her. She wanted to tell him to get the fuck on, but she knew a man like that wouldn't be in a place like this if it weren't for business.

"Please, join me," she hollered over the music.

"My name is Chino Rossi." He extended his hand, causing the diamond-encrusted Rolex to start a light show on his wrist.

"I'm Markita. Thanks for coming to celebrate the life of my brother." As Kita introduced herself, she fought the urge to display her recognition. Not long ago, she'd heard Marlowe and Bernard discussing the drug titan, so she knew exactly why he was there that night.

"I watched your brother for quite some time until his demise." Chino sipped from the Heineken beer in his hand. "Young Marlowe has been missed."

"You can say that again." Kita used her finger to trace the rim of her cup filled with orange juice. She wasn't old enough to be drinking yet, and she honestly had no desire to. The higher they got to the top, Kita knew how important it would be for her to stay on her game. She'd even decreased her marijuana intake because she didn't need anything altering her mind-set.

"I've been watching you too." Chino leaned close to Kita. "I see what you and your friends have been doing lately, and I must say, I admire your work. You remind me a lot of your brother." He paused. "If you're interested, I would love to have you on my team. We offer our affiliates top-grade products, affordable pricing, and domination over a large portion of territories in their respective regions."

Kita didn't know if she should scream excitedly or just play it cool; she chose the latter. The Rossi brothers were the alpha and the omega of the heroin and fentanyl business in Michigan and Canada. The only way into their organization was by invitation.

"Mr. Rossi, I'm elated, and I mean no disrespect when I say this, but I have to talk it over with my friends first. Can I get back to you?"

Chino's thick brow furrowed as he stood from his seat. He was used to people jumping at his offers because they were rare. "You have forty-eight hours."

"How can I reach you?" she asked.

"A man like me is not reachable, Markita, but rest assured that I will find you," Chino winked.

"Thank you so much for the opportunity." Kita watched Chino as he left the section, disappearing into the sea of faces beneath her.

Instantly, dollar signs danced in her eyes as she began to think of all the money she and her girls would be making if they added heroin and fentanyl to their inventory. Before Kita could dive too far into la-la land, she was snapped into reality by her friends. "Bitch, who the fuck was that?" Alexis quizzed.

"Let me find out your ass is into sugar daddies now," Kenya teased.

"That was Chino Rossi, one of the Rossi brothers. He's a major fucking player in the dope game." Kita talked freely because she knew no way could anyone on the dance floor hear what she was saying over the music. "He wants us to join his team and push fentanyl and heroin."

"We don't know shit about pushing dog food or fentanyl either, for that matter." Kenya shook her head.

"We didn't know shit about pushing cocaine either, but look at as now," Alexis stated as a matter of fact, and Kita nodded in agreement.

"I told him we needed time to discuss things, and he gave us forty-eight hours." Kita scratched her head. "This could be a good opportunity to take our hustle to the next level, but heroin and fentanyl are big business both on the streets *and* in the legal system. Do we want to take that risk?"

"People die off that shit." Kenya shook her head.

"People die every day, nigga. That's life," Alexis rebutted. "Look, the way I see it, we're already in too deep. Ain't no turning back, so we might as well move full steam ahead."

"If we're going to do it, then we need to bring in a whole separate team for that shit," Kenya demanded. "I want to reap the benefits but not get my hands dirty."

"Breeze and his boys already dabble in it, so they'd be the perfect people to kick it off with." Alexis began to scan the crowd for her man.

"Lex, you know how I feel about mixing business and pleasure. It's bad enough we let you talk us into selling discounted coke to him. I don't know if supplying him with the other shit is a smart idea. We need to spread out our business, or our profit margins will never increase." Kita spoke up for herself and Kenya, who'd had a few private conversations with her on the matter. They disagreed with Alexis's decision to tell her man about their business, yet didn't harp on it. Then she asked if they could offer him a special price on cocaine, and they relented. Now, though, they had to draw the line.

"I know tonight isn't the time to talk business, and this isn't the place." Alexis wrapped her arms around the necks of her friends. Staring down at the crowd, she said, "Let's enjoy Marlowe's birthday and talk more tomorrow."

# CHAPTER FORTY

As the party neared its end, Kita hugged those of importance, told her friends good night, and went to retrieve her car from the valet. While she waited, she took some time on her phone to capture a few selfies for the gram.

"My, how you've grown into a fine-looking young woman." The voice of a man came from behind her.

"Excuse me?" Kita whipped her around to see a white man wearing blue jeans, a white shirt, and a tan blazer.

"You're Markita Jones, right?" The man's blue eyes were dark and cold.

"Who are you?" Kita looked around to spot someone she knew, but she and the stranger were outside alone.

"My name is Detective Douglas. You might remember me from the night your brother called after getting pulled over," he reminded her. "You were sick in the passenger seat that night."

Instantly, Kita began to recall the occasion. Although she couldn't remember everything, she remembered the officer from that night being crooked. "Nah. It doesn't ring a bell," she lied.

"Well, let me introduce myself again." He paused. "I'm the motherfucker you pay when you want to move weight in or around my city." His voice grew stern and menacing as he pulled a Newport cigarette from his jacket pocket and lit it with the engraved, refillable lighter he'd gotten for his fifteenth year of service.

"Weight?" Kita innocently looked in the air like she was trying to find the answer.

"Ms. Jones, I'm not the one to fuck with, so I would caution you against it." As the two engaged in the ultimate game of mind chess, the valet arrived with Kita's car. Douglas looked from the BMW back to Kita with a raised brow. He sighed, "I know every player in this city, believe me. I've let you off long enough to play this game without paying. Now, it's time to pay the piper."

"Detective, I'm not sure what you *think* you know, but I assure you, you're mistaken." As Kita paid the valet attendant, other partygoers began to exit the club.

"A mistake would be not paying me, Ms. Jones." Douglas flicked his cigarette to the ground. "I'll be in touch."

Without a word, Kita watched the detective until he disappeared into the parking lot. Silently, she wondered how real his threats were but decided not to worry about it until there was something to worry about.

It took Kita approximately an hour and thirty minutes from the club to her place. She'd driven the entire way in silence as she reminisced about Marlowe; she missed him. She desperately wished heaven had a phone so she could call him and hear his voice again. Never did she think her life would go like this. She wished she could've put on some red shoes like Dorothy, clicked them three times, and woke up to find everything the way it used to be.

Finally, she reached her town house and pulled into the driveway. A glance at the digital dashboard told her the time was two a.m. She grabbed her phone and began to dial her mother. It was late, but she knew her mom would probably be up thinking about Marlowe too. It saddened Kita that they hadn't spoken in so long, but a hearty knock on the window jolted her from her seat before she could get too far into her feelings.

Instinctively, Kita reached for the gun tucked on the side of her seat and then pointed it out the window. "Davit!" She looked up, grateful to see a familiar face, yet worried at the same time. He was dressed to the nines in tailored, white pants and a yellow collared shirt. Cautiously, Kita opened her door and stepped out. "Where the fuck did you come from?"

"I'm going to give you a pass because it's your brother's birthday, but if you don't want to end up like him, I suggest you pay more attention." Davit shook his head in disapproval. "Not only did I follow you all the way here, but I was also at the club tonight too, and you didn't even see me."

"So, you're stalking me now?" Kita smiled.

"My uncle likes to keep eyes on his acquaintances." Davit glanced down to the ground, "And I liked your brother. So, it was only right to come and pay my respects to his life on his birthday."

"I appreciate that, Davit, but I know you've got something else to say. Otherwise, you wouldn't be here." Kita quickly scanned the street, making sure no one else had followed them.

"I saw Chino there tonight, and it didn't sit right with me that our biggest competition was conversing with our upcoming protégé in a very intimate way." Davit rubbed the hairs on his chin. "My uncle probably would have jumped to the conclusion that you're working both sides of the fence and had you at the bottom of the Detroit River by now. However, I don't assume, Markita, so I came here for the facts."

"Chino approached me tonight, asking me to join his roster selling heroin and fentanyl. I told him I'd think about it and let him know." Kita leaned against her car, trying to read the expression on Davit's face. "The product would bring us new customers and more money. I don't think it's a bad idea."

"It's a very bad fucking idea!" Davit hit the side of Kita's car.

"You guys don't sell the same products, so I don't see the problem." Kita restrained herself from turning up because she didn't want Davit to shoot her in the driveway.

"Markita, in this industry, working for your boss's enemy is *never* a good idea. Let's start there." Davit sighed. "Second, heroin and fentanyl come with bigger penalties and stiffer punishments. If you get knocked for selling fentanyl, who's to say you won't roll over on my uncle to gain leverage in your plea deal?" Adamantly, he shook his head. "No! You either with us all the way or you're out. As a matter of fact, I think we should terminate this arrangement now because I'm beginning to have second thoughts about you. I thought you were like your brother, but Marlowe went to his grave being loyal. He would've never allowed Chino to think he had a chance of snagging him from us."

"Davit, please accept my apology. Maybe my judgment is off today because I miss my brother, or maybe I'm just too green at this shit, but it was never my intention to offend you or your uncle. My loyalty will always remain with you guys. I was just trying to make more money, that's all." Kita did her best to convey how sincere she was.

"Based on the strength of my relationship with Marlowe alone, I will not share the details of tonight with my uncle. However, I *will* be watching you very closely. If I feel like your loyalty is questionable at any time, I won't hesitate to make it known." As swiftly as he'd come, Davit walked down the darkened street, disappearing into the night.

# CHAPTER FORTY-ONE

Before bed, Kita sent an emergency text to her friends asking for a meeting at their favorite Coney Island for breakfast in the morning. Sleep hadn't come easy that night; she tossed and turned. Not only was Davit's warning on her mind, but so was the thought of having to decline Chino's offer. A man like that couldn't possibly be okay with hearing the word no. When she woke the next day, she showered and dressed in a black running outfit and a pair of tan and black gym shoes. After pulling her hair into a simple half-up-half-down style, she grabbed her keys and was out the door, preparing to make the long trek back to Detroit.

As soon as she got into the city of Southfield, Kita pulled into the parking lot of a popular coffee and donut spot. Though she'd be eating with her friends soon, she needed caffeine ASAP. Quickly, she parked the car, stepped out, and flew toward the building. As she approached the door, she was nearly knocked over by someone who just spilled iced coffee on her outfit.

"What the fuck! Slow down."

"I am so sorry, miss." The man frantically grabbed napkins from his bag and handed them to her. "Markita?"

She looked up, and immediately, her frown became a smile, exposing all of her teeth and one of her dimples. "Rico Richardson. Long time no see."

"Damn, girl, you look good. How have you been?" He was dressed in a fitted white collared shirt and some navy blue slacks. His body was chiseled to perfection and more toned than when they dated a few years ago.

"You look nice yourself. I'm good, just maintaining. How are you?" Kita fought hard to keep her composure. However, the butterflies she felt years ago after first laying eyes on his were still there like they never left.

"I'm doing good. I returned to the city six months ago to start training at the Detroit Police Academy. I'll get a notification any day now that my training is complete." Rico pointed at the engravement on his collared shirt that said DPA.

"So, you're the po-po?" Kita tried not to let her feelings come across in her facial expression.

"Yeah, something like that," Rico laughed. "After my dad died in the line of duty, my mom moved us to Atlanta, seemingly overnight. She said she didn't want me to live in a place that killed my father. For a while, I respected her decision, and I also began to despise law enforcement for failing to protect my dad, but then I thought about it. The only way to make a difference is to be the difference. I reached out to some of Dad's old buddies and inquired about joining the police force. My godfather, a senior detective, sent me the information, and now, I'm here ready to fight crime and make the world a better place," he joked. "Enough about me. I know you're doing big things. Tell me what's going on in your world."

The cell phone in Kita's hand began to ring. Without looking, she knew it was Alexis or Kenya telling her she was late. "Well, I got accepted into my dream school, but I've put off going for a while. I started a business with my friends and need to tie up a few loose ends." Her phone rang again. "Hey, I hate to rush, but

I'm late to a business meeting as we speak. Let me give you my number, and we can set a time to link up soon." Every fiber in Kita's being told her *not* to exchange numbers with her ex, but her heart had its own agenda.

"Okay, cool. My apologies again for spilling the coffee, but I am glad I ran into you, no pun intended." Rico laughed at his corny joke, and Kita did too. Being corny was something she loved the most about him.

After exchanging numbers, Kita hopped back into her car and sped to Brenda's Coney Spot. When she arrived, Kenya and Alexis had already ordered and were talking shit to each other over cups of orange juice.

"Well, look who decided to show the fuck up." As always, Alexis was the first one to give Kita a hard time.

"I know, right? Who the fuck is late to a meeting they called?" Kenya added.

"Are y'all hoes through?" Kita took a seat. "Anyway, before I get into the real business at hand, let me tell y'all the tea." She began to laugh when her friends both leaned in closely to listen. It was apparent that hearing gossip could quickly end their attitudes. "I ran into Rico this morning on my way here. We exchanged numbers."

"Rico, as in *your* Rico from sophomore year?" Kenya smiled.

"Yes," she confirmed.

"Rico, as in the one who got your nose wide open, Rico?" Alexis teased.

"Whatever that means, yeah. *That* one." Kita exhaled. "He is even finer than he was back then. He got this grown-man quality about him now." While giving them the rundown, she'd intentionally omitted the part about him working for the police. There was no need to get their panties in a bunch when all they did was exchange numbers.

"Damn, I guess that nigga is your soul mate. He came back to you just like they do in the movies." Alexis sat back in her seat.

"I know, right?" Kita waved the waitress over and placed her order. "Anyway, enough about that. We need to talk about Chino."

"I'm ready to get to this bag!" Alexis began to dance, moving her shoulders from side to side.

"Well, last night after the club, our plug followed me home. He very sternly explained to me that doing business of *any* kind with his competition might result in me being unalive and dropped into the Detroit River," Kita exclaimed.

"So, he was at the club? You should have said something." It was no secret that Alexis was still hurt about being excluded from knowing who they did business with.

"I didn't know he was there until he told me," Kita snapped. "Anyway, Chino is out."

"Hold the fuck up." Alexis dropped her hand on the table. "I'm getting just a tad sick of you being in control of decisions that the group should make. First, you withhold the identity of *our* plug. Now, you say we can't work with Chino. Seems to me like you want to be in control. You are Mr. Ruffin, and we are the Tempts."

"Lex, I've been playing everything aboveboard. It's not me. The plug doesn't want to be known, and excuse me if I don't want to get killed behind doing business with Chino." Kita looked to Kenya for support.

"You both have valid points here, but a win is a win, Lex. Until last night, selling anything besides cocaine never crossed our minds. We are making more money than we've ever made, and as long as we are making money, who gives a fuck about that petty shit?"

Kenya's attempt to come off as neutral had failed.

"Kenya, you can be this bitch's sidekick, but I'm good." As Alexis finished her sentence, the cell phone in front of her began sliding across the table. Without another word to her friends, she grabbed it, stood, and abruptly left the restaurant, leaving them speechless.

# CHAPTER FORTY-TWO

As Kenya worried about Alexis and tried to call her, Markita ate her food and enjoyed every bite. She knew Alexis was being dramatic as always. After finishing the last of their meals, Kenya and Kita's phones chirped, notifying them of a group message with Joey. He'd sent all the girls a coded message about a new client needing an urgent delivery.

"Come on; let's go make this money." Kita wiped her mouth and prepared to slide out of the booth.

"What about Lex? Should I call her again?" Kenya began to dial.

"She didn't answer the first ten times. I doubt she's going to answer now." Kita rolled her eyes. Though she never wanted to lose Alexis as a friend, she wasn't one to kiss ass. Her motto was to give people space and trust that things would work out how they were supposed to.

"*Leave a message.*" Alexis's voice blared through the phone.

Kenya looked at Kita and shook her head before doing as instructed. "Hey, I don't know if you saw the text from J, but we are headed there now if you want to meet us."

Together, Kita and Kenya went to the stash house to collect what the message said the client needed, and then they headed to The Westin Hotel. A minute after pulling the car off of the service drive and into the valet lane, Kita grabbed a black overnight bag from the backseat, and they exited the car.

"I wonder who the client is?" Kenya hated being out of the loop. "I couldn't tell by Joey's message what the hell he was talking about . . . larger than life . . . bigger than a nickel . . . what the fuck does that mean?"

"The good thing is, if we can't figure the shit out, then neither can the police." Kita sashayed through the hotel's entrance like she owned that bitch. "Just chill, though. We'll find out soon enough."

Kita approached the receptionist and asked her to call the penthouse to inform the hotel guest of her arrival.

While the ladies waited in the swank lobby decorated with ceramic tile, recessed lighting, and a baby grand piano, neither Kenya nor Kita said a word. Instead, they exchanged random glances at each other whenever someone came their way. Luckily, the guessing game didn't last long before the bronze elevators opened, and a white guy wearing a red blazer, white shirt, black tie, and pants greeted them. "Are you here for the penthouse?"

"Yes, we are. Are you Auzzie?" Kita referred to the nickname in Joey's text message.

"Yes, I am. Right this way, ladies." He held the elevator door open, and the girls hopped on. "I'm glad you could make it on such short notice."

"No problem," Kita replied while Kenya stood there trying to figure out what the hell was happening.

The elevator ride was long. When the doors opened, both Kenya and Kita marveled at all the security guards standing at their posts. "Shit!" Kenya counted four men right away. "Who's up in this bitch, Lil' Wayne?"

"Close." Kita winked. She'd already deciphered Joey's text but didn't want to ruin the surprise for her friend.

"Right this way." Auzzie bypassed the muscular plainclothesmen, leading the girls toward his client. "Silver Dollar is back here."

"Did he say Silver Dollar?" Kenya whispered, and Kita nodded. "Oh my God!" she mumbled, trying hard to contain herself.

Silver Dollar was a rapper who turned mogul seemingly overnight. With hits like "Down for You" and "Girl Stop Playing with My Feelings," he was arguably one of the best rappers alive. After his sophomore album, Silver Dollar began to apply his street knowledge to the boardroom. This proved to be a smart move that garnered several lucrative deals between him and major corporations. He had come a long way from his days on the streets of Harlem, or so everyone thought, but truth be told, this nigga was still up to no good.

"Who the fuck is this?" Dollar stared at the two women with a grimace. He was sitting in a chair, being massaged by a small Asian woman.

"They've got what you asked for, sir." Auzzie shifted nervously. Dollar had been known to rough up a few people occasionally. So, Auzzie didn't like being on the short end of his temper.

"Oh shit! These bitches got the work?" Dollar looked from Kenya to Kita. "Neither of them looked like dope dealers. Y'all bitches look like the arm candy me and my partners fuck on before and after our performances." His laugh was heavy and loud.

"You can kill that 'bitch' shit!" Kita bucked. "Your man called my people and said you needed four bricks of the good shit, and it doesn't get better than this." With a stone-cold grimace, she unzipped the overnight bag, removed its contents, and set the items on the table, never removing her eyes from Dollar. He stared her down just the same.

"All right, fuck it. I can respect that. So let me get a sample to see what you got." He motioned for the masseuse to take a ten-minute break.

"The sample is fifty dollars." Kita reached into her bag and pulled out a small bag of white powder.

"We're talking about making a major deal here. Are you going to charge me for a sample?" Dollar laughed.

"Let me see the money, my nigga." Kenya jumped in, not missing a beat.

Dollar liked these fiery bitches, but he still gave them a hard time. "I'm Silver Dollar, baby!" He laughed. "Google my net worth. It proves that I'm good at it."

"Look, I ain't trying to be rude or no shit like that, but we got better things to do with our time. Give me the money, and I will give you a sample. Ain't nobody trying shit for free around here." Kita was annoyed.

Aussie looked like he could've shit a brick, but Dollar was amused.

"All right, little mama; relax." He licked his lips before reaching toward the floor. On cue, Kita and Kenya pulled pistols, prepared to pop off if need be. This caused his security guards to do the same. Everyone in the room had some heat except Aussie, the masseuse, and Dollar. He dropped the briefcase onto the table and raised his hands in surrender. "Damn, I was only grabbing the money. Y'all bitches . . . I mean, y'all ladies don't play."

"Open it," Kenya instructed Aussie, who nervously approached the table. The lid popped open after he fumbled with the combination lock on the briefcase. There were three rows of crisp, stacked, rubber-banded money all the way across. Two hundred and forty thousand dollars, to be exact. Kita tucked the gun into her waist, grabbed three stacks, and flipped through them all to ensure there were no imposters in the bunch. She wasn't one for taking losses.

"Is everything OK? Can I put my fuckin' hands down now and get your fifty?" Dollar asked. "It's in my pocket."

"Yeah, but do it slow, motherfucker," she laughed, indicating that it was now her turn to joke. "Here's your shit." Kita slid the bricks and the sample across the table.

Dollar smiled. He was like a kid in a candy store, inspecting the contents. He grabbed a container from the floor and retrieved a small jar filled with a clear liquid. Carefully, he poured the sample into the jar and turned it upside down three times before setting it on the table. Within seconds, the clear liquid turned pink, then dark blue. Kita and Kenya knew he was testing their product's potency, but they didn't sweat.

"Y'all got some Grade-A shit here. My little homies back home will have this sold in no time. I'll probably be back in a month for more." Dollar lay back on the sofa and signaled his masseuse to return.

"Thank you, ladies." Aussie smiled. He always felt accomplished when his client was happy. "Now that your business is complete, I'd be happy to see you out."

"Yes," Dollar clapped. "Thank you, ladies." He gave the girls a thumbs-up as Kenya began dumping the money from the briefcase into their luggage.

"How long are you all in town?" Kita asked as they followed Aussie back to the elevator.

"Two days." He stopped and pushed the button. "Dollar is in town to make a guest appearance at a show tonight. Would you like tickets?"

"No, thank you," Kenya and Kita replied in unison, which meant they were on the same page.

"I wonder how old Dollar's little homies are that sell for him?" Kenya asked once the elevator doors closed.

"Not our problem, just our profit; remember that!" Kita extended her fist, and Kenya bumped it with hers.

Unbeknownst to them, their meeting with Silver Dollar would put them in a whole other league. Celebrities shared many things, like who did the best hair, for instance. Now, every time there was a concert, stage play, or star-studded event in or around the city of Detroit, the Get Money Girls would be first on the list to supply some big names in the entertainment industry without having to go through Joey, which kept more money in their pockets.

# CHAPTER FORTY-THREE

"Good morning." Breeze wiped sleep from his eyes as he greeted Alexis, who'd shown up at his door unannounced. Instead of replying, she barged inside and dropped her purse on the sofa. "What's going on?"

"Kita really pissed me off today, and Kenya too."

"Lex, this seems to be a continuous thing lately. What happened?" Breeze walked over to the bar cart in the corner of his sparsely decorated bachelor pad and poured a small cup of cognac. He took a sip and handed it to his girl, who needed to relax.

"Chino Rossi approached Markita at the club last night. He told her he wanted to work with us, but you know we don't dabble in heroin or fentanyl. So, I told her we could bring you and your crew on and get the shit popping." Alexis paused to take a drink.

"Let me guess. She had a problem with that," Breeze interjected.

"Not only did she have a problem with it, but this morning, she also decided that we won't be working with the Rossi brothers at all."

"You don't turn down a guy like Chino Rossi." Breeze took a seat on the arm of the sofa. "Why would she do that?"

"Well, according to her, our plug threatened to kill her if she did business with Chino, but if you ask me, she's lying." Alexis reached down on the coffee table and grabbed a prerolled blunt that was resting on a weed tray.

"She might not be lying, bae. Nobody wants their top earners working for the competition." Breeze leaned over and began to rub her back. "You've got to calm down and take your feelings out of this hustle game. Ain't no room for attitudes."

"I just get so irritated with her, and then Kenya always chooses her side, which pisses me off even more." Alexis lay back in her man's arms and sparked the blunt. "We started this shit together, but now it feels like I work for Kita." Immediately after inhaling the smoke, she gagged. "What the fuck is this?"

"Relax, baby. It's what I like to call 'middle man.'" Breeze laughed. "It's a combination of an upper and a downer."

"I know weed is the downer, but what's the upper?" She pulled on the blunt again, becoming more comfortable with the effects.

"A sprinkle of coke," Breeze said nonchalantly while continuing the conversation. "Have you ever thought of splitting your business? People do it all the time." Breeze removed the blunt from Alexis's hand and put it to his mouth. "You and me can do our thing, and they can do theirs. As long as y'all still cut the profit three ways, you shouldn't care who looks like they're calling the shots. Besides, once you're not in the mix every day, Kita and Kenya will see who's the brains of the operation."

"You're right." Sparked with fresh energy, Alexis sent a message to the ladies and requested a meeting tonight. "These hoes got me hot!"

"The only one that should have you hot is me." Breeze began to nibble on her neck. "I've told you a million times to stop playing with them little girls and come join forces with a real. With your product and my skill set, we can take over the world, baby. Just tell daddy the word, and it's on."

"I don't want to compete with my friends, though. You know I'm loyal to them."

"Alexis," Breeze placed the blunt into the ashtray on the table, "I've told you a thousand times that loyalty in this game ain't shit but a seven-letter word."

Later that night, Kita and Kenya waited over twenty minutes at Shyla's house for Alexis to arrive. Just when Kita stood to leave, the sound of keys jingling could be heard as the side door was opened. "About damn time. One more minute, and I was out of here," she said with an attitude.

"It's cool for you to have us wait, but God forbid we keep the queen waiting." With an attitude of her own, Alexis dropped her keys on the table and took a seat. "Anyway, this won't take long. The reason I called the meeting is to discuss separation."

"What?" Kenya looked around the room. "You don't want to work with us anymore?"

"I think we all need space. When we started, it was fun being with y'all all the time, trying to find our way. Now, it doesn't feel like that, and I'm afraid if we don't separate the business soon, our friendship will suffer." Alexis stared at Kita, who returned the gesture.

"Actually, I agree with that." Kita nodded in approval.

"I didn't sign up to be solo!" Kenya yelled. "Yes! The money is good, but it was never about the money for me. I did this shit for y'all. Without y'all, this doesn't matter to me."

"Are you about to cry?" Alexis joked, but Kenya was as serious as liver failure.

"We said we would never let this game change our friendship, and that's exactly what's happening." Kenya dabbed at her eyes.

"We ain't ending the friendship. We are just splitting the business." Kita wrapped her arms around Kenya, and Alexis did the same.

"Let's try it for a while and reconvene in ninety days," Alexis suggested.

"Okay, so what's the plan?" Kenya wiped her face. "Where is everyone going to trap from?"

"We can still take turns trapping from Shyla's spot and doing deals with Joey, but mainly, everyone will hustle their way in separate parts of town. We can meet weekly to divide profit and talk shop." Kita broke the embrace and went to take a seat.

"I'm going to take the East Side because Breeze is there. Kita can take the West Side, and you can take the middle because your school is there, Kenya." Alexis added, "It's hella college students looking to get high."

"I guess that's settled then." Kenya grabbed her things and prepared to leave.

"Well, there is one more thing we didn't get to discuss this morning." Kita walked over to the window and looked outside. "There is a guy named Detective Douglas who's known for collecting 'street tax.' He tried to shake me down after the party. I don't know how much of a threat he is, but I wanted y'all to know he's lurking."

"All right, thanks for the heads-up. Y'all be safe out there." Kenya exited the house.

"Yeah, thanks." Alexis followed behind Kenya, with Kita hot on their trails. Without a joke or any light banter, the women each got behind the wheels of their respective vehicles and pulled off in opposing directions.

# CHAPTER FORTY-FOUR

For nearly four months, things had run as smoothly as everyone hoped, and the trio's friendship appeared stronger than ever. Kenya was killing the game with sales around campus and other colleges, while Kita and Alexis held down their prospective areas. As the profits from the street sales grew, Kita talked her girls into opening up a legitimate business. She thought it would be great to have a way to launder the dirty cash into clean money. They all agreed that opening a hair salon would be a great first business. After tossing around a few names, they settled on KAM's Hair Co. Neither of the ladies knew a thing about hair or nails besides Alexis. However, they'd grown up and gone to high school with plenty of girls who did.

It took some time to find the perfect location and get through the red tape of zoning for remodeling improvements. However, once everything was done, Alexis agreed to host interviews for prospective stylists, nail and lash techs, and an office manager to oversee the day-to-day duties of the business. Applicants arrived in record numbers and showed out in true Detroit fashion. After careful consideration, she hired ten stylists, three nail techs, one lash tech, and her grandmother as the office manager. Tonight was the grand opening, and all the stops were pulled for this event. There was a red carpet, photographers, a strobe light out front, and the local radio station was broadcasting live with a popular DJ.

"I can't believe we did this shit!" Alexis peered out of the tinted glass window as the stretch vintage Jaguar cruised down the block. The line outside of the salon extended for almost two blocks. "Finally, a business Mommy would have been proud of." Alexis laughed while nudging Talia, who was in aww, taking everything in. Recently, Alexis has begun spending more time with her sister. Though she didn't want Talia in this lifestyle, she did want her sister to know that college wasn't for everybody, but if you worked hard and applied yourself, you could still live the life of your dreams.

"How did you get so many people to show up?" Kita was amazed.

"I offered discounts to everyone that came tonight and booked a future service." Alexis was proud of herself.

"I'm not going to lie. It does feel good having something legit!" Kenya squealed with a sense of accomplishment. It felt good to see something she helped to create getting so much shine. This was a much different feeling than selling cocaine in the dark.

"Let's do this, ladies." Kita took a deep breath as the limo came to a stop. The driver got out and opened their door.

The crowd of family, friends, supporters, and clients met them with a barrage of applause. Kenya's mother and Alexis's grandmother stood at the door to greet them. They were beside a giant red bow tied in front of the door.

"We're so proud of you three." Mama Ella wiped tears of joy as she handed the girls a pair of massive scissors. Kenya, Kita, and Alexis smiled at the cameras recording the moment.

"Is your mom coming?" Alexis spoke in a lowered tone.

"I invited her, but she didn't respond to my text," Kita said with a plastered smile. "It's okay if she doesn't. Let's just enjoy our moment." After cutting the ribbon, the ladies walked inside, welcoming their guests to enjoy what they'd been working on.

Instantly, everyone began to admire the 1,800-square-foot salon decorated in silver, white, and blue, with posh pieces of furniture, valuable wall art, and a six-foot fish tank strategically placed in the center of the lobby wall. Each styling suite was equipped with leather reclining chairs that massaged clients and a grass wall with an LED light that said, "*Hello, Gorgeous,*" to capture content. The floors were custom-made with marble tile to match the décor. It was apparent to everyone in the building that the trio had spared no expense on their first baby, and it showed. The place was stunning.

"Hey, beautiful." Rico walked up behind Kita and lightly kissed the side of her face. Since their encounter at the coffee shop, the pair had gone on several dates and rekindled their flame.

"Hey, baby." With a smile, Kita turned and greeted her man. He was holding a beautiful bouquet of red roses.

"I know the décor is blue, but red means I love you, and I wanted my message to be clear." He laid on the charm.

"Damn, Rico, that almost got *my* panties wet," Kenya, who was standing nearby, joked. "Not for nothing, but I'm happy to see you two back together. You bring out the best in my girl."

"I try," Rico smiled. "Well, baby, I will let you entertain your guests while I head to my shift. I'll bring breakfast when I get off in the morning to finish the celebration. I'm so proud of you."

After kissing her man and seeing him out, she began to work the room. Her mission was to meet several vendors while securing potential clients. Someone lightly tapped her shoulder as she talked with older women about the benefits of natural hair versus straightening products.

"Congratulations, Kita." Jackie lovingly hugged her daughter. Behind her smile was a combination of admiration and a twinge of sorrow. She wished her son were here to see the woman Kita had become; she knew Marlowe would've been proud of this moment.

"Thank you, Ma." Kita wrapped her arms around her mother and held on tight.

"This place is beautiful!" Jackie wiped the tears from her eyes as someone handed Kita a microphone. Instantly, the tender moment was placed on hold.

"Thank you all for coming out to support us, our new salon, and our awesome team of stylists." Kita addressed the crowd and handed the mic over.

"It feels amazing to have a business in a community that we love so much," Kenya added before passing the mic to Alexis.

"Don't forget to meet the stylists and schedule those appointments before you leave. Now, let's party and enjoy the surprise we have planned!" Alexis turned the microphone off.

As the guests waited for the miniature surprise hair show to take place, they were served champagne and hors d'oeuvres. Kita was about to take a seat when Breeze and his crew entered the building, sticking out like a sore thumb. "Aye, I want to make a toast to my girl and her friends!" He walked into the center of the room holding a gold bottle of Ace of Spades champagne.

Kita eyed Kenya, and then Alexis, who wasn't the least bit bothered. With a smile, she met her man where he stood and planted a wet, sloppy kiss on his lips. "Give it up for my man, y'all. He's my rock!" The crowd awkwardly started clapping at her request as Kenya and Kita cringed.

"I won't take too much time because I know there is a schedule to keep, but," he fumbled with something in his pocket, "I love this girl, and I want to ask her to be my wife in front of all of y'all on her special day." Breeze got on one knee and popped the question with a large diamond ring.

Immediately, people pulled out their cameras to record as the room filled with women began oohing and clapping. Forced not to want to look jealous or angry on video, Kita and Kenya clapped and congratulated their friend too. However, neither of them thought a proposal from Breeze was a good thing, especially at their grand opening.

# CHAPTER FORTY-FIVE

After the party ended, Kita hung back with her mom, Ms. Barbara, and Shyla to put the shop back in working order. Normally, she would've complained about being left to do the work, but Alexis had gone early to celebrate with her man, and Kenya had gotten too tipsy and had to be driven home by her mom. Since there was no one to go home to, Kita used the time to catch up with Jackie. As they talked about the latest television show drama and current events, Kita couldn't help but smile. It felt so good being back in the presence of her mother. Though they still had things to hash out, it was amazing for the world to seem right again.

Within the hour, everything in the salon was tidy and ready for business the following day. Once outside, Kita waved goodbye to everyone, then unlocked her car. Seconds after placing her purse inside, she saw a black town car rounding the corner. Kita stared at the car until it stopped horizontally to hers. The back-tinted window rolled down, and Chino leaned forward. "No pretty girl like you should be out here at night alone."

"I'm never alone, believe that," Kita bluffed.

"Good to know," Chino smirked. "I know it's been a while since we last spoke. I've been away on business, but I'm back now, and you were the first person I thought of the minute I landed. Do you have an answer for me?"

"I do have an answer, but it's not one I think you will want to hear." Kita paused, trying to read his expression while casually placing her hands on her hips. This was an attempt to have her hand in reach of the concealed gun in her waistband. "As grateful as I am for your offer, I'll have to decline."

"Markita, you're right. This was not what I wanted to hear, and quite frankly, I pegged you to be smarter than that."

"*Excuse* me?" Kita remained calm in an attempt to de-escalate the situation. However, she wasn't going to tolerate disrespect.

"Markita, the goal of this business is to make money—lots of it—and leave before the time on your clock runs out. You are limiting yourself in a major way here. You need to diversify your portfolio, you know . . . dibble and dabble in a little of everything. That's the only way to see a real increase in profit margins."

"I appreciate the knowledge, but I'm good where I'm at." Kita entered her car, a gesture letting Chino know the conversation was over.

"You be well, Markita!" Chino's car pulled off into the night. Seconds after starting her car, the dashboard lit up, indicating she had an unknown call.

"Who the fuck is this?" The irritation in her voice couldn't be missed.

"I wanted to congratulate you on a well-put-together grand opening tonight and say thank you for keeping your word when it came to Chino." Davit's voice sounded rough yet sensual.

"Damn, are you stalking me again?" With a laugh, Kita surveyed the street. She spotted a man standing in front of a nearby corner store. He was holding a cell phone, but his head was down. He wasn't there before, so Kita knew it was Davit playing his usual game of keeping her on her toes.

"Keep doing what you're doing, but please, be careful. It's smart to have legit businesses, but understand that being in the spotlight can bring lots of unwanted attention to you and your colleagues. Are you prepared to handle that?"

Without responding, Kita drove slowly down the street. With her window down, she made sure to peer at the man standing on the corner. Just as she passed him, she blew the horn and waved her hand out the window. Kita wanted him to know that she'd seen him.

Kita was awakened with breakfast in bed the following day, just as Rico had promised. After indulging in a triple stack of pancakes, bacon, and cheese eggs, he broke her off with his magic stick and then showered. The moment she reached for her phone, prepared to gossip with Kenya about the prior night's events, it rang.

"Good morning, Ms. Barbara," Kita sang into the phone after seeing the salon name appear on the caller ID.

"Hey, Kita, are you busy, baby?" The tone in her voice was concerning.

"What's wrong?" Instinctively, Kita began pondering the millions of things it could've been, like loss of power or no hot water.

"I think you need to get down to the salon." Barbara's voice was unsteady. "An unwanted guest here refuses to leave until he speaks with the owner. I offered to take down his number and have someone call, but then he demanded to speak with you specifically," she whispered.

"Call the police!" Kita was frustrated at the thought of someone causing trouble at her place of business when everything was so beautiful last night.

"He *is* the police, Kita."

"OK. I'll be there in twenty minutes." Without hesitation, Kita ended the phone call, threw on clothes, and put on her black Nike running shoes. She didn't have time to tell Rico bye. On the way to the shop, Kita called her lawyer to keep him on standby. Then she texted her girls, whom she knew were probably sleeping off hangovers. Her stomach fluttered when she pulled up to the door of the salon. She didn't know why the police were there, but sure as shit, a police car was parked in front of her.

After calming herself, she hopped out and entered the building. "What's going on?" she asked aloud. Barbara was standing behind the desk with her arms folded. Officer Douglas sat with his feet propped up on the coffee table covered in various magazines.

"Please excuse us, ma'am. I need to talk to your boss alone." Douglas dismissed Barbara before addressing Kita. "This is a nice little spot you got here."

"What can I do for you?"

Officer Douglas stood from his seat. "Where the fuck is my money?"

"*Your* money?" Kita folded her arms and shifted her weight to one foot.

"This is my second time telling your black ass that it costs to be a player in this game. Now, are you going to pay the piper, or will we have a problem?"

"Tell me, Detective, what makes you the piper?" Kita patiently waited for the answer.

"Have my money by Friday, or you will discover what makes me the piper." Douglas walked toward the door. "Miss Jones, you better ask about me before deciding not to pay me on Friday. I'm not someone you should fuck with, but I told you that already."

"Are you going to pay him?" Barbara came from the back once the coast was clear.

"This is a legal business. I ain't paying shit!" Kita meant that too. "Once you start paying one, you might as well prepare to pay them all."

# CHAPTER FORTY-SIX

Things for Kita and her crew felt settled for the first time in a long time. Business with Arman was better than ever. Detective Douglas had finally gotten it through his head that Markita was no easy target, and with a growing number of clients coming to the salon, the girls could easily clean up their money. Everyone was so busy living their lives and working in their respective corners of the city that it was sometimes hard to make time for linkups. However, tonight was New Year's Eve, and it was also Alexis's birthday. She'd rented the ballroom at the Roostertail and hosted an all-white party. She splurged to have the place decorated from top to bottom in white, metallic silver, and light blue accents. In addition to the crisp linen, fine china, and floral centerpieces, images of Alexis abounded around the room, as well as a vinyl decal in the center of the dance floor. Guests indulged in various foods from vendors around the city as the DJ filled the room with trendy music.

"This is nice!" Kenya mimicked a popular comedian as she and Kita walked into the room. Since Rico had to work and couldn't come, the two women had decided to ride together.

"You got that right." Kita took in every inch of the room, scanning the crowd until she found the birthday girl. "There she is, looking as gorgeous as ever," she pointed toward a photo area where Alexis, Breeze, and Talia posed for a picture. Alexis's hair was pulled up in a cute ponytail with curls, and her makeup was beat to perfection. The fabric of her dress was mesh, covered in rhinestones. From a distance, she almost looked tastefully naked.

"There's some fine-ass people up in here tonight." Kenya eyed a beautiful, brown-skinned girl waving from across the room. "Where do you think she knows them from?"

"Girl, there is no telling. Knowing Alexis, she probably invited everybody she ever met in life." Though Kita laughed, she couldn't help but think of Davit's warning about the spotlight. She made a mental note to ask Alexis to tone it down some but dared not say anything until after the party was over.

"Hey, y'all," Alexis hollered over the music before waving them over to where she was.

As Kita and Kenya walked through the crowd, they couldn't help but notice the familiar faces of Breeze's crew. In the midst of them was Al, who immediately tensed up as they got closer. However, Markita paid him no mind as she approached her friend for a hug.

"Girl, you look so beautiful! Happy Birthday!" Kita handed her a gift bag. Without looking inside, Alexis gave it to Talia, who took it to the gift table. "She looks so pretty too, but I am surprised you let her come to this adult shindig tonight."

"Yeah, that's my mini-me. She's been attached to my hip lately, but I don't mind. Besides, I want to spoil her and expose her to the glamorous life the way Marlowe showed you," Alexis said while hugging Kenya. As the trio conversed, Joey approached them with a large group of people, three of whom were their clients. With her brows furrowed, Kita watched Joey and his group chopped it up with Breeze and his group like they'd known each other for years.

"Do you think having Joey and our clients here mixing and mingling with everybody is a good idea?" Kita whispered. "There should always be a line between business and personal."

"A party ain't a party without people, Kita. Damn." Alexis rolled her eyes. "Why do you *always* have to be a killjoy?" Dramatically, Alexis stormed away. Though Breeze didn't hear what was said to make his girl angry, he gave Kita a look that could kill. Sensing the energy shift, Kenya inquired about what happened.

"We'll talk about it later." Now, with an attitude of her own, Kita decided that it was time to leave the party. However, as she approached the door, someone began tapping on the microphone, causing her to stop and listen. It was Breeze; he was standing beside Alexis and Talia. All eyes were on them.

"Before the clock strikes midnight, I wanted to take a moment to tell my lady that although it's her birthday, she's been a gift to me. She is the woman I never knew I needed. She is my rock, my lover, and my friend. She is the queen of my team, and I wouldn't be the nigga I am without her. Bae, fuck them haters. As long as you got me and I got you, we gon' take over the world. Everybody, please raise your glasses and, on the count of three, wish my girl a happy birthday. One . . . two—"

Sickened to her stomach and irritated to the max, Kita left the room before Breeze could make it to three. Just when she stepped outside to call an Uber, she was met with the familiar face of the man whose presence she wasn't expecting.

"Rico, what are you doing here?" Markita smiled hard to conceal her anxiety as her man walked up. He wore an all-white suit and an expression that told her he'd missed her.

"I got off a little early, and it's almost midnight," he whispered into Kita's ear. "Do you want to go back inside for the countdown?"

"Nope. We can stand right here. As long as I bring in the New Year with you, it doesn't matter where we are." Kita planted a wet kiss on her man to distract him. The last thing she needed was for him to walk into the ballroom full of dope boys, fly girls, and would-be criminals. Internally, she'd been struggling for quite some time with the fact that she and her man were on opposite sides of the law. She loved Rico so much and didn't want to lose him again, so she stopped at no cost to keep him from knowing the *real* her.

"Get a fucking room," a drunk partygoer teased.

"Kita, if it's okay with you, I want to spend every New Year together." Rico smiled.

"No problem, baby. I'll put it on my calendar," she giggled.

"I asked Alexis if I could do this in the ballroom, but right here is as good a place as any. I love you and want to spend the rest of my life with you." Reaching into his pocket, Rico started to speak again, but inside the ballroom, the crowd started yelling.

"Ten. Nine. Eight. Seven."

"I love you, and I'm not going anywhere," Kita yelled back.

"Five. Four. Three," the crowd continued.

"I'm not going anywhere either, so let's make it official." Rico removed a Cartier box from his pocket and dropped to one knee. "Will you marry me?"

"Happy New Year!" The crowd had drowned out Kita's answer, but the tears pouring from her eyes indicated that she had said yes.

After sharing a passionate kiss beneath the stars, Kita looked back to see that most of the crowd from the ballroom were now standing in the doorway watching them. Some clapped, while others cheered. This was the best surprise Kita had ever received, but the moment was bittersweet when she realized that Kenya was front and center . . . but Alexis was not. Markita knew they'd have to talk and make things right, but for now, she decided to enjoy her moment.

# CHAPTER FORTY-SEVEN

It had taken nearly two weeks for Kita to convince Alexis to meet to address the elephant in the room. She'd arranged for the meeting at Kenya's campus apartment at noon. Not only did she live alone, but also, as the neutral party, it made sense that her place would be the perfect space for mediation.

Kita was the first to arrive. After knocking, she entered the bare home with a basket of goodies. Things had been so busy that she hadn't found time to visit Kenya before now. "Hey, girl, hey!" Kita placed her basket on the kitchen counter and glanced around the home. It was small, but just enough. The walls were bright white with recessed lighting. The floor was covered in a gray laminate tile resembling wood, and a sliding patio door led to the balcony. Aside from a mounted television, sofa, and coffee table with a few pictures in frames, the apartment was empty.

"My bad, girl. I was in the back, lighting candles." Kenya came into the room holding a pink, three-wick candle that she set on the coffee table.

"What scent is that? It's making me feel sick." Kita sat and placed the back of her hand on her head. "Forget the candle. Your ass better start locking that door."

"I usually do, but ain't nothing in here to take. Shit, I still keep all of my stuff at my mom's house, so I ain't too worried about it."

Someone knocked on the door, and Kita's heart dropped because she knew it was Alexis.

"What's good?" Alexis walked into the apartment and copped a squat on the floor, choosing not to sit on the sofa with Kita.

"Okay, I called this meeting because there is an elephant that we need to remove from the room before we can move forward." Kita cut right to the point.

"Girl, I'm sick of you and these meetings. *You* are the fucking elephant!" Alexis yelled.

"If stating the obvious or asking questions that make you think makes me the elephant, then it is what it is." Kita shrugged.

"Everybody, take a chill pill. Damn." Kenya clapped her hands. "We are too close for this. Now, let's talk without all of the hostility. Alexis, I can see in your face that you are hurting. Please tell us what's wrong so we can fix it."

"It doesn't matter. You always side with Kita anyway." Alexis crossed her arms.

"Please, Lex, talk to us," Kenya begged.

"I just don't like how Kita always seems to be in control. With her condescending judgment, she always makes me feel like everything I do is wrong." Alexis dabbed at the tears coming down her face. "When her nigga asked me days ago if he could propose to her at *my* party, I said yes without hesitation. Though I wanted my night to be all about me, I was delighted to share the moment with my friend because that's what friends do when they are happy for one another. However, the minute she walked in, she had a problem with Talia being there, and then Joey, etc." Alexis took a deep breath. "And I know she doesn't like Breeze, so she's definitely not as happy about my proposal as I am for hers. I didn't miss her stank face on the night we got engaged."

"Alexis, I love you and am very happy you are living the lifestyle you've always wanted. I truly apologize for hurting your feelings. We are equals, and I need to learn to stop making you feel less than that." Though Kita sincerely apologized, she had to keep it real too. "Now, with that said, I disagree with the flamboyant shit because it draws too much attention. The higher we get, the more enemies we make, which means we must be careful with how much access we give the world. Lastly, I have no problem with Breeze. I just don't like how deep you've brought him into our business against our will." She sighed. "If you want to supply him with product, that's one thing, but introducing him to our clients and affiliates is another. Once he puts all the puzzle pieces together you've given him, he won't need you anymore."

"*Boom*—there is it!" Alexis stood from the floor. "You heard that, right, Kenya?"

"Girl, what are you talking about?" Kita frowned.

"You just said that after giving someone all the pieces, they won't need you, right? Well, now we know why you don't want us to know who the plug is! You don't want us not to need you anymore."

"Lex, are we *still* on that?" Kenya rolled her eyes, which further agitated Alexis.

"You know what? I'm done. You two can have this shit and the fucking cocaine connect. Me and Breeze have something lined up anyway." Alexis stormed toward the door.

"Please, sit back down." Kita had about enough of the theatrics. "It ain't that simple. We have a legit business in all of our names. You can't just walk out."

"Watch me!" With the middle finger held stiffly in the air, Alexis left the apartment like it was on fire.

With her mouth agape, Kenya looked at the door in amazement. "Is she for real right now?"

"I don't know, but let her be. I'm done for real." Kita sat back on the couch and crossed her leg, which began shaking profusely. "If she wants out, then so be it. She and Breeze can have at it."

"So where does that leave us?" Kenya took a seat, exhaling loudly.

"There is no doubt that Lex is going to reclaim Shyla's spot for her own since that's her cousin, and she's probably going to try to poach Joey too, but we can cross that bridge when we get to it. In the meantime, we can head over to Shyla's spot and clear out what's left. If Alexis wants it, she will have to start with nothing like we did."

"I got class in less than an hour. I can't go right now." Kenya glanced down at her watch. "Speaking of class, when are you enrolling?"

"Girl, I've seriously been thinking about starting this summer." Kita laughed when she saw the side eye Kenya was giving her. "To prove I'm serious, I will go by the student admissions office before going to Shyla's. Have a good class, and call me later."

# CHAPTER FORTY-EIGHT

True to her word, Kita went by the admissions office and began the process of enrolling for the summer semester. After filling out a stack of papers and paying tuition in full with a personal check, she was allowed to meet with an advisor and select classes. When she finished, she called to tell her mother the news and used the drive time to Shyla's house to discuss the upcoming nuptials. Unbeknownst to Kita, her mother had begun planning the wedding the same day Rico called asking for permission to have her daughter's hand in marriage three weeks ago. Jackie had a binder almost full of ideas. "What date are you thinking? We need to lock down a location. I think November is a good month. Everybody else does the summer."

As Jackie rambled off questions without pause, Kita pulled her car to stop several doors down from Shyla's home. She did so to prevent anyone from hearing the intimate details of her conversation, and she also felt like she needed to throw up. However, all that went out the window after noticing a familiar car in Shyla's driveway. On cue, her heart skipped a beat.

"Ma, let me call you right back." Kita didn't wait for Jackie to respond before ending the call through a button on her dashboard. "What the fuck is he doing here?" Quickly, she began to take pictures of the car on her phone before exiting her vehicle. Inconspicuously, Kita made her way down the block, through the alley, and then she crept up to the back of the house. She knew that Shyla sometimes left her kitchen window open.

"Bingo!" Kita whispered as she approached the window in a crouched-down position. It was a good distance above her head, so she had to grab a lawn chair, push it up to the exterior of the house, and slowly inch her way up. Just as her head became level with the window, she could see Detective Douglas and Shyla in the hallway. Neither was looking in her direction.

"Come on, now. Is that any way to treat an old friend?" He rubbed Shyla's arm.

"I told you we are not friends, and you can't be here." Shyla's body was tense and appeared as stiff as a board. "Why are you here anyway? I haven't done anything!"

"You might not have done anything, but I'm hearing from some of the people you party with that you know something." Detective Douglas moved past Shyla and went into the kitchen. Kita almost fell, trying to hide from view.

"Know something about what?" Shyla's voice could be heard through the open window. Kita was so still that she could've passed for a mannequin.

"Bernard Jackson." Douglas opened the fridge and went through it as if trying to find something specific.

"I coped from him a few times, but that's about it." Shyla's voice trembled.

"Stop fucking around with me. I know you have information about the night of his murder."

"I don't know shit!" Shyla screamed.

"I bet you don't know anything about this money or coke an informant of mine purchased from here either, huh?"

"That shit ain't mine!" As Shyla began to cry, Kita forced herself to inch back up to the window. She saw Shyla bent over her kitchen table with a Ziplock bag of money near her face. Instinctively, Kita pulled out her cell phone and began to record.

"Put your fucking hands behind your back!" Forcefully, he placed handcuffs on Shyla as she continued screaming, denying knowledge of anything he was asking. "Your ass is going to jail today unless you talk or you do something else for me."

"Well, tell me what I need to do because I don't have shit to say." It was admirable how Shyla handled her situation like a G. Kita made a note to reward her for being solid as soon as this shit was over.

"You already know what I want." Douglas reached into his pocket and retrieved a condom, then unzipped his pants.

"No! Not that. Please, just take me to jail. I'm not fucking you." Shyla's screams turned into cries as she was forcefully raped from the back, with her hands still in handcuffs. Kita couldn't stomach what was happening. She wanted to barge inside, but her hands were tied. After turning off the camera, Kita carefully got off the chair without making a sound. She was back in her car within minutes, pulling off before Douglas was done busting his nut.

With tears, she drove like a madwoman the hour-and-a-half trip back to her home. She was sad and pissed. She didn't know who to call or what to say. She didn't want to disturb Kenya in class, and hitting up Alexis was definitely out of the question.

"This motherfucker has to go." Furiously, she hit the steering wheel. Not only did Douglas have to be dealt with for how he'd handled Shyla, but Kita was also afraid that he might have enough dirt on her to do something about it. Her mind was still racing when she pulled into the driveway, so much so that she didn't see Rico sitting on her porch. When she didn't come to greet him, he came down to her with concern on his face.

"Kita, what's wrong?"

"Nothing. I'm sorry I didn't see you." She tried to straighten up, but it was useless.

"You're lying." Rico spoke lovingly as he opened Kita's car door and pulled her into his arms. "Whatever it is, you can tell me, baby. If we are going to spend the remainder of our lives together, then we have to keep it a buck."

"Rico, I—" Kita was cut off by the ringing sound of her cell phone. She was stunned to see that the caller was Alexis, but then she thought it might've been about Shyla. "Give me one second. I have to take this in private. It's girl-talk about Lex and her boyfriend," Kita lied with a straight face and walked toward the street. "Hey, what's up?"

"Somebody took my fucking sister!" Alexis sobbed into the phone.

"What? Where are you?" Kita was completely caught off guard by this news. "I'm on the way." Without an explanation, she jumped back in the car and pulled off, leaving Rico just as confused as she was.

# CHAPTER FORTY-NINE

Temporarily putting the impending drama with Shyla and Detective Douglas on hold, Kita drove the long distance back to Detroit to be with her friend. "I didn't want to ask on the phone, but what do you mean somebody 'took' Talia? Took her where?" Kita asked after entering Alexis's grandmother's apartment. Kenya was sitting in the kitchen with her head in her hands.

"I don't know." Alexis was crying hysterically. "My grandmother called me and said she didn't come home from school today. We went to the school, and they had no record of Talia attending class. This shit is not like her." Alexis's voice had grown raspy.

"Do you think Talia has a boyfriend or something?" Kita hated to ask, but she knew how girls her age became a little fast when they began to notice boys.

"No." Alexis sniffed, "I talked to a few of her friends who usually walk with her in the morning. They said she realized she'd left her project at home, so she turned around and returned to get it. They haven't seen her since."

"Did you guys call the police?" Kita asked the obvious.

"Yeah, but that was not helpful. She has to be missing for forty-eight hours before we can formally file a report." Alexis blew her nose. "Do you know what can happen in forty-eight fucking hours? Why does no one care about our missing Black girls? I bet if she had blond hair and blue eyes, her story would be on the news right now."

"I know this is hard, but we've got to trust God. We *will* get Talia back." Silently, Kita began to pray that nothing happened to Talia before they could find her. "I think I know somebody who can help."

"Who?" Both Alexis and Kenya stared in anticipation.

"Rico." She felt nauseated having to say his name because she knew they'd feel a way about her withholding his occupation from them. However, Kita wouldn't be able to live with herself if she had a way to find Talia and didn't use it. "He's a cop."

"Come again?" Alexis snapped and looked at Kenya. "See, this bitch is a trip! I hate I even called your conniving ass for help. Please, just leave."

"Lex, you have every right to be mad, but please, let's work on finding Talia first." Kita tried to appease her friend, but it was useless.

"Bitch, get the fuck out!" Alexis pointed toward the door as tears poured down her face. "She's been so worried about mixing business and personal, yet she's fucking with the gotdamn law!" With anger, Alexis slammed the door in Kita's face. Seconds later, it opened, and Kenya appeared in the hallway with an unreadable expression and her arms folded.

"You have to admit that this is fucked up! I mean, had this not happened to Talia, were you *ever* going to tell us that your fiancé was a cop?" Kenya didn't give Kita time to respond. "We had a right to know that you've been sleeping with the enemy. Who knows if your ass has been pillow-talking and telling our business. You know—this shit that can send us to prison."

"Kenya, everything you're saying is right. From the bottom of my heart, I'm sorry, but Talia needs to be the focus right now. Do you guys want me to ask Rico for help or not?" On one hand, Kita wanted to make the call and bring him in. On the other hand, she didn't want to violate her friend's right to choose.

"You can do whatever you want. Seems like you're good at that these days." Kenya returned to the apartment, and the door closed again in Kita's face.

With a pounding headache and the consistent urge to throw up, Kita decided not to call Rico, choosing to instead go on a solo mission through the city, retracing Talia's steps. For the better part of four hours, she knocked on doors like the police and questioned everyone she saw. Besides a wino telling her that he believed he saw Talia get into a black car with a man whom she seemed familiar with, Kita was no closer to solving the case than she was when she started.

The clock struck seven when Kita returned to Ms. Barbara's building. Kenya's vehicle was parked in the same spot it had been when she left, and Alexis's car was there too. Kita knew they were probably still upset with her, but there was no way she could go home tonight. She had to be with them the way they had been with her the night she awaited updates after her brother was shot.

*Bzzzzz*

Before Kita could cut the engine, her phone vibrated. It was a text message from a foreign number with a picture attached. Her first instinct was to delete the message without reading it because she hated spam. However, curiosity got the best of her, and she opened it. It was a picture of Talia, gagged and bound to a chair. "Oh my God!" Kita grabbed her chest. Although Talia didn't appear to be hurt, it was gut-wrenching to see her like that.

Immediately, tears gathered in the corners of Markita's eyes. She wondered what the young girl was going through and if she had been assaulted in any way. There was a text message below the picture demanding $100,000 by midnight . . . or Talia would die.

Quickly, Kita grabbed her purse, flew up to Ms. Barbara's, and banged on the door frantically until it opened. The look on Alexis's and Kenya's faces told her everyone must've gotten the same message. Her heart broke as she noticed Ms. Barbara in the living room. She was sobbing uncontrollably. "I don't know what the hell y'all got going on, but Talia better be home tonight! I don't care how much money you've got to spend."

"Don't worry. We're going to get her back." Kita did her best to sound reassuring.

"What if we give them the money . . . and they hurt her . . . or worse." Alexis had a valid point, but none of that mattered.

"You can't think like that." Kita shook her head.

"I'll call the number and see if I can get someone on the phone." Kenya hit send and placed the call on speaker. The phone rang three times before someone answered.

"You must be calling about my fucking money." The voice on the other end of the phone was concealed with a voice disguiser.

"You will get your money, but how do I know Talia is safe?" Kenya eyed Alexis and Kita. While waiting, they could hear some shuffling before someone spoke again. This time, it was Talia.

"Is my sister there?" Her voice shook like she had been crying.

"I'm right here," Alexis yelled. "Are you okay? Did they hurt you?"

"I'm okay. I'm just scared." The phone made another shuffling sound, and then the robot was back on the phone.

"I want my money in large bills. Bring it in a garbage bag to the school yard at Beaubien Middle School. When you get there, leave it in the center of the field. Don't fuck around. My shit better be there on time too!"

"Where will my sister be?" Alexis screamed.

"Once the money has been collected, I'll call you with a location to pick her up."

*Click!* Just like that, he ended the call.

Alexis slammed her fist hard on the glass table, causing it to crack from edge to edge. "That nigga is going to kill my sister."

"At this point, all we can do is what he asked." Kenya sighed.

"She's right, Lex." Kita agreed. "I'd rather give it to him than to hold out and see what happens."

"After what I spent on my party, I don't have that kind of money," Alexis admitted. "I probably have like fifteen thousand in a safe."

"What about Breeze?" Kita asked.

"He's been trying to bounce back from the money he spent on this ring. Part of what I have is his." Alexis admitted.

Kita wanted to scold Alexis about not saving money, but tonight was not the time for any lectures. "I've got about seventy thousand to spare. Can you do fifteen, Kenya?"

"I got about ten Gs in a safe." Kenya had been dipping into her rainy-day funds more than she wanted to admit.

"I have the other five thousand." Without hesitation, Ms. Barbara went to the hiding spot in her bedroom and grabbed some money.

"Okay, so we're good then." Kita was relieved that they were able to come up with what they needed, but she was pissed that she had to carry the bulk of the bill.

"I swear I'll pay y'all back every dollar," Alexis sniffed. "I swear on my mother."

"We'll talk about that later. For now, let's go get Talia." Kita glanced around the room to make sure everyone was prepared for the mission.

# CHAPTER FIFTY

After putting their money into a duffle bag, the girls headed together to the drop-off location. The school park was dark and deserted. They tried to see if anyone lurked in the shadows but found nothing. Alexis wanted to stay and wait, but her girls advised her that the kidnapper probably had eyes on them too. It was best for Talia's sake to return to Ms. Barbara's to wait for the call.

The ride back was a silent one. Everyone feared the worst, but no one said so. Things like this didn't usually turn out well. Once the bad guys had the money, there was no reason to keep Talia alive. What if she had seen or heard something that could be used to identify them? Everyone in the car knew that kidnapping typically led to sex trafficking rings, and with more than twenty thousand cases a year, no one had a good feeling.

To break the ice, Kita blurted out, "I went to Shyla's spot earlier, and that detective I've been telling y'all about was there. He was asking her questions about Bernard and who'd been selling drugs from her house."

"Did Shyla say anything?" Taking her eyes off the road, Kenya peered at Kita.

"No, but her silence came at a price, y'all. He raped her." Kita looked down at her ringing phone. It was Rico. He called back-to-back, but Kita didn't answer. She texted him that now wasn't a good time but that they would talk in the morning. He didn't reply. The remainder of the ride went back to being silent as everyone processed what was happening. Though she knew they would find out anyway, Kita wished she would've kept her big mouth closed about Shyla. Things were already tense enough.

Within thirty minutes, they were at Alexis's condo, sitting with their phones in the middle of the kitchen table. They'd decided not to return to Ms. Barbara's house in case things had gone sideways. They didn't want to spook the older woman until they had solid information.

"Where's Breeze?" Kenya stood to use the restroom.

"I don't know, and I don't care. Why aren't they calling?" Alexis picked up her phone and tossed it across the room.

"Maybe we should just try to call the number back." At the end of Kita's sentence, the sound of screeching tires outside caught their attention. They all bolted to the door, damn near knocking each other down, to find Talia sprawled out on the front lawn. Aside from a few bumps and bruises, she appeared untouched.

"Thank you, Jesus!" Alexis screamed, dropping to her knees.

"Are you okay?" Kenya inspected the young girl for additional wounds. "Did they hurt you or touch you inappropriately?"

"No, but I did hurt myself trying to get away." Talia's little face glowed beneath the street lights.

"Fuck all of that!" Kita snapped. Now that Talia was back home, only one thing mattered at the moment. "Who is this nigga, Talia? Tell me what you saw and what you heard. We need to find this motherfucker tonight." Kita's blood boiled at the audacity someone had to kidnap one of their own.

"I was walking to school with my friends when I remembered leaving my science project in the fridge. I turned around and started running home. I saw the guy from your birthday party coming from the store, and he asked me why I was running. I told him, and he said he would give me a ride so I wouldn't be late to school." Talia began to cry. "Instead of taking me home, he took me to somebody else's house, where he tied me up to a chair in the basement."

"Do you remember his name?" Alexis bit down on her bottom lip so hard it began to squirt blood.

Talia shook her head, "I think they called him Al." She paused. "It was Breeze's friend from your birthday party." No one said a word as the revelation of what she'd said hit each of them like a ton of bricks.

After Alexis instructed her sister to go inside the house and call their grandmother, she stood on the lawn processing the story with Kenya and Kita. As they tried to make heads and tails of the matter, Breeze's SUV pulled into the driveway, and everyone became tense. "Bae, I have been out there looking, but I can't find any information on T."

Kita rolled her eyes and looked at Kenya, who stared at the ground. In a calm voice, Alexis said, "Nigga, just tell me why!"

"Why what?" Breeze scanned everyone's face to see what he was missing.

Alexis lost it. Within a split second, she went full Mayweather on his ass, punching and screaming. He didn't hit her back, but he had to exert his force to stop her blows after a while. "Why the fuck are you hitting me?"

"Breeze, where is the fucking money?" This time, it was Kita who got the drop on him when she pulled her gun and pointed it at his chest.

"What fucking money?" he barked, "Would someone tell me what the fuck is going on?"

"Nigga, Talia is back!" Kenya screamed. "And she said Al was the one who took her for ransom."

"Al?" Breeze scratched his head.

"You got two seconds to prove you had nothing to do with this, or you will lose your life on this lawn tonight." Kita saw red.

"Bae," Breeze turned to Alexis, "you know I would never do anything to hurt you or Talia. We are family! I swear I didn't know shit about Al's plan but," with eyes pleading to be believed, he took a moment to stare at each of them, "if you take me to him, I will kill that nigga myself. Y'all don't even have to get your hands dirty."

"Not for nothing, but I don't trust this nigga." Kita shook her head.

"How do we know he didn't help Al execute this plan, Lex?" Kenya spoke without removing her eyes from Breeze.

"I know him. If he said he didn't do it, then he didn't." Rubbing her temples, she continued. "Look, we need Al gone anyway. If Breeze wants to do it, I say we let him."

"That's less blood on our hands." Kenya looked at Kita.

"Fine," she relented, "but we all have to go to make sure the job is handled right."

# CHAPTER FIFTY-ONE

After spending an hour cultivating a plan, Breeze and the girls dropped Talia off at Ms. Barbara's. As they drove away from the apartment, Kita's cell phone rang. It was Rico again. Without answering, she powered off her phone and instructed everyone in the car to do the same. Though she'd meant to leave her phone at Ms. Barbara's, she knew they couldn't be traced if the phones were off.

The first stop of the evening was to one of Breeze's rented storage units, where they loaded up on guns and ammo. "Hell yeah, it's on now!" Kenya playfully pulled an AK-47 from its space in a box on the shelf, posing like she was one of Charlie's angels.

"Damn, nigga, you got an arsenal. Are you expecting a war?" Kita had to admit the unit was quite impressive.

"Aye, we are living in perilous times. If the government doesn't start a race war, then aliens will attack, so I figure if I stay ready, I won't have to get ready." After grabbing what he needed, Breeze locked up his shit and led the ladies back to the car. Each of them had blood in their eyes. Their adrenaline was on overdrive. Kita hadn't felt a rush like this since she bodied Bernard. Although she tried to suppress the feeling of satisfaction, she had to admit that she loved the way a gun felt in her hand. It made her feel powerful and in control.

Just after midnight, Breeze brought his vehicle to a slow creep down Al's block. Though some houses had their lights on, the block was mostly dark. After pulling his car to a stop, Breeze secured two guns into the waist of his skinny jeans. "Let's do this."

Alexis and her friends pulled down the ski masks on their heads and followed Breeze toward the two-story home with a brick exterior. He filled up the back door entryway with his large body to conceal the women behind him before knocking in code. Seconds later, the door opened, and Al appeared. "It's pretty fucking late to be making a house call, my nigga. What's good?"

"Man, some shit went down today, and we need to talk about it." In one swift motion, Breeze pulled his pistol and put it up against Al's chest, forcing him backward into the home.

"What the fuck is this?" Al's question was not only in reference to the gun being pointed at him but also to the three masked intruders behind Breeze. "Nigga, I know this ain't what I think it is."

"Shut the fuck up!" Breeze used the butt of his weapon to cold cock Al in the face. "I'm the nigga in charge of the questions here."

After coming into the house, the group moved through the kitchen and into the dining room, where they instructed Al to sit with his hands lying flat on the wooden dining table. One by one, each of the ladies sent blows and body shots Al's way. Breeze stood in the corner with his gun, ready to shoot if Al attempted to defend himself. "Why did you take my fucking sister?"

"I didn't take no fucking body." Blood dripped from Al's face as he struggled to hold his head up.

"Where's the money?" Kita began to ransack the area where they were standing.

"What money?" Al's voice was barely above a whisper.

"You thought you could cross me and get away with it, nigga? I treated you like family." Alexis walked into the kitchen and retrieved a large knife. Without hesitation, she raised it in the air and dropped it right into the center of his left hand. He screamed in agony.

"I didn't do shit to your sister; you have to believe me. Someone is setting me up." Al's pain had brought him to tears. "Please, you have to believe me."

"Nigga, she said it was you." Breeze didn't have time to listen to any more lies. Talia had identified her assailant, and that was good enough for him. Before Al could say another word, the hot lead from Breeze's gun exploded in his face. The flash of bright fire was the last thing he ever saw before the bullet entered his skull, ending his life right then and there.

"Gotdamn, could you have at least waited until he told us where the money is?" Kita wiped blood splatter from her arms.

"He wasn't going to say shit." Breeze wiped the gun using the bottom of his shirt and tucked it back into his jeans. "Y'all can comb the house and look for it, or we can slide. The choice is yours, but I've done my part."

"We don't want to risk leaving prints and evidence behind. I say we leave." Alexis sided with her man.

"That's easy for you to say when the bulk of the money was mine." Attitude dripped off of Kita like a leaky water faucet.

"Kita, I said I would pay you back, and I mean that," Alexis snapped.

"We don't have time for this shit right now. Fuck the money. We did what we came to do. We'll figure the rest out later. Let's bounce before a nosy neighbor calls the police." Kenya walked toward the door, and everyone else did the same.

# CHAPTER FIFTY-TWO

The sun was coming up when Kita put her key in the door. She was exhausted and ready to shower, but no sooner after dropping her purse and removing her shoes than someone knocked on the door. Briefly, she hesitated on whether to answer it, but she knew no one would be knocking if it wasn't someone important. Upon checking the peephole, Kita could see Rico standing with an agitated expression. She opened the door and stepped aside for him to enter. "Good morning."

"I've been calling your phone all fucking night, Kita. What's the deal?" Rico was on twenty. "I mean, you flew out of here like a bat out of hell and didn't say shit. What am I supposed to think?"

"Baby, I'm sorry. Something came up with Talia, and I needed to be with Alexis and Kenya until we figured everything out."

"Markita, please don't baby me right now." Rico hollered, "Something is off with you and your friends. I need you to be honest and tell me what's happening."

"Nothing is going on, Rico." Kita clung to her lie like it was the truth and nothing but the truth.

"Kita, I'm not stupid! Your business is doing well, but not well enough for the three of you to live the way you are. Are you into something that you shouldn't be into?" Rico stepped closer to Kita and stared into her eyes. "I saw the people at Alexis's party, and I recognized her boyfriend too. Most of them niggas are on the board at the precinct for drug operations."

"No, Rico! In fact, I'm a little offended that you would even come at me like that!" Kita snatched away. "When my brother died, he left my mom and me a lot of money, and contrary to what you believe, our business is doing great, so miss me with that other shit. Until you've seen my name on a fucking board, then you should know better."

"Markita, I'm sorry for accusing you of lying, but you got to admit that things have been a little off with you lately. My head is telling me that you're into some street shit, but my heart is begging me to believe it when you say you're not." Rico took a seat on the sofa. "Ever since my father was killed in the streets by some punk-ass dope dealer trying not to get busted, I just have a no-nonsense policy on that shit. No weed, alcohol, or other harsh substances for me or anyone I deal with."

"I can appreciate where you're coming from, but please understand that everyone in the streets ain't a bad person. Sometimes, hustling is the only way for people to have a chance at a better life."

"There are plenty of ways out of the ghetto that don't consist of selling drugs or killing each other," Rico huffed. "Everybody claims to be woke, but nobody has their eyes open, and when you do, you only see what you want to see."

"What the fuck are you talking about?" Kita was beginning to lose her cool.

"The drug trade is modern-day bondage. The plugs are the new masters, dealers are the new slaves, and cocaine is the new cotton. How can't you see that? Every time these dealers sell that shit on these streets, we're making the noose around the necks of our people tighter."

"Rico, I love you, but I think it's clear we are on different pages right now." Kita walked over to the door and pulled it open. "I think it's best that you leave."

"Are you serious?" Rico stood.

"I love you, but I need a little space right now. I'll call you in a few days." Kita couldn't look at him as he walked toward her. With her head down, she pulled off her ring and held it out for him to take.

"You're making a mistake, baby. I'm sorry." Without taking the ring, Rico exited the door before stopping abruptly. "Is that blood on your arm?"

"Goodbye, Rico." Choosing not to answer his question, she closed the door and broke out into tears. Kita hated that she'd had to be like that with him, but she knew if she didn't cut him off now, he'd keep digging until he found something.

Kita spent the next two days held up in her home alone with the blinds closed. Aside from replying to text messages to let everyone know she was okay, she had no desire to talk. The situation with Rico was devastating, but it was Al who was heavy on her heart. Kita couldn't help but replay the events leading to his death, and something just didn't sit right with her. However, she didn't know what it was. On top of all of that, Kita had continued to feel extremely sick throughout the day, which prompted her to order the delivery of a slew of pregnancy tests. They had been dropped off at her door twenty minutes ago, but she couldn't bring herself to take them. "Fuck it." She finally gave in and took all four tests in the bathroom.

The phone rang as Kita sat patiently on the toilet, awaiting her results. It was Jackie calling, so Kita decided to answer to kill time. "Hey, Mama."

"Several hours and event spaces later, your aunt Gwen and I have found the perfect wedding venue." Jackie was excited as she told Kita about the grand ballroom with an upscale spiral staircase, several oversized chandeliers, and a dance floor perfect for a Soul Train line. "Kita, this venue is every girl's dream. I hate you've been too busy to go scouting with us."

"Mama, I haven't been busy; I've been sick." Kita glanced at the time on her phone to see how long it would be before she could check the results.

"Do you have COVID?" Jackie gasped.

"No, Mama." Kita laughed. Ever since 2020, people assumed COVID-19 was the culprit for everything.

"Well, what is it? I've noticed you've been extremely quiet these past few days."

"It's nothing major. My stomach is just upset, and I've been nauseated," Kita explained.

"Are you pregnant?" Jackie gasped again.

"I don't know, but I'll tell you in about thirty seconds." Kita placed the call on speaker and began to inspect her test. One by one, all four of them told her what she already suspected.

"Kita, you there?" Jackie tried not to sound as anxious as she felt.

"Mama, I'm pregnant!"

# CHAPTER FIFTY-THREE

"**K**ita, your ass got three seconds to open this fucking door, or I'm kicking it in." Alexis had been banging on Kita's door for the better part of ten minutes.

"Please, Kita, just open the door because you know Lex is crazy enough to do it." Kenya placed her ear to the door to listen for movement.

"Damn, what part of the concept 'call before you show up' do you *not* understand?" With a smirk, Kita opened the door. Her friends barged in and made themselves comfortable. Kenya was holding a pizza box and carrying a two-liter bottle of Vernors Ginger Ale. Alexis had a giant pregnancy pillow and a grocery bag of food for sick people. "My mama can't hold water."

"I knew something was off when you' said my candle nauseated you the other day." Kenya placed her items down, then began rubbing Kita's nonexistent belly. "No offense, but I always thought Lex would be the first one to make me an auntie."

"Me too," both Alexis and Kita said in unison. They all erupted in laughter.

"Have you told Rico yet?"

"Not yet, and I probably won't." Kita flopped down on her couch. "I broke it off and gave him the ring back the other day."

"Bitch, what? Why did you break it off?" Kenya took a seat.

"Fuck that, why did you give the ring back?" Alexis began removing groceries and putting everything up.

"We live in two different worlds now. It's never going to work."

"I think he deserves to know about the baby, Kita, even if you don't want to marry him." As usual, Kenya spoke the truth. "You've got to talk to him."

"Talking to him makes it real, so I guess that's why I'm stalling." Kita sighed. "I've loved that boy since I first met him. All I ever wanted was to marry him and have his babies, but he's a cop, and I'm a criminal. We would never be able to live a normal life, and I know that."

"Why is life such a double standard? I bet if you were the cop, and he was the drug dealer, you'd be made to feel like you *have* to make it work." Alexis opened the pizza box and grabbed a slice.

"I know, right? Anyway, it is what it is." Kita shrugged.

"Are you going to keep the baby?" Kenya reached for the remote and turned on the television.

"I'm not sure." Ever since finding out she was pregnant, she had begun reevaluating her life. Although a good deal of time had gone by since killing Bernard, Kita knew that she didn't get away with murder because God saw everything. Even though she didn't technically kill Al, simply being present didn't sit well in her soul either. Ultimately, both men had gotten what they deserved, but Kita was beginning to feel like she should've just let God handle them. Maybe it was her motherly instincts kicking it, but she should've left it alone instead of trying to settle the score. Street retaliation was a vicious cycle that never ended, and she didn't want her child to get caught up in her mess.

"Whatever you decide, we will be here for you, and I'm sure Rico will too." Kenya clicked through the channels, trying to find her favorite television show.

"Yeah, we got your back, girl." Alexis joined her friends on the sofa. "Speaking of having someone's back, I appreciate y'all having mine. Give me a little time, and I will—" She was cut off by the ringing phone.

"Hey, Grandma. What's wrong? Calm down. Is Talia okay?"

While Kita eavesdropped on the call, Kenya stopped clicking the buttons on the remote and pointed to the television. A news broadcast was on, and a reporter was standing on the corner of Shyla's block. Her home was in view as officers walked in and out of the front door. "Turn it up!" Kita's eyes widened in anticipation of the story.

*"Police were called to this Detroit home around nine a.m. this morning after a concerned neighbor felt something was wrong."*

The video cut to an audio call to 911. A lady's voice said she'd stopped by her friend's house for a scheduled card game, but her friend never came to the door, although her car was in the driveway. The woman said she peered into the living room window and saw the body of her friend on the floor.

*"When the police arrived to do a welfare check, they discovered the body of the thirty-four-year-old female resident, whom they initially suspected had overdosed."* The reporter resumed. *"Upon further inspection, police now report that the woman appeared to have been sexually assaulted and strangled to death several days ago. They do not plan to release her name at this time due to impending investigations with both the medical examiner's office and Detroit Police Department."*

The room fell silent as the broadcast went to another story. Alexis ended the call with her grandmother and stared at her friends. "Shyla didn't deserve this."

"There is no investigation needed. It was that Detective Douglas that I've been telling y'all about." Kita instantly began to wish she'd done something when she saw him raping her.

"He has to be dealt with!" Alexis leaned forward, ready to put a plan in motion.

"There's enough blood on our hands. God will handle Douglas." Kita liked Shyla, but ultimately, this battle was not hers.

"Well, God better get to that motherfucker before I do!" Alexis was ready and willing to go to war for her cousin.

# CHAPTER FIFTY-FOUR

With so much going on and a lot to think about, Kita had decided to take some time away from the business. She wanted to focus on her pregnancy and weigh her options with her mom. However, upon visiting today, it was apparent that Jackie had already decided for her. "Kita, did you hear me? I asked if you wanted the nursery painted green or yellow." Jackie rambled, "Really, since both colors are gender neutral, you could do either, or you could just go with a classic white and pull in colors with the décor."

Kita was beginning to regret her decision to stop by. "Mama, I don't know about any of that right now. Please, can we talk about something else?"

"Fine." Annoyed, Jackie placed the paint samples on the table before her, sat back, and folded her arms. "Let's talk about the wedding, or do you not know about that either?"

"Let's talk about you, Mama. What's going on in your world?" Kita was lying across the sofa, staring at the ceiling.

"Well, not much. With Marlowe gone and you out of the house, my world is quite boring these days."

"Aww, you miss having me here, don't you?" Kita joked.

"Hmm. Let me think. With your dirty dishes, messy room, and all that attitude . . . No, I don't miss having you here." Jackie tossed a sofa pillow at her daughter. "Just kidding. I miss you a lot, Markita." She paused. "Hopefully, when you have my grandbaby, you'll bring them by so I can fill this house with laughter again."

"There you go. You just had to bring the baby up again, and this time, you're trying to play on my heartstrings. You just couldn't help yourself from playing dirty, could you?" Kita tossed the pillow back at her mother.

"This baby is a blessing, Kita. I think, in some way, this is Marlowe's soul finding its way back to us."

"Ma, you know better than to make a pregnant woman cry." Kita stood and walked toward the bathroom, making her third trip within the hour. Just as she washed her hands, she heard a knock at the door. "Are you expecting company?"

"Okay, don't be mad." Jackie walked to meet her in the hallway. "Rico called me this morning and said he wanted to talk. I told him to come by at noon, but I had no idea you were coming over."

"Ma." Kita stomped her foot.

"You need to talk to him, Kita." As the doorbell rang for the second time, Jackie walked over and opened it with her best smile. The room was silent for several seconds after Rico entered the house. He and Kita stared each other down. "Rico, please, have a seat and make yourself comfortable. I need to go make a phone call." Before Jackie could fully exit the room, her doorbell rang again.

"Any more surprises?" Kita rolled her eyes as she gestured for Rico to sit on the sofa opposite her.

"None that I know of." Jackie casually opened the front door, fully expecting a deliveryman or something.

"Hi, Ms. Jones. My name is Detective Douglas. May I have a word?"

Instantly, Kita's heart began to feel like it would explode into pieces. Rico leaned forward on the sofa but didn't move. His mouth was agape like he wanted to say something but couldn't find the words.

"How can I help you, Detective?" Jackie moved into the door frame, blocking Douglas's view of her living room.

"Well, I just wanted to ask some questions about your daughter, Markita." Detective Douglas did his best to peer past Jackie and get a glimpse of the interior of her home.

"Now is not a good time, sir."

"This is pretty serious, Ms. Jones. The sooner we can talk, the better. I swear, it'll only take a few minutes." Taking a step forward, Douglas put his foot into the doorway.

"You've got five seconds to get your fucking foot off my doorstep." Jackie was growing more irritated by the second.

Knowing the treachery that Detective Douglas was capable of, Kita stood from her seat, prepared to end the madness. However, Rico was up and at the door in no time before she could move. "Hey, is everything okay?"

"Rico! What the fuck are you doing here?" Douglas slid his foot out of the doorway.

"This is my girlfriend's mother." Rico paused. "But what are *you* doing here?"

"Your girlfriend?" Douglas sounded as if someone had knocked the breath out of his body. "Markita Jones is a dangerous criminal, son. It would be in your best interest to cut ties with this drug-dealing murderer immediately."

# CHAPTER FIFTY-FIVE

Douglas had been gone for a good twenty minutes before Rico could find the nerve to speak to Kita, let alone look at her. His emotions were all over the place as he tried to process the information his godfather had just given him. "Can we talk in the backyard?"

"Right here is fine." Kita sensed that the conversation was about to get heated. She found comfort in knowing someone was nearby in case it reached a boiling point.

"I've got some questions you might not want to answer in front of your mother." Rico's nostrils were flared, and his chest rose and fell rapidly.

"At this point, I've got nothing to hide from either of you. I'm sick of running from the truth, so let's get to it."

"Why would my godfather call you a drug dealer? Don't fucking lie to me like you did the last time I asked if you were into some street shit, and you had the nerve to get offended." Rico's eyes were turning glossy. "I chose you to be my wife. I thought we had something. Why lie to me, Kita?"

"It wasn't intentional." Kita walked toward him, but he jerked away, so she continued. "When you came back into my life, I was knee-deep in the dope game, and shit was complicated."

"Why didn't you just stop?"

"Contrary to what you think you know about the streets, they don't work like that." Kita couldn't help but to antagonize his privileged ass. She knew he'd never gone to bed hungry or had the utilities turned off. Most people hustled because they didn't have a choice.

"Why did he call you a murderer?" Rico began pacing the floor as Jackie looked on because she too was waiting for the answer.

"I have no idea!" Markita snapped. "But I think it's funny that your crooked-ass godfather can come here with that accusation when *he* is an actual murderer." Reaching into her pocket, she retrieved her cell phone and pulled up the video that she had captured of Detective Douglas raping Shyla. "This was the girl they found dead in her house the other day. He assaulted her and then killed her to cover his tracks."

Rico's eyes widened in surprise. He'd never known his godfather to be anything but a stand-up guy. Hearing Douglas's accusation of Kita and her accusation against him was too much for Rico to handle. His ears began to ring, and his palms became clammy. His knees felt like they were going to give out at any moment. Without another word, he turned and headed for the door. The sight of Kita was nauseating him.

"Rico, I'm pregnant!" Kita shouted just before he reached the door. He turned and looked at her with disdain in his eyes.

"Bitch, how dare you use something as serious as this to try to get me to feel bad for you." He laughed. "Don't ever call me again, and if you see me in the streets, you better not look my way. We are done!" Though Rico was screaming at the top of his lungs, the tears on his face indicated that he was more than angry; he was hurt.

"Rico, I'm sorry I lied to you before, but I am not lying about this." Kita was now the one crying. "I don't know what I'm going to do about the baby, but according to everyone's advice, the right thing to do was let you know. Now, you know." Hurriedly, she grabbed her purse and tried to rush past him and out of the house before she broke down. Before she could leave, though, Rico grabbed her and held on for dear life as they cried both tears of joy and pain together.

The waterworks continued for several minutes before either of them said a word. Kita was the first one to break the silence. She wanted to know how Rico felt about her pregnancy and what he wanted to do about it.

"Markita, I love you with all of my heart, and I want nothing more than to have a life and start a family with you." He wiped his face. "But I can't do that while you live in the streets."

"What does that mean?" Kita stared at the ground. "Do you want me to get an abortion?"

"Kita, I want nothing in the world but for you to be my wife and have my children." He grabbed her hand. "But you've got to be done with this lifestyle first. If you can't leave the streets alone, I will be forced to seek full custody the second you go into labor."

"Rico, I'm tired and want to leave the game, but I need some time. Can you give me that?" Kita placed her head on Rico's chest. "I've got to settle things with my connect and break the news to the crew. Then I need to figure this shit out with Detective Douglas."

Placing his hand over Kita's belly, he lovingly kissed her forehead. "I'll handle my godfather. You just handle everything else before the baby is born."

"I don't want you involved in my shit." Kita shook her head.

"I'm already involved." He pointed to her stomach. "We're in this together." Pulling Kita's face up to look at him, he kissed her lips. "I love you."

"Rico, I've got one more secret," Kita blurted out as guilt nibbled at her heart. She was done hiding things from her man.

Sensing that Kita's secret needed spousal privilege, Rico whispered, "Baby, you can tell me after we get married. For now, let's just live in this moment."

# CHAPTER FIFTY-SIX

After spending the day with Rico, planning the next steps, and discussing their future, Kita went to be with her friends. Alexis held an intimate card party in memory of Shyla. Though the timing was off, and Kita dreaded being the bearer of what they might consider bad news, she knew it was now or never.

"Kita, did you hear me?" Alexis's long fingernails clicked as she snapped her fingers. "I said, I bet Kenya $5,000 you have the baby on December 12th." She was shuffling a deck of cards. "As a matter of fact, I bet another $5,000 it's going to be a boy." This time, she slammed the deck down on the dining room table, disturbing Kita from her somber thoughts.

"Girl, bye!" Kenya countered the wager from the kitchen. "I bet you $20,000 Kita has a baby girl on Christmas."

"I can't believe what I'm hearing. Y'all bitches are something else." Kita laughed lightly, unwilling to believe her friends had nothing else better to do with their time and money than to place bets on her child's gender and due date. "Alexis, you don't need to bet on shit until you give me back my money."

"Girl," Alexis smacked her lips, "there ain't no real money on the table. It's just a friendly wager. Relax."

"Fuck that. I want to bet for real. You got a couple of months before the baby comes." Kenya grabbed a piece of fried chicken from a bucket on the kitchen counter and then returned to her chair at the dining table.

"As soon I pay y'all back and get my money up, I got you." Alexis turned to face Markita, who was sitting with her feet up on the couch. "What's up with you? Your ass has been looking sad since you got here."

"Well, for starters, Detective Douglas showed up at my mom's house today calling me a drug-dealing murderer while Rico was there." Kita watched her friends grab their chests and gasp in unison.

"That motherfucker is at the top of my shit list," Alexis announced. "I just need to find the right time to get at his bitch ass for what he did to my cousin. Speaking of which, let's take a shot for Shyla." She poured some tequila into cups for her and Kenya.

"Don't move on him just yet. Rico said he'll handle it," Kita advised.

"What is Mr. Goody Two-Shoes going to do with his lame ass?" Alexis looked at Kenya for backup, but she remained silent.

"They have some history. Maybe he knows something that we don't." Kita intentionally omitted the fact that Douglas was her man's godfather because she knew better.

"Girl, this is good news." Kenya cut the deck of cards on the table. "So, why are you so quiet then?"

"Honestly, I don't know." Markita sat up and sighed. "I've just felt like I need to get out of the game before something bad happens."

"That's those hormones talking." Alexis blew her off.

"What do you think is about to happen?" Kenya never looked up while dealing out the cards.

"I can't explain it. It's just a feeling." Kita could tell that her friends thought she was crazy.

"Girl, ain't nothing going to happen to us. This shit with Douglas got you spooked, that's all. Once your man handles it, that feeling will pass." Alexis collected her cards and began organizing her hands for the spades game.

"It's not just Douglas. It's Marlowe, Bernard, Shyla, and Talia too." Kita rubbed her stomach. "I would lose my shit if something happened to one of y'all or this baby." She paused. "I'm out."

"Out of your mind, that's what you are," Alexis teased. "We got more money coming in than we've ever seen. We got guns, and we got each other's back," Alexis stated as a matter of fact.

"That's right!" Kenya reached out and gave her girl a high five. "Y'all my bitches until they lay me down. Get Money Girls for Life!"

Usually, Kita would've joined in on the moment, but she wasn't feeling it.

"So, you ain't down with us no more?" Alexis eyed Kita suspiciously.

"I'll always be down with y'all, but after this next shipment, I'm done." Kita mustered a smile, but truth be told, her days of riding with her girls were over. Now that she was about to become a mom and a wife, she had to leave the street life alone. Sure, the money was good, but what about the consequences? Kita was tired of looking over her shoulder and living in fear. She was ready to enjoy life the right way, with her man and their child.

"So, if Kenya and I wanted to keep the hustle going, would you at least introduce us to the connect?" Alexis slapped an ace onto the table and took the book.

"I told you he doesn't operate like that. Sorry, but you'll have to find your own plug."

"We've been buying coke from *your* connect for a while now. That shit has to mean something! Can't you just ask?" Alexis was beginning to wonder if Kita was holding out on purpose.

"What if you became our plug?" Kenya scanned her hand, looking for a card to play. "You can get the shit from your guy and then sell to us. That way, you can still make a few dollars, and we can keep quality product."

"Oh, I like that idea, Kenya." Alexis nodded before looking over to Kita. "You'd be the fly'est, pregnant plug the streets have ever seen."

"I'm out, y'all, and that's that." Kita lay back on the sofa.

"Look, I understand your reasons, but why do you have to leave us hanging?" It was apparent that Alexis was growing more annoyed by the minute.

Kita didn't respond because she knew her words were going into one ear and out the other. The game had been good to her, but everything in her being told her it was time to bow out gracefully. She'd be a fool if she didn't listen.

# CHAPTER FIFTY-SEVEN

Markita impatiently made a drumming sound on the steering wheel of the rented moving truck as she glanced at the clock for the fifth time in two minutes. Just as she sat up in her seat, preparing to start the engine and back out of her parking spot, she spotted a white maintenance van rapidly approaching from the rear. Instinctively, she reached for the gun tucked under her seat but decided not to grab it when the van's driver came into view.

"Kita, my apologies for being late. I got stopped by a train." Davit exited the car wearing an all-black cashmere sweater and a pair of black slacks. Quickly, he opened the back door of his vehicle and began unloading boxes to place in Kita's truck. When the transfer was complete, Kita handed him two overnight bags filled with money. Before leaving, Davit stopped to access Kita. "What's wrong? You seem different."

"I'm pregnant." Kita knew there was no point in beating around the bush, so she came right out with it.

"Oh shit. Um, congratulations, I guess." However, Davit didn't smile. "Sorry, that's just not something I'm used to hearing in my line of work."

"I won't be doing any more shipments," Kita blurted.

"Markita, things don't work like that. Once you're in, you're in until my uncle says otherwise." The coldness in his eyes couldn't be missed.

"Davit, your uncle is not my boss." Kita began to walk away. "And before he thinks of coming after me, please remind him of the time I saved his daughter's life. Technically, he still owes me."

"We'll be in touch soon. In the meantime, be safe." Davit stood firm with his hands tucked into his pockets.

"That sounded more like a warning than concern, but yeah, you be safe too." Kita got back into her truck and pulled away.

A million thoughts crowded her mind as she drove back toward the city. Kita tried to relax as the music from the radio played the electric sounds of smooth jazz. The last thing she wanted was for her stress to harm the baby, but as soon as her cell phone rang, she immediately tensed back up. Chrissy, a salon stylist, called to inform her that the cops were there harassing customers. She told Kita that they'd done this several times this week. Chrissy feared that clients would begin to cancel appointments if no one put a stop to the madness.

The thought of her legit business failing because of some bullshit had Kita livid. Within thirty minutes, she was pulling up on practically two wheels.

"What's the problem?" She stepped from the truck and approached a black police car; it was double-parked in front of the salon door.

"This is some bullshit! They gave me a ticket while I was in there getting my hair done." A customer pointed at two Black female officers leaning up against their car and laughing.

"It appears your customer parked at this meter for two hours instead of the hour and thirty minutes she paid for," Officer Howard said, walking up to Kita.

"Since when did the police become meter maids?" Kita rolled her eyes. "Don't you have something else better to do with your time?"

"I'll be whatever I have to be until I collect that fucking money," the officer exclaimed.

"Who sent you?" Kita frowned. "Never mind. I already know who it is. You can tell that dick sucker that I ain't paying shit!" Kita stood her ground.

"You know what?" Officer Howard looked back at her partner. "I think we should call our friends down at the DEA and recommend they come get serviced at this salon."

"Yeah, I'm sure they would love the opportunity to snag some dope dealers and get a manicure at the same damn time," her partner laughed.

"Tell your bitch-ass boss I will have his money on Friday!" Kita rubbed her temples. The last thing she needed was more police in her business.

"Nah, bitch. I'm leaving here with something today for my trouble." Officer Howard looked beyond Kita toward the truck.

The direction of the officer's glance wasn't lost on Kita. "How about you ladies go inside and get serviced on the house?"

Howard looked like she wanted to decline, but her partner chimed in. "Hair and nails?"

"Yeah, whatever you like," Kita relented.

"Okay, but don't get shit twisted. We *will* be back Friday." The officer tapped her partner, and together, they headed inside the salon.

Once the ladies were inside, Kita unlocked her phone and texted Rico. It read: Handle that shit today! To her surprise, he responded right away.

His message read: It's done.

Kita was confused by this news because two of his blue goons had just tried to shake her down, but she knew better than to ask for details over the phone. Therefore, she put that business on hold for now and made sure the shipment got to Kenya and Alexis, who were ready to break it down and get back in the grind of things.

It was just before eight in the morning when Rico slipped into bed with Kita, who was snoring lightly. Gently, he began to nibble on her neck until her eyes opened. "Hey, you."

"What's the update on Douglas?" she yawned.

"Well, damn, good morning to you too," he laughed, but Kita did not.

"This is serious! He's fucking with me and my business." Kita sat up in bed and grabbed her phone. Rico placed his hand over hers and removed the phone. He lifted the television remote and turned on the news without a word.

The reporters talked about the weather and the toxins in the air for nearly a minute. Kita was about to give Rico a piece of her mind for wasting her time, but then the story changed. Rico turned up the volume just as a male reporter came into view. He was standing in front of the courthouse.

*"Recently, we brought you the story of a Detroit woman found dead in her home. At the time of our report, the woman had been sexually and physically assaulted before death. The police claimed this case was at the top of their priority list. However, last night, our station received a shocking video that placed one of their own at the top of the suspect list. Our viewers should be advised that this video may be hard to watch and that viewers with small children should remove them now."*

The reporter was replaced by the cell phone footage from Kita's phone. Though the video is blurred in some parts, it's apparent that Officer Douglas was forcing himself on Shyla, who was screaming and crying with her hands behind her back. Once the video finished, the reporter continued. *"The state's prosecutor, Dalyn O'Shea, told us that formal charges have been filed against Officer Wayne Douglas, and he is being detained in 1300 Beaubien as we speak. If you have any additional information, please dial the number on the screen."*

With tears of gratitude, Kita hugged her man tight. It felt good to know that Douglas was off the streets, not just for her sake but so he would never darken the doorway of another woman like Shyla again.

"Thank you, baby. This means more to me than you'll ever know." When Rico didn't respond, she looked up to see his eyes glossy. "Are you okay?"

"I've known Wayne since I was born, so this was hard for me, but wrong is wrong." Rico sighed. "Anyway, the video was encrypted before I turned it in. That means it didn't disrupt the integrity of the data like time and date, but it does remove anything traceable to you."

"Rico, I just want to thank you again. I truly appreciate the sacrifice you made for me."

"Kita, I will go jump through rings of fire for you. I just pray you'd do the same for me." Lying back on the bed, he closed his eyes.

"Baby, you and me are stuck like glue." Kita began to leave a trail of kisses on his body. On cue, Rico's manhood began to react. Already knowing what time it was, Kita pulled her man's boxers down and began to lick his penis like it was her favorite popsicle. She gagged and spit on that dick like she was preparing for the Blow Job Olympics.

# CHAPTER FIFTY-EIGHT

Three months had gone by since Kita told Davit she was retiring from the dope game, and Detective Douglas was arrested for Shyla's murder. True to her word to Rico, she completed the obligations to her crew, and tonight was her retirement party/baby shower at Alexis's condo. The three of them decided to hold a business meeting before the baby shower guests arrived.

"We made one hundred grand each!" Kenya counted the final dollar from the large pile on the table. "Not fucking bad for our last go-round. Damn, I'm going to miss this shit!"

"It was fun, but I'm ready for a change." Kita never thought she'd see this day, but, boy, was she happy she did. As she slid her portion of money toward her and looked around Alexis's condo at all of the baby shower decorations, she had to admit it felt good to be putting that street shit to bed. She was ready to get married, have the baby, and start school to live the safe life her brother always wanted for her.

"Here is every dollar of y'all money, just like I promised." Alexis came into the living room with two large manila envelopes.

"Bitch, do I need to count this?" Kenya opened hers.

"Nah, you ain't got to count it, but now that I got money again, let's finalize our bet on the baby."

"Do y'all realize this will be one of the last times we will chill like this?" Kita was smiling at her friends as she admired the glow-up. "A little less than two years ago, life was so different. Now, look at us."

"I know, right? I can't believe we are done with this shit!" Alexis grabbed her money off the table and fanned herself. "We've been through some shit, but I wouldn't have wanted to go through none of it with nobody but y'all."

"Look, bitch, don't be trying to make me cry and ruin my makeup." Kita grabbed her belly, which was still small, and stood to use the bathroom. She peered down the hallway and saw that the door to the lower-level bathroom was closed. With a sigh, she ascended the stairwell to the second level. As soon as she placed her hand on the bathroom door, Talia jumped out of her room, startling Kita.

"*Bang!*" Talia held a black gun with an orange tip in her little hands.

"Girl, you scared me." Kita grabbed her chest.

"You don't have to be scared. It's just pretend, Kita." Talia laughed while showing her that the gun was a toy.

"It looks pretty real. Does Lex know you have that?" Kita was perplexed.

"No, but we play pretend all the time. Me and her played pretend the day I got kidnapped, remember?" Talia made air quotes with her fingers.

"Huh?" Kita needed clarification. However, Alexis called Talia's name from downstairs, and without responding, she skipped away. Kita was utterly confused but decided to put the little girl's make-believe stories on the back burner . . . for now. She used the bathroom and then headed across the hall into one of the guest bedrooms to give herself a once-over in the full-length mirror.

The minute she entered the room, her cell phone rang. A glance at the screen let her know her boo was calling. Smiling, she said, "Hey, baby, how are you?"

"Hey, beautiful." Rico's endearing voice made Kita's heart melt. "I know the baby shower is set to start soon, so I just wanted to call and tell you that I love you so much. I wish I were there with you, but I get it that it's a girls' thing, so enjoy yourself, and I'll see you tonight when you get home."

"I love you too." Kita blushed. "Keep my spot warm; see you tonight." After ending the call, Kita looked at herself in the mirror. "Well, little one, it's almost time for us to meet officially." Markita Jones rubbed her round belly while staring at her glowing reflection in the mirror on the dresser. "Mommy is very nervous, but I know things are going to be okay," she smiled. "You are so loved and spoiled alr—" The tender moment was cut short by a loud sound coming from downstairs.

Instinctively, she walked toward the bedroom door to assess the situation. Initially, she thought her two best friends, Alexis Walker and Kenya Lewis, had dropped something as they made space and moved furniture to prepare for the baby shower they were about to host. Just as she was about to yell downstairs and tell them to be careful, the sound of gunfire erupted through the two-story town house like booming thunder. Fear gripped Markita's heart as she internally processed what was happening.

A barrage of bullets ricocheted off the walls and windows, tearing up everything in their path. Markita dropped to her knees, fearful for her life and the others in the house. That's when she heard her friends screaming for help. They were still downstairs in the living room, where she had been no more than ten minutes ago. Had it not been for the baby pressing on her bladder, she'd still be down there.

"Fuck!" Frantically, she searched the bedroom for anything she could use for protection. Unfortunately for Markita, her quest yielded no results.

Scared to make a move, yet fearful of being trapped, she crawled toward the bedroom door. Her heart raced erratically as she tried to calm her breathing.

"Where the fuck is the cash at?" A man's deep voice bellowed from the living room.

"I don't have any fucking money in here!" Alexis screamed in agony. It was apparent to Kita that she was injured.

"Bitch, I'm going to ask you one more fucking time. Lie to me again, and you won't like what happens next."

"I'm not lying," Alexis cried. "Please, just leave. Let me call the ambulance before we die in here. I swear to God I won't say nothing . . . just let us live, please."

# CHAPTER FIFTY-NINE

Though Markita desperately wanted to go downstairs and help her friends, she had an unborn child to think about first. She slowly closed the bedroom door and retrieved her cell phone from the bed. It was lying next to her black Yves St. Laurent Cassandre purse. Quickly, she dialed for help.

"911, what's the emergency?" With a stiff tone, the operator sounded more like a robot than an actual person.

"My name is Markita Jones. I'm at 906 Chene Dr., unit number three. Please send the police and a few ambulances," she whispered through labored breaths.

"What seems to be the emergency?"

"Oh my God, he's coming!" Kita's voice oozed in panic as the sound of heavy footsteps headed in her direction. The pattern of their stride matched the beating in her heart. She felt like she was seconds from passing out. "I'm at my friend's house. Someone just came in shooting!"

"Do you know how many assailants there are? Do you know what they look like?" The operator bombarded her with questions.

Frustrated and afraid, Markita dropped the phone onto the bed. That's when she saw the knob on the bedroom door jiggle. She thought her life was over, but right on cue, the headlights from a car outside illuminated the bedroom window, giving Markita the sign she needed to use the only escape route accessible. Though Markita didn't exactly want to jump two stories to safety, she knew desperate times called for desperate measures.

Quickly, she pried the window open and kicked out the screen. With one leg dangling over the edge, she looked back at the door just in time to see it crack open. Before the assailant could fully enter the room, Markita closed her eyes tight . . . and jumped. Thankfully, she landed on her knees instead of her stomach or back. However, her victory was short-lived as the sound of two gunshots whizzed past her head. Without hesitation, she jumped up and frantically ran toward a neighbor's house. *POW!* A missed shot hit the headlight of a burgundy Nissan parked nearby.

"Help!" Markita screamed . . . just before the next shot hit its target. The bullet successfully tore through her left calf muscle and dropped her where she stood. Within seconds, she forced herself up from the ground and shifted her weight onto her right leg, determined to keep pushing. Though hurt and tired, she willed herself to fight for her child, if nothing else.

*BANG!* However, the fourth blast was the shot that inevitably put Kita down. The bullet had entered her back and exited through her chest. The scene seemed theatrical as pieces of her flesh opened and flew out in front of her, sending thick, red blood squirting everywhere.

Seconds after the shot, Markita felt a burning sensation so hot that she wondered if she was on fire. The pain was unbearable. She wanted to scream in agony, but her lungs were full of something . . . blood perhaps. She tried twice to get up from the concrete, but it was useless. Her limbs were no longer listening to her brain as she lay there unmoving. Her eyes fluttered as she tried hard to keep them open. Within a matter of seconds, her body grew cold. Internally, she knew she was losing her fight to stay alive.

"Oh my God!" a lady screamed while another person hollered for someone to call 911.

As Markita lay outside dying beneath the stars, she thought about her mother, Jackie, and how she would feel after receiving the news. She wondered if Jackie would blame herself and go into another bout of depression the way she did when her brother Marlowe was killed. Markita wished she could comfort her mom and let her know that none of this was her fault.

Next, she thought of her fiancé, Rico Richardson, and large tears gathered in the corners of her eyes. Without a doubt, the police would report the incident as being drug-related, and she knew he'd be mad at her for bringing shame to his name and tarnishing his reputation. Markita also knew Rico would ultimately hate her for losing their child to a street hustle she should have never been caught up in.

Markita wanted to make things right with everyone. She wanted desperately to start over, but there were no second chances in life. It was time to meet her maker and face judgment for how she had been living lately. She wondered if Alexis and Kenya would be at the crossroads to greet her when she arrived. With her friends in mind, she managed to muster a faint smile.

How did three innocent girls from the ghetto get caught up in a life of crime? This simple question triggered a movie to begin playing in Markita's head. With her eyes closed, she began to relax and allow herself to be transported through what felt like multiple dimensions. Flashbacks of her life began in childhood when things were rough for her family. Markita knew this period was the catalyst that undoubtedly turned her from an innocent, sweet girl into an infamous street gangster.

# CHAPTER SIXTY

"I guess it's true what they, bad bitches do die slow!" Alexis stood over Markita's cold body as she faded in and out of consciousness. She was still lying on the concrete, bleeding to death, where she lay riddled with bullets. "Kenya took a whole five minutes, but your ass is going on ten." Looking down at the bloodstained wristwatch on her left arm, she spat, "Just go ahead and die already!"

"Lex?" Kita gasped. "Why did you do this?" Kita hated to waste any ounce of breath she had left, but she needed to know why her best friend would do her so dirty.

"Well, I figured since this was our last pack, there wasn't no need in splitting that shit three ways," Alexis admitted. "I need all that money to make up for the loss I'm going to take when I no longer have *your* supplier supplying me." As she squatted over Kita, she made air quotes to be sarcastic.

"Were you behind the Talia thing too?" Markita coughed. She was beginning to put two and two together.

"Oh yeah, that was me," she laughed wickedly. "How genius was it to have my sister kidnapped for ransom? You bitches came through, though, and my pockets appreciated that shit. I only paid it back to look good because I knew y'all wasn't leaving with it."

"What about Al?" By now, Markita was so cold she was trembling.

"Me and Breeze set that nigga up to take the fall for the whole thing." Alexis smiled at how easily her plan had come together, but unfortunately, her joy didn't last long.

Without warning, a single bullet entered the back of her head, blowing off half her face. Instantly, her lifeless body fell on top of Kita. Now, standing in her place was Breeze, holding a nickel-plated nine-millimeter.

"Breeze," Kita's eyes bucked. "I thought you loved her." The realization of everything going on was beginning to make her feel crazy.

"Ain't no love in the dope game." After plotting with Alexis to take the money from her friends, he decided plans needed to change. That large sum of money would be a major come-up for him if he didn't have to split it.

"What about Talia? Please spare her," Kita whispered as tears rolled down her face. There was no use in begging for her life because she knew Breeze was about to seal her fate the same way he'd done Alexis. That was the law of the streets.

"That little bitch is no longer my concern, and neither are you." Cold and methodically, Breeze raised his gun and squeezed the trigger. Kita didn't close her eyes. She accepted her fate with no attempts to shield herself. But ... nothing happened. So Breeze squeezed again and again, but it was clear the gun had jammed. "Fuck!"

He paced back and forth briefly before deciding to leave well enough alone. With sirens blaring in the distance, Breeze tossed the hood of his jacket over his head and ran away, disappearing into the night.

Kita remained stiff as a board on the ground while internally fighting hard not to succumb to her injuries. Though her body was ice cold, her pants felt extremely warm. She didn't have the strength to reach down and inspect the situation. However, the woman who had run off earlier was now back with her cell phone. "Hang in there, baby. I think you're in labor," she said while stroking Kita's head. This gesture brought Kita to tears, and she began to cry in the arms of the stranger. Sensing that she wouldn't make it before help arrived, the stranger asked, "Is there anyone you want me to call?"

Mustering every ounce of strength she had, Kita began rattling off her mother's number. As the woman dialed the final number, Kita said, "Tell her I love her."

"Hello?" Jackie answered on the second ring.

"Hi, I am here with a young lady." The stranger hesitated. "She's been shot, but the ambulance is close."

"Oh Lord! Is her name Markita?" Jackie's voice was full of horror. "If so, that's my daughter."

"Sweetie, is your name Markita?" the stranger asked, and Kita nodded. "Stay with me, Markita. I see the lights on the ambulance, baby. They are right here."

"Lord, please don't let my baby die!" Jackie could be heard screaming on the phone. "I'm on the way to the baby shower. Is that where you are?"

"I don't know about a baby shower, but we are in the parking lot of the condos on Chene, near Vernor St." The woman began waving her hand in the air for the ambulance to locate them in the dark.

"Please, can you put the phone to her ear, ma'am?" Jackie was crying hysterically as the stranger did as she was instructed. Once given the okay to speak with Kita, she said, "Baby, please fight with everything you have. Mommy is on the way! I love you and my grandchild. Please, fight!"

"Mama," Kita began to cough up blood. "I love you too. None of this is your fault—" Kita stopped talking midsentence. When the woman looked down, it was clear that Kita's life was no more. She'd died still holding on to the stranger's hand with her eyes open.

# EPILOGUE

For nearly fifteen minutes, the EMTs worked to get a pulse on Markita as they loaded her into the back of the ambulance and drove to the nearest hospital. On their last attempt, before calling her time of death, she came back to life. However, her heartbeat was extremely weak. Without hesitation, the ambulance team passed her off to the staff at the emergency room, who worked twice as hard to get her in and out of surgery successfully. Not only did they have to repair her flesh wounds from the gunshots, but they also had to perform an emergency C-section to remove the baby. Kita's injuries were so severe that she had to be placed in a medically induced coma for two weeks.

Today, the doctors decided to bring her out of the coma.

"Ma'am, it's been two hours, and she hasn't woken up yet." Rico sat at the foot of Kita's bed, rubbing her feet.

"Please don't be alarmed. It could take twenty-four hours before some patients regain consciousness." A young nurse gave Rico a reassuring smile as she checked Kita's vitals on the machine.

Kita began to stir as if she'd heard the conversation about her. First, she moved her feet, then her fingers. Next, she blinked rapidly before pulling her lips apart. "Rico?"

"Kita! Oh my God, baby, I'm right here." Instantly, he was on his feet, throwing himself over the top of his fiancée to hug her and kiss her face.

"The baby?" Kita mumbled.

"He is with your mom in the NICU." Sensing the fear in her eyes, he placed his hand on top of Kita's. "Michael is fine; just a little premature. They want to get his weight up, and then he can come home." Rico pulled out his phone and showed her pictures of the cutest baby she'd ever seen.

Kita's eyes became glossy at the revelation that she'd had a son. "His name is Michael?"

"Yes, his full name is Michael Marlowe Richardson." Rico paused. "I didn't know if you were going to make it, and I didn't like him being referred to as Baby Doe, so I named him after my father."

"It's okay. I like the name Michael." Kita wiped her eyes. "How long have I been here?"

"Two weeks." Rico placed his phone down and stared at the nurse. She got the hint and walked away.

"Where are Kenya and Alexis?" Flashbacks of that night began to intrude on Kita's brain.

"Only you survived." Rico sighed. "Talia's funeral was on Monday. Alexis and Kenya had a double funeral last week."

"Alexis and her boyfriend set this whole thing up, but then he double-crossed her." Kita's blood began to boil. "That bitch was dishonorable! *She's* the reason Kenya and Talia are dead."

"Wow, we didn't know." Rico was stunned at her revelation. "When officers arrived on the scene, it appeared that you all were ambushed in the house but that you and Alexis made it outside, where she threw herself on top of you to protect the baby. She's in all of the papers as a hero."

"Hell no! We need to correct that narrative ASAP! People need to know the truth." Kita was beyond pissed.

"Baby, why does it matter?" Rico stood and walked over to the window overlooking the parking lot. "Fuck her, fuck that story, and fuck this city. Let's just focus on getting you and Michael out of this hospital. After that, we're leaving and never looking back."

Without a word, Kita closed her eyes. She didn't know what to say or how to feel. Her friends were gone, her brother was gone, and she had too many fucking skeletons in the closet. However, Rico was right; she knew it would be best to leave well enough alone. Kita knew most people only left the game in cuffs or a body bag, but God had spared her life. She didn't know why, but she vowed to make something of this second chance.

# THE END

# ACKNOWLEDGMENTS

First, I want to thank God for giving me the ability to share my writing talent with the world. Second, I want to thank my family and friends for always having my back and cheering me on no matter what. Next, I want to thank the Boss Magnet and Black Odyssey Media team for bringing this dope story to life, on film and to book shelves around the map. Last, but certainly not least, I have to send a special thank you to everyone who has supported my work in any way over the years. Thank you for believing in my ideas and pouring into my dreams. It's because of each of you that this black girl from Detroit shines bright.

Much love always,

India

# BOSS CHAT WITH INDIA

Friends,

We could not let India leave without a quick sit-down with our Boss Magnet Media family to get another scoop of greatness from this talented creator.

**BOSS MAGNET MEDIA:** India, you have been on the urban scene for a while now. How does it feel to have your literary works adapted to film?

**INDIA:** Honestly, it still feels surreal. Though, I've always envisioned my literary works being adapted to films, I really didn't think it was a possible without help from Hollywood.

**BOSS MAGNET MEDIA:** What was the first thought that ran through your mind when you were told the one and only Jason Mitchell would be in YOUR debut movie?

**INDIA:** The minute I received the news, I began to cry and pray... hard! I just wanted to thank God for being such a way maker and game changer in my life. Though I've had many big moments in my career, this one takes the cake. I've been a fan of Jason Mitchell's work since the beginning. It was hard to believe he'd be one of my characters, reciting words that I wrote.

**BOSS MAGNET MEDIA**: How does it feel to have had a hand in producing the *Dishonorable* movie, and being featured in it?

**INDIA:** The experience was nothing short of amazing! Being on set for hours, helping the actors get into character, and cooking for the cast and crew because we were snowed in really ignited a fire in me that craves scripts and set life.

**BOSS MAGNET MEDIA:** Now that you've officially crossed over into film, where do you see yourself in five years?

**INDIA:** I'd like to start a production company with my family and bring more characters to film. As a licensed mental health professional, I'd like to return to writing novels and using my pen game to bring increased awareness to mental health, human trafficking, adverse childhood experiences, intimate partner violence and more.

**BOSS MAGNET MEDIA:** What advice would you give aspiring authors?

**INDIA:** Never stop dreaming! I tell everybody, the sky is the limit. All it takes is for opportunity to meet preparation and you'll reach heights you never thought existed.

**Stay connected with India at:**
FB: India Johnson-Williams
IG: @InkDivaIndia
Email: gradeapub@gmail.com

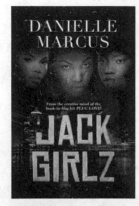

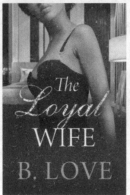